AND THEN CAME THE DARKNESS

Sara Henderson sensed that somebody was watching her every move. That, and the eerie phone calls she'd been getting, made her terrified to cross fog-enshrouded Balboa Park at night. Determined to patch her life together after her divorce, Sara was attending night classes at the university. Getting there, though, meant crossing the park where a vicious killer was reported to be stalking young women. They called him the San Diego Strangler — and all his victims had red hair. As Sara set off, the fog swirled around the trees, thick and heavy, stifling her cry when a hand snaked out and touched her red hair — then fastened on her wrist . . .

Books by Jane Toombs
Published by The House of Ulverscroft:

HARTE'S GOLD
NIGHTINGALE MAN

JANE TOOMBS

AND THEN CAME THE DARKNESS

Complete and Unabridged

ULVERSCROFT
Leicester

First published in the
United States of America

First Large Print Edition
published 2005

British Library CIP Data

Toombs, Jane
And then came the darkness.—Large print ed.—
Ulverscroft large print series: adventure & suspense
1. Serial murderers—California—San Diego—
Fiction 2. Suspense fiction 3. Large type books
I. Title
813.5'4 [F]

ISBN 1–84395–544–X

Published by
F. A. Thorpe (Publishing)
Anstey, Leicestershire

Set by Words & Graphics Ltd.
Anstey, Leicestershire
Printed and bound in Great Britain by
T. J. International Ltd., Padstow, Cornwall

Prologue

They'd forgotten to leave his door ajar again, so he lay in darkness. His heart pounded in fear; the dark wasn't his friend. And he sensed evil.

He didn't think that they'd closed his door all the way on purpose. One or two were mean, their harsh hands shoving him this way and that when they took care of him. The others, mostly, were nice, even if only one or two really cared about him.

Despite how frightened he was, he lay quietly. He could do nothing else. Unable to move or speak, he had no way to change what happened to him. Or what happened to anyone else.

He knew he hadn't always been this way. A long time ago, he'd talked and walked and even ran. But it was dangerous to think about that, and so he tried not to.

He closed his eyes to shut out the dark. It might not be any lighter behind his lids, but at least this was a dark of his own choosing. Sometimes closing his eyes helped. Tonight it didn't. The evil was still there, waiting.

Not near him, no, but that didn't matter,

1

because if he was supposed to see and hear the evil, he would. Nothing could stop it.

If only he had someone who could understand. Not Daddy. Daddy didn't like him anymore, he could tell. And there wasn't anybody else. No one loved what he was now.

I don't want to see, he screamed inwardly, silently, hopelessly. I don't want to hear, don't want to know. Please stop making me know.

It was no use. Suddenly he wasn't lying in the bed, he was somewhere else, he was outside in the night. In the fog. Shrouded in gray mist, he floated over dimly glimpsed trees, finally dipping down to hover over a clump of bushes. He recognized a pink oleander flower. Daddy always used to make sure he knew the names of trees and plants and birds. And that he knew about music and painting, too. That's 'cause daddy was a teacher.

But it didn't do any good to try to keep his mind on other things, like what his father had taught him. Evil filled the night; he could feel the badness lurking in the fog.

He dipped lower, among the bushes, and there it was. He couldn't close his eyes to shut out the horror of what he saw, 'cause when he was away from himself like this, he didn't seem to have any eyes. Or any body, either.

2

When it first happened, he'd tried to think it was like watching TV, only it really wasn't. TVs could be turned off.

A man stood among the pink flowers, wiping a knife. At his feet, something, all bloody, lay scrunched up on the ground. A lady. She was dead. He couldn't see the man's face 'cause of the fog, but he could feel the evil pulsing from him.

'So long, bitch,' the man whispered.

The sound of the man's voice chilled him, even though he'd learned by now that he couldn't be seen. That's 'cause he wasn't really there, only some kind of invisible part of him was. He didn't understand how or why.

What he saw and heard scared him, but the worst of all was knowing that something awful bad like this was going to happen to someone he liked. Maybe even someone he loved.

'Cause sooner or later it always did . . .

1

The fog drifted in from the ocean like a great gray bird, spreading misty wings over the gorges and mesas of Balboa Park. The man crouched among the pink oleander bushes lifted his head to breathe in the welcome dampness.

Time to go. He eased free of the oleanders and slogged across the grass, his movements heavy and slow, feeling as though he was making his way through thick mud. Not Nam jungle muck, but red adobe, California clay made soggy by rain.

The kind of mud that built up on the soles of shoes but, like Hank used to say, not inside the souls of men. If men had souls. Women didn't, no more than dogs did, he was sure of that.

Afterward was always the same — the low, the bottomless down. Glancing back toward what he'd left in the fog-shrouded mass of shrubbery behind him, he tried to remember how good it had felt. As usual, he failed. The high never lasted; he could never bring back the feeling. Until the next time.

The fog slithered along the city streets as

he left the park. Tonight's full moon, visible in the eastern-most suburbs near the desert, couldn't be seen in this vast park so close to the ocean. He lived on the park's east side and counted on the fog as a part of his life. As a friend. He hadn't had many.

Hadn't had any friends, really, until Nam and Hank. Now he had none. Except for the fog. And, sometimes, the dogs. But they were expendable. They had to be expendable, or they were of no use to him.

Concealed within the fog's embrace, he slipped into the alley leading to his rear apartment, relishing the feeling of invisibility. No one saw him; no one knew him. He moved as silently as the fog, as stealthily as an owl drifting on the night wind.

Inside, the shower drained what meager vitality he had left, and he fell into bed. If he was lucky tonight, the dreams wouldn't plague him. Sometimes, afterward, he didn't dream for as long as a week.

With his left hand he fingered the golden heart on the gold chain around his neck, and with his right he rubbed his left upper arm, stroking the tawny owl needled into his skin. Night's heralds, Hank used to call owls. Before he'd met Hank he always thought guys who talked fancy were showing off. But not Hank.

Better stop thinking about Hank, or he'd be risking a nightmare. Sleep, he needed sleep. He was depleted, nothing left of him. Way down, too spent to even look up, much less climb out. It was all over — the search, the excitement of the chase, the careful collection of a specimen without being caught, the juggling of each detail so everything would be perfect. Then the final ecstatic rush of release.

He needed to rest now, needed to prepare himself for the time he'd find it necessary to begin the hunt again.

2

Sara Henderson crossed the dark parking area toward the lighted school buildings, not quite running. She'd almost decided not to come. The UCSD extension class was at a junior high school close to Balboa Park, right next to the zoo. And spring was still months away; this time of year the dark came early. But she'd convinced herself it was silly to worry about being attacked every time she went out alone at night. Or almost convinced herself.

She glanced to each side as she hurried, unhappy about the large hibiscus bushes lining the sidewalk. Impossible to spot someone hiding behind or between them. Fallen eucalyptus leaves crunched under her feet, covering the sound of possible footsteps behind her.

Increasing her pace, she resisted the urge to turn her head for a quick scan behind her. She wouldn't be here if Dr. Zimmer hadn't urged her to find a way to make contact with other people. Easy for him to say, he wasn't a woman. Wasn't a red-haired woman. He didn't have to worry about anybody stalking him on a foggy autumn evening. Or any other time.

But it was partly her own fault. If she'd been on time, she might have found others to walk with. Instead, she'd dithered about going or not going until almost too late.

She was breathless by the time she opened the door to Room 24 and slid into a seat. No way was she going to walk back to that parking lot alone after the class was over.

Sara wasn't certain why she'd chosen a mythology course. An introduction to computers would've taught her a useful skill. Or she might have taken a refresher in her field of special education. What good would mythology be, when she dredged up the courage to go job hunting?

'We all practice procrastination, Sara,' Dr. Zimmer had said, 'but reality can't be postponed forever.'

Her lips curled in wry amusement. Perhaps she'd chosen mythology because he stressed reality.

Why were the others in the room with her taking this class? She was looking them over, when a man in a brown corduroy jacket with leather patches on the sleeves came up the aisle and leaned on the lectern.

'I'm Ralph MacDuffy,' he announced, running a hand through his ginger hair, artfully disarranging the curls. His smile seemed a deliberate attempt to call attention to the contrast of even white teeth against tanned skin — to say nothing of the dimple in his right cheek.

Sara looked up at him with mixed appreciation and cynicism. There was certainly no question of his good looks, or his awareness of them. Still, he seemed young to be an assistant professor, so he must have something going for him other than being a gorgeous hunk.

As she listened to Ralph MacDuffy extol the heroes of myths around the world, she grew more and more uncertain of her subject choice. Did she really want to wallow in legendary heroes, after trying to live with one for seven years and failing miserably?

Sara shrugged. Heroes were the vaunted men in all civilizations, no one bothered to laud losers. Certainly C.W. had gotten his share of adulation — so much so that he came to believe he truly was as heroic as the media claimed he was.

' . . . and, of course, we must not neglect the *Kalevala* of the Finns,' MacDuffy went on. 'Longfellow, one of our early American moralists, thought it good enough to steal from for his 'Song of Hiawatha.' Meter, cadence — a direct theft.' He raised his left eyebrow engagingly and paused for effect.

Though competent in her own area, Sara had never felt herself to be an expert in any field whatsoever, but she did know the *Kalevala* — Grandpa Saari used to recite it in Finn, yet — and she knew something about Chippewa Indians, because she'd gone to school with them when she was growing up in Michigan's Upper Peninsula.

She raised her hand. 'Mr. MacDuffy?'

'Ralph — we're contemporaries, after all.'

'Well, about 'Hiawatha.' Don't you think Longfellow might have been struck by the resemblances in the myths of the American Indians and those of the Finns? Both emphasize magic and trickery. Perhaps he felt it was fitting to borrow the same method to tell about an Indian hero.'

'My dear — what is your name?'

'Sara Henderson,' she murmured, already sorry she'd spoken.

'My dear Sara, 'Hiawatha' is a fake from beginning to end. *Gone With The Wind* gives us a truer mythology of the Old South than 'Hiawatha' does of the Chippewas. Even the name of the hero comes from the Iroquois — deadly enemies of the Chippewa. Longfellow created a fake hero and coupled him with a direct steal from the *Kalevala* for his cadence. I'm sorry if it shocks you to think of him as a plagiarist.'

Some of the younger members of the class tittered, and Sara felt her face burn. She shook her head and looked down at her hands, unable to defend her position, but unwilling to agree. She'd never had any defense against ridicule. Her ex-husband, the famous, the wonderful Charles William Gallion, had discovered that fact early in their marriage.

'If you don't want to be trampled on, stop being such a doormat,' he'd say, while at the same time knocking her down verbally every time she tried to stand up to him. C.W., the legend in his own time.

' . . . a point here.' Sara belatedly realized the voice didn't belong to MacDuffy and raised her head to see who was speaking.

'I'm no authority on either the Finns or the Indians,' the man went on, 'but if they both used magic and trickery to explain the ways of nature, then how can you arbitrarily say Longfellow stole from the *Kalevala?* No reason the man couldn't have borrowed a primitive verse form. Maybe he thought his readers would be smart enough to see why he'd used the meter and cadence, and they'd praise his cleverness.'

MacDuffy threw his arms heavenward in a dramatic gesture. 'Unfortunately, he's up there now, so we can't ask, can we?' And he went on to other lands and other heroes.

Sara eyed the tall man in the gray sweater and faded jeans who'd spoken for her. Championed her cause. He glanced her way, and she managed a faint smile before she ducked her head again. Ridiculous to be so flustered at being put down by that ginger-haired egotist. After all, she'd been put down far more expertly in the past.

Never again, she told herself. No more being chivvied through life by an ex-pro halfback who had to trample down all competition on or off the field. Never again. MacDuffy was no C.W., but he was of the same breed. Weren't all men, if given half a chance?

She owed the man in the gray sweater, though. At the break she caught up to him on the way to the coffee machine. 'Thanks for the support,' she said.

He slowed and spoke without looking at her. 'Our Ralphie is full of crap. Knows his stuff, they tell me, but demands center stage at all times. Don't let him bother you. Besides, I think you were right.' He glanced at her and smiled briefly. 'I'm Ian Wilson.'

'You've heard my name. It's Sara without the *h*.'

He raised his eyebrows slightly but said nothing.

She examined him more carefully. Rather an ugly man, actually. A few years older than her twenty-eight, face hilled and furrowed, nose slightly askew, possibly broken once. Defenseless brown eyes looked out at the world, at her. Eyes that didn't seem to belong in the dour, craggy face. Sara turned away, conscious of staring.

'How do you like your coffee?' His voice was pleasant, almost soothing.

'Sugar only, thank you.'

'You aren't related to MacDuffy, are you?'

Sara was astonished. 'Me? Good grief, no.'

Ian waved an apologetic hand. 'Well, your hair's the same color as his. And there's a general resemblance.'

She blinked at him, rather dismayed at being linked with Ralph MacDuffy.

Ian handed her a coffee and asked, 'Are you an English teacher like most of us?'

'No. That is, I'm a teacher — though not of English — but I'm not working at the moment.' Involuntarily she touched her ringless finger, reminded of how C.W. refused to hear of her keeping her job once they were married.

'Don't tell me you're taking the class for pleasure.'

14

Sara half-smiled. 'I hadn't thought of it as pleasure.' More as therapy, though she wasn't about to admit it. 'Where do you teach?' she asked.

'I'm on a sabbatical until next fall.' He answered readily enough, but she had the impression her question had disturbed him and she wondered why.

She noticed the groups around the coffee machine were breaking up and thought, now or never.

'Please don't think I'm crazy.' She spoke quickly, wanting to get it all said before he had a chance to respond. 'I'm really nervous about walking to the parking lot after class is over. Because of the strangler. We're so close to the park, and it's so dark in the lot, and I don't know anyone to walk with yet. Would you mind — are you parked there, too?'

'Yes. I'll walk with you.' His words were abrupt, even begrudging.

Back in class, she fumed at herself. He must think she was coming on to him when, God knows, it was the last thing she intended. She should have asked one of the other women to walk with her.

'Get out of the house,' Dr. Zimmer had said. 'Find an outlet.'

'The shrinks are crazier than the people who go to them,' C.W. had insisted. 'And you

15

have to be pretty damn nutty to go to one in the first place.'

C.W. was, of course, perfect.

So here she was out of the house, enrolled in, of all things, a mythology course, and already one man had done his best to humiliate her and another thought she was chasing him. On top of it all, she might well be risking her life by walking alone so near the park at night. For what? To learn about heroes when she hated heroes.

What she should do is sell the house and rent an apartment. She'd thought she'd relish living alone, but sometimes she felt afraid and isolated. Especially since the strangler. She had no friends; everyone she knew lived back east. In an apartment she'd meet others in the same complex. Make friends. But she loved the house as she loved San Diego. She treasured every Spanish tile in it, even liked the overgrown foliage in the yard. Besides, how could she keep her three cats in an apartment?

Ian Wilson walked with her to the parking lot after class. He didn't speak, and she found nothing to say that didn't sound inane, so she, too, was silent. Don't worry, I don't want any part of you, she felt like telling him. Only the protection of your company on the way to my car. Only your presence so I don't feel

16

eyes in the dark watching me, waiting for a woman alone. A redheaded woman.

★   ★   ★

Ian Wilson yanked his car door shut with unnecessary force. He was acting like a damn fool. The woman was only scared of the dark — nothing wrong with that. He pulled onto the road with a screech of tires, realized he was driving too fast and eased his foot off the accelerator. Speeding was no good. Drinking was no good. And he was taking too many of those little red capsules.

Nothing was any good. Might have known the class would be worthless with that idiot MacDuffy involved. He'd heard about MacDuffy. Did his best to screw all the women in his class under fifty, and couldn't stand contradiction. Especially from a female.

MacDuffy had gone out of his way to humiliate what's-her-name; he'd embarrassed the hell out of her for no good reason. What *was* her name? Oh, yeah, Sara without the *h*. She reminded him of one of those little birds that fluttered around houses back east. The ones with red heads. Sparrows or wrens, something like that.

She was an unusual-looking little thing,

17

with that red hair and her eyes and skin all wrong for it — both a golden brown. Her skin should be fair, and her eyes bright blue like MacDuffy's. Or maybe green. Like Moira's. Except no woman could ever have eyes as green as Moira's.

Oh God, not Moira. Don't dig up the dead. Don't think about the living dead, either. Stop it. He forced his foot up from the accelerator again.

He had no intention of involving himself any further with Sara. Already he could tell she was the kind of woman who needed tenderness, and he had none left in him. He'd forget the class, stop going. What an ass MacDuffy was — Longfellow a thief, for Christ sake.

'The day is cold and dark and dreary
It rains and the wind is never weary . . . '

That was Longfellow. A New England poet. Though it wasn't always sunny here, Southern Californians knew nothing of the weather Longfellow had in mind for that poem. Still, the dark weather of the soul was universal.

★　★　★

Ralph MacDuffy left the last of his admirers in the parking lot and got into his silver Porsche. He evaluated the blonde in the tight white jeans from the rear as he flicked on his headlights. Provocative ass. Eighteen, she'd said. And she'd been all over him on the short walk to the car. Oh, yes.

He smiled, then the smile faded as he remembered the redhead in the class — what was her name? Sara something. His eyes narrowed. Thought she knew more than the instructor, a damned nuisance to have a woman like her in his courses. Not that he didn't know exactly how to deal with her. The smile returned. Oh, yes, he quite looked forward to taking care, in his own special way, of Sara what's-her-name. First. The blonde could wait, eighteen-year-old blondes were a dime a dozen. Recalcitrant redheads, on the other hand, were rather rare.

★ ★ ★

Three Thursday nights later, Sara stood by the coffee machine on the edge of a group of women, with them yet not quite with them. They all knew one another and spoke of mutual acquaintances and problems, maybe not meaning to intentionally exclude her, but effectively doing so.

19

Didn't anyone except English teachers and teens take this course? Ralph was surrounded by all the pretty young girls, she noticed. Should she feel flattered he'd singled her out for attention lately? Favorable attention. Actually, it rather alarmed her. It took a lot of effort to cope with a man as persistent as Ralph, effort she didn't care to expend. She needed all the energy she had just to keep going from one day to the next. Looming before her was also the frightening necessity of looking for work before she ran out of money.

'Hi.'

Sara spun around and saw Ian Wilson, who hadn't been to class since that first night.

'I thought you were a dropout,' she said, unaccountably pleased to see him and wondering why.

He shrugged. 'I wasn't sure I could take our Ralphie for an entire quarter, but I decided to give him another chance.'

Sara sought but didn't find a casual way to inform him that she and Ralph were no longer enemies.

'Also, I figured I'd better come back so you'd have an escort to the parking lot,' Ian added. 'If you haven't replaced me by now.'

She stared at him in surprise, then smiled. 'I trail after a few older women who seem to suspect me of trying to overhear their conversation. Lord knows why.'

She'd chosen the women over Ralph, not wishing to join his retinue. Not that he'd offered to walk with her; the class beauties kept him well occupied. She really didn't understand why he'd called her at home, ostensibly about the *Kalevala*, but actually pushing to come by and see her.

'I take it we've finished with Finnish mythology by now,' Ian said.

She nodded. 'Currently it's the 'Nibelungenlied' and, frankly, I prefer Finn to German myths. Maybe because I'm half-Finnish. What's your preference?'

'I've never read more than a summary of the *Kalevala*.'

'The only way to really experience the story is to hear it aloud. The runes are meant to be sung to the *kantele* — a five-stringed Finnish harp something like a zither. Longfellow may have used the same cadence, but he really didn't do humor — the anonymous parody on Hiawatha's mittens comes closer to the Finn's love of the ridiculous. You know:

'made them with the skin-side outside
with the outside, furside inside . . . ' '

Ian grinned.

She smiled back. 'That's what I mean. The *Kalevala* is fun. Silly, sometimes, like its hero. Who isn't like most of these supermen we're hearing about in class. He doesn't even have a proper hero's name, like Seigfried or Ulysses or Beowulf. How can you not smile at a hero named Vainamoinen?'

Sara grew so involved in convincing Ian he should read the *Kalevala*, that all the others were in their seats by the time the two of them slipped back into the room. She felt like a truant schoolgirl when Ralph raised his eyebrows at her.

Ralph had suggested he tape her reading the verses of the *Kalevala*, while he played guitar in the background. She'd explained the *runo* singers were usually men, but that was an unimportant detail to Ralph. She could be wrong in thinking he was using the tape recording as an excuse, that he had a hidden agenda. Perhaps he thought it was as important as she did that more people should be made aware of the great Finnish folk epic. But she doubted it.

One of her grandfather's favorite verses came to mind, the classic tale of the uninvited wedding guest taking his revenge. When knives are drawn, the men move outside the house because:

'In the yard the blood looks better,
In the yard it looks more lovely
On the snow it looks much better . . . '

Grandfather Saari had found the words grimly amusing, but Sara, thinking of the rapist-strangler, shivered as though the chill November fog had slithered into the classroom. He was out there somewhere. Was he already stalking his next victim?

After class she was glad of Ian's company on the walk to the parking lot.

'I suppose you think I'm the typical nervous female, afraid of the dark,' she said.

He glanced at her and shook his head. 'No, not really.'

'I know it's silly to believe this strangler has singled me out, but I can't overcome my fear of walking alone at night so close to the park. I hope and I pray they catch him soon.'

'Since you *do* have red hair,' he said, 'I can see why you'd be nervous.'

Sara looked at him. 'Why do you suppose he always chooses redheads?'

'They're distinctive. Over the ages redheads have been subjected to all kinds of harassment. I'm sure you've heard the superstition about the devil having red hair.'

'My grandfather used to tell me the devil had a red beard. *Punaparta*, the Finns say.

23

Redbeard. Also known as the devil.'

One of the big cats from the nearby zoo roared, a menacing sound in the thickening swirls of fog. Sara started and involuntarily clutched Ian's arm. He eased away from her, and she dropped her hand immediately. Did he think she was pursuing him like those girls who went after Ralph? Sara increased the space between herself and Ian.

'Thank you for your trouble,' she said formally. 'I do appreciate your walking with me to my car.'

'Unless I happen to be the strangler,' he said.

What a thing to say! Sara stared at Ian, unsettled and upset by his comment. Ian a murderer? She laughed a trifle shrilly.

'You don't have a killer's eyes,' she said.

He edged farther away. What was he reacting to now? Did he feel she was being too personal in mentioning his eyes?

Ian shut Sara into her car, turned to leave, then swung back, and tapped on her window. She rolled it down.

'What?'

'I've come up with an idea. Where do you live?'

'North of the park. Why?'

'I drive down University Avenue to class,' he said. 'If you'd like to ride with me, I'll pick

24

you up — it's really not out of my way.'

'Well,' Sara began dubiously, the words of Dr. Zimmer flashing on and off like a neon sign in her mind. *Meet people. Relate to others.*

Did that include accepting rides to class with strangers? Still, Ian Wilson wasn't exactly a stranger.

'It sounds all right, I guess,' she finished, peering at him, unable to see his face clearly. 'You're kind to offer.'

His laugh was short and unamused. 'Don't worry, a ride is *all* I'm offering.'

She made up her mind. 'Okay, thanks. I'll see you next Thursday at 6:45.'

'I'll need your address.'

It crossed her mind to say she'd meet him on the corner near her house, but she decided if she was going to ride with him, what difference did it make if he also knew where she lived? She told him.

'That *is* close to the park. It won't be hard to find.' He sketched a wave and turned away.

Her nerves jangling, Sara drove off, unable to dismiss how he'd joked about being the strangler. It *had* been a joke, of course. Or had it? What did she know of Ian? Not very damn much. Had she made a mistake in agreeing to ride with him? In giving him her address? Maybe that's how the strangler

25

worked — picking a victim, getting her to trust him, and then . . .

She shook her head violently. Next she'd be convincing herself that the real reason MacDuffy wanted to drop by her house was to kill her. She didn't know him any better than she knew Ian.

While she'd learned the hard way that men weren't to be trusted, that they were bullies who lied and cheated, there was no reason for her to begin picturing every man she met as a killer. It'd been in poor taste for Ian to tell her he might be the strangler but, deep down, she didn't really believe he was.

So why worry about riding to class with him? Not that she wasn't making a mistake, because chances were that letting him or any man even that far into her life could be her biggest mistake of all time. She wasn't ready to deal with a man except in impersonal — and distant — encounters.

She still hadn't worked through Dr. Zimmer's comments about victims. Lately he'd been hinting her problems might be as much due to her own lack of insight as to C.W. Some people, he'd said, become victims through chance, some through choice. And while it might be difficult, if not impossible, to control chance, no one was required to remain a victim by choice.

She didn't yet understand how anyone could choose to be a victim. She certainly never had and never would.

What about those four women the rapist-strangler had murdered? They sure as hell hadn't chosen their fates. Or had it been pure chance they'd become the killer's victims? Suppose there was something they'd done to attract his attention, or suppose they'd somehow made it easy for him to get to them. Like going out at night near the park. Or maybe simply living alone.

Sara grimaced. If she was trying to work herself into a state of panic, she was doing a damn good job.

He isn't after you, she told herself firmly. No one is. Now that you're rid of C.W., you're not anyone's victim, by chance or by choice.

3

He didn't like the new dog, Sheba. She'd been the only black bitch available, and he wanted to get started, so he'd taken her rather than waiting for a better one. A smaller one. For everything to go right, the dogs had to be black. And female.

Sheba kept a wary eye on him at all times — like now, when she was eating the food he'd set out for her. She never slept when he was awake. Damn bitch didn't trust him, but she obeyed him. She'd do well enough, though he'd be glad to be rid of her. He preferred more tractable animals.

He needed her. Without having a black bitch handy, he couldn't begin the hunt for the woman.

He'd done his forty push-ups before breakfast, and when Sheba finished her food, he'd take her for a walk in the park. Keep himself fit. He flexed his biceps, picturing his father slumped in a kitchen chair, fat bulging over his belt. He was in better condition than the old man had ever been. His fists clenched. He'd been glad when his son-of-a-bitch of a father had died, not understanding what the death would mean. He found out soon enough. From bad to worse.

He forced himself to relax by taking deep breaths. His father had been dead twenty years. Dead and buried. The muscles of his arms rippled, the wings of the owl undulating as though in flight. No getting even with the old man now. Forget him.

But that was easier said than done. He could almost smell the sour stink of stale beer and dead cigarettes that had always surrounded his old man. He'd never been able to stomach beer. Hank used to kid him about his preference for wine, saying there must be some Italiano in his ancestry.

There wasn't. He was Welsh on one side and Irish on the other, and Hank knew it. Hank was pure Welsh himself, could even speak some of their crazy lingo. Like the night they got stewed and tattooed.

'Hell of a thing to choose *aderyn y corff,*' Hank had protested when he decided on the flying owl. 'Why not pick a dragon like mine?'

But he'd stuck with the owl, even after he discovered the Welsh words meant corpse bird. He'd never been sorry. The owl was a night hunter, like he was. Owls existed, were real. They protected a man. Hadn't he survived Nam?

Dragons weren't real. Dragons were myths.

29

And Hank was gone.

Sheba growled, and he came back to himself, belatedly realizing he'd been repeatedly ramming the point of his knife into the wooden tabletop. He glared at the dog and she subsided. Just as well she'd warned him by growling; memories of Hank unsettled his mind and he needed to be calm. He couldn't afford to slip up while he was hunting.

He'd think of the park and the woman he'd find there. A small one, he preferred them little. He liked small dogs better, too — Sheba was too damn big. He scowled at her, and she lifted her head from her food to stare at him. Her hackles rose.

He shrugged. Sheba was afraid of him; he was her master and she knew it. She'd never jump him. He'd put up with her for the six or seven weeks it'd take.

He wouldn't make a hasty choice. He'd made a couple of mistakes in the past, but this time he'd wait until he was sure he'd picked exactly the right one. Then he'd show the other bitch who *her* master was.

4

Sara woke too early to get up and continued to lie in bed with her three cats, thinking about Ian Wilson and his sad brown eyes. For some reason she hadn't deciphered yet, she liked him better than Ralph MacDuffy. Not that she could trust her judgment concerning men — after all, she'd chosen C.W.

The cats wouldn't be inside the house if C.W. still lived with her, much less in the bedroom. But they kept her company in her queen-sized bed, and she'd far rather share it with them than with him.

Namath bit Violet on the ear. She wailed and retreated to the bottom of the bed, leaving her warm spot next to Sara for Namath to usurp. He was a large black and white tom who, until his neutering, had been the terror of the neighborhood in Western Springs, Illinois, where she and C.W. used to live.

Namath dominated the other two cats, though the tortoiseshell, Friedan, held her own. Violet was as afraid of Namath as she was of everything else — people, noises, any new object brought into the house. C.W. had

31

labeled her Shrinking Violet, and had even less use for her than he did for the other two cats.

Someone had abandoned Violet when she was a half-grown scrawny kitten who, because her fur was varied shades of off-white, always looked dirty. A cat no one would want. Sara felt responsible for her after finding her crouched by their garbage can in terror with Namath glaring at her. The placid Friedan was friendly enough toward her, but Violet saw every approach as menacing.

Like me? Sara wondered. Am I as reclusive as Dr. Zimmer seems to believe? The hermit of St. Hubert Street?

Enough of that, she told herself and slid from the bed, yawning. She fed the cats and put them out into the fenced backyard. She eyed the tangle of shrubbery and decided she'd have the man who cut the lawn hack away at it. When he left, C.W. had taken all the garden tools as well as every hammer and screwdriver they owned. Why on earth he needed garden tools in his Chicago condo, she had no idea.

She thought of their first house back in Illinois, where they'd lived for five years — sold in the divorce settlement. She'd never really liked the two story colonial, or the friends she and C.W. entertained there.

It'd been a mistake for C.W. to move to California. All his friends, his contacts, were in the Midwest — he'd played six years for the Bears before his retirement — and he soon realized he shouldn't have left the Chicago area. Luckily they hadn't bought, only rented. When he informed her they were going back, she told him she was staying in California. Alone.

She'd loved San Diego from the first. She still did, despite her loneliness. She couldn't imagine living in that condo on Lake Michigan with C.W. In fact she couldn't imagine living with C.W. again under any circumstances.

Okay, so how was she going to arrange her finances so she could stay in San Diego in the house she loved? By going back to work, that's how. The trouble was, even the thought of looking for a job filled her with panic. When they got married, C.W. had wanted her available for him at all times, so she'd given up her special ed position at the county center, and she hadn't worked since.

It wasn't a question of not being able to find a job, because special ed teachers were always in demand. And it wasn't that she didn't like helping handicapped kids — she did. The job at the county center in Illinois had been her first one out of school; because she'd gotten married, she'd stayed less than a year, and she hadn't worked since. She wasn't any too sure she even could.

Dr. Zimmer had suggested she ease back into the working world by becoming a volunteer.

Meet people. Relate to others.

She shook her head. How could she help anyone else when she was doing such a lousy job of helping herself?

Enough of going round in circles. What she needed was to shower, get dressed, and go for a walk in the park to soak up some of that winter sun.

Her house was on a corner lot less than two blocks from Balboa Park, screened from the side neighbor by two sets of hedges, and from the alley by red and white oleanders. She strode along rapidly, seeing no one in the front yards except a Siamese cat at the end of her block, sunning himself on the porch rail.

As she crossed Upas Street to enter the park, a big blond man in a gray sweatshirt jogged past her and she gasped, staring, afraid for a moment he was C.W. But, of course, he wasn't. C.W. didn't live in California anymore. Thank God.

As she entered the park, a young woman, a girl, really, came toward her along the sidewalk with a fat baby carried on her hip in a side-sling. The girl smiled and said good morning, while the baby regarded Sara with round blue eyes. Sara took a deep breath, unable to return the greeting as she fought back the grief she thought she'd buried.

Behind the woman and child, a stocky man walked with his dog. To exorcise her painful memories, Sara forced herself to smile and say hello to the man. He flashed her a surprised glance, and the dog, a black German shepherd — as if astonished, too — stopped to watch her pass. The man nodded briefly and jerked on the leash.

Why had she spoken to that stranger? Was it to be rid of the greeting the woman with the child had given her? Sara smiled ruefully. She'd given the poor man an unwished-for greeting and stuck him with it. Now *he'd* have to find a way to pass it along.

She walked faster, tired of her endless analyzing of her every action and reaction. If only she could stop thinking, and begin doing things instead. Right or wrong things, do them without lengthy pondering and take the consequences, instead of investing every possibility with so many 'what ifs?' and 'why dids?' that she couldn't enjoy anything.

'You're a young woman, barely twenty-eight,' Dr. Zimmer had pointed out. 'Yet you've taken on the protective coloration of an old-fashioned spinster. Why? Think about it.'

Sara felt old. Older than the exuberant MacDuffy, though she couldn't be. Picturing Ian's furrowed face and unhappy eyes, she decided maybe he felt as old as she did. Neither man seemed to be married, at least they didn't act married.

Not for the first time, she wondered how C.W. had behaved when she wasn't around. The pro players had their own set of camp followers. How many of those girls and women had he slept with before their marriage was dissolved?

Dissolution. A strange word. The legal action wasn't what severed the bonds — the acid of hatred did that.

When Sara got back home, she heard the phone ringing before she unlocked the door. Hurrying inside, she grabbed it. Her hello was breathless.

'This is Ian Wilson. Are you free for lunch?'

Surprised, she couldn't think of any excuse not to go. 'Well, I — ' She bit her lip, aware that she wasn't ready to face a man across a small table in an artfully darkened restaurant, nor was she ready to begin the ritual of moves leading to a new relationship.

He waited for her to go on, until she found the silence embarrassing. 'All right, I'll go,' she blurted finally.

'I'll pick you up in an hour. Okay?'

Sara agreed, hung up, and went to survey her closet. Somehow she'd managed to commit herself to something she wasn't at all sure she wanted to do. Why couldn't she assert herself more?

She changed to gold knit pants and a matching sweater that C.W. had never liked. He'd preferred her in dresses. In green. She loathed green. It came from Grandma Saari's superstition about green being an unlucky color, she supposed. As it certainly had been for her.

She shifted from one foot to the other by the front window, until she saw Ian's red Firebird pull to the curb, then slipped out the door and down the walk. She wasn't ready to invite Ian or any other man into her house. Not now, not yet. Maybe never.

They went to Kelly's in Mission Valley.

'A drink?' Ian asked after they'd been seated at the usual small table. He was to her left in a chair, while she sat in the corner of a padded bench that ran along several small tables to the right. For some reason this made her more confident. Not vis-à-vis, after all.

'Screwdriver, please.'

Ian ordered a vodka martini without the olive.

Sara raised an eyebrow.

'Calories,' he explained. 'They creep up on you, when you begin to creep up on forty.'

'You're far from fat.'

'Doesn't hurt to watch it.' His eyes were as she remembered, soft, sorrowful eyes looking out from an otherwise forbidding face.

She found the contrast intriguing.

'Well, Sara without the *h*,' he said, 'I didn't know if you'd come. Why without the *h*? I've been wondering.'

Sara seized on the question with relief. 'It's Sara without the *h* and Ann without the *e*. My mother didn't believe in complicating things. She didn't foresee I'd find myself always explaining.'

'Moira had that problem, too. My wife. Her name was totally unfamiliar to a lot of people.'

As soon as he spoke, Ian raged inwardly. Damn his tongue. He'd had no intention of mentioning Moira to Sara. He never meant to say her name again. The doctor had made him talk, vomit it all out, wanted him to see a shrink, for Christ sake.

'You're married, then.' Sara's voice was cool.

Did she think he was a misunderstood husband out for a fling? For a moment Ian was tempted to let it go at that. His throat fell full, nearly choking him.

'My wife's dead,' he managed to say.

'I — I'm sorry.'

'It's been over six months. Car accident. Our boy was with her. He didn't die.'

Sara said nothing.

'Jamie's in a nursing home,' he added reluctantly. 'Head injuries.'

He felt a light touch on his arm, then her hand was gone. She still didn't speak, and he glanced at her, appreciating her silence.

'The doctor says grief has to be worked through, but grief is for the dead,' Ian said. 'Jamie's a vegetable lying there mindless. He's there and yet gone.'

'I know,' she said softly.

You don't, he thought. No one knows. Why am I telling it again? He stared deliberately into Sara's gold-brown eyes until she leaned away from him, retreating. What was he doing with another woman? What was the use? She'd make him forget in bed, maybe, for a time. But she wasn't Moira, could never be Moira.

'Moira's an Irish name, isn't it?' Sara asked.

'Yes. She was Irish. With true Irish black hair and white skin and shamrock green eyes. You don't see the real green very often.'

'She must have been lovely.'

'The most beautiful woman I've ever seen. I couldn't understand why she wanted to marry me.'

'But you — you're an interesting man.'

He forced himself to put aside Moira and smile at her, at red-haired Sara, small and tanned and solemn. 'Thanks. You're looking very nice today. I like you in gold — it turns your eyes yellow, like a cat's.'

'My cats all have green eyes.'

'Yellow eyes like the big cats in the zoo.' The thought amused him, comparing Sara with her fluttery butterfly movements to a wild animal. Moira, on the other hand . . .

'Have you always lived in San Diego?' Sara asked.

'Native, born and bred. When I was ten, my parents moved to Massachusetts for a couple of years. But we came back, and now I can't imagine living anywhere else but here.'

'Was your wife from San Diego, too?'

'No, she came from the East, oddly enough from Massachusetts. Moira never quite lost that Eastern accent.'

'Does it bother you to talk about her?'

'No,' he lied.

'You must have loved her very much.'

Without warning his head began to pound and he felt the room tilt. He lowered his head to the table, closing his eyes.

40

'Ian, what's wrong? Are you sick? Ian?'

Sara's voice faded in and out of his comprehension, while everything inside his head spun in a dust devil of chaos. He gripped his hands together under the table and waited helplessly.

It didn't last long. Be thankful for small favors. Bad enough to have it happen at all — he thought he was over that trouble. Caused from too many reds, according to his doctor. But he hadn't blacked out altogether this time, anyway. He raised his head slowly, cautiously. He seemed to be all right.

Sara was staring at him anxiously, her hand on his arm.

'What's the matter, Ian?'

'I'm okay now.' He looked around. Thank God he hadn't attracted attention.

'You scared me to death. Are you sure — ?'

'Don't worry. It's something I've had before. I'm getting over it.' He finished his drink and looked at her. Trying to keep his voice from revealing his intense need to get into the open, he asked, 'Are you terribly hungry?'

'Not really.'

He thought relief must be written all over his face. 'Let's drive down to the ocean then. I could use some fresh air.'

'That's fine with me.'

He took a deep breath when they came out of the restaurant, wondering if he could have coped if Sara had insisted on staying there. Noticing her anxious sideways glance at him, he smiled reassuringly at her, at the same time certain this was one lunch date she wouldn't risk repeating.

You've fixed yourself with her really good, Wilson, he told himself sardonically.

The sun shone in Mission Valley, but as they neared the beach, fog cloaked the blue sky and the shoreline wavered in and out of the mist. Ian parked the car and they walked along the edge of the water. Seagulls, hidden by the fog, mewed forlornly somewhere above them.

The briny air made him feel more alive than he had in months. He ought to do this more often. Moira hadn't cared for the beach, and he'd gotten out of the habit.

'What about you, Sara?' he asked.

'What about me?'

'Do you have a past or have you just sprung to life this minute, born here in the fog?'

'I — it's not very interesting,' she said. 'I've lived in San Diego less than a year. Before that doesn't matter.'

'Why?'

Her glance at him was almost desperate, he

thought, curious as to the reason. But her past was none of his business.

'Forget I asked,' he said. 'We'll agree you're a fog maiden, right?'

After a moment she gave him a tiny smile. 'There's a Finnish myth about *Terhan Neiti*, the Fog Maiden. How she'll come to show you your way, if you use the right incantation to call her from her home in the gray waters where the mists hide. But if she comes to you, there's often a penalty. She may carry you off to the rocks, to the crags where *Kivi Kimmo*, the Rock Spirit, dwells. And he steals your memories, so you have no past.'

'That's not necessarily a penalty.'

She glanced at him. 'Everybody has unhappy memories. But we live with them because they're ours.'

'So why not turn *Kivi Kimmo* loose? Then we'd all be rid of the past.'

'But we'd lose the memories of the good times along with the bad. Not to mention what we learned from our past mistakes.'

He'd be willing to give up everything to be able to forget once and for all. Didn't she understand?

'I'd hate to think I might have to make the same mistakes over and over,' she continued. 'Once is bad enough.'

Would he do it over again if he had the

chance? Make the mistake of marrying Moira and go through the good and the bad times?

'I used to love the fog when I was a little girl,' she said, obviously changing the subject. 'But he's made me afraid of it — the strangler, I mean. He always chooses a foggy night. Which reminds me, I didn't think that joke of yours the other night about being the strangler was very funny.'

He forced himself back from the past and tried to make sense of what she'd said. Joke? Oh yeah, he sort of remembered.

'I was trying to warn you that you're too trusting,' he said.

'I'm really not especially trusting. It's just that I'm trying to do what Dr. Zimmer tells me I should — meet people and relate to them.'

Zimmer must be a shrink. Thank God he'd had the sense not to get tangled up with one.

'Shrinks don't know everything,' he muttered.

'But he's right. I can't stay home with my three cats for the rest of my life.'

He couldn't help smiling. 'So here you are on a foggy beach, with a guy who's a hell of a lot crazier than you are, and one who's not as good company as your cats. That's an improvement?'

'Come to think of it, you and Namath do

have a few traits in common. He's the tom.'

'Namath? You must like football.'

'I detest football.' She snapped the words out.

It sounded to him as though she hated more than the game. He glanced at her and noticed her covering her ear with her hand. 'Something wrong?'

'My ear hurts. The wind's cold.'

'Let's go back.'

Once inside the car Ian pulled up his sweater, then unbuttoned his shirt. He took her arm and pulled her to him, placing the side of her head against his bare chest. 'My mother used to ease my earaches this way when I was little. You'll be surprised at how effective it is.'

The move had been too sudden for Sara to protest, and though the intimacy unsettled her, the warmth of his skin did feel good, just as he'd claimed. His hand went over her other ear as he pressed her head closer to him. The pain was easing, but she was far from relaxed. She could hear his heart beat, and it seemed to her the rhythm speeded up as she listened. Hers had, she knew. Earache remedy or not, this was not a good idea. She tried to move away without obviously struggling, and wound up with her head tipped so she was looking into his face.

45

He bent and kissed her without any finesse at all, hard and awkwardly. He held her too tight and she couldn't breathe. She should have hated it, but somehow she didn't.

She should have ended the kiss immediately, but somehow she didn't do that, either.

His embrace was like a drowning man clutching at a life preserver. His lips weren't gentle or coaxing, they demanded. At the same time, she sensed a desperation in the demand and it was this that got through her defenses, unexpectedly arousing her.

Ian needed her.

Shaken by the intensity of her response, Sara finally pulled back. He let her go reluctantly but without fuss, and they stared at one another without speaking. He looked, she thought, as confused as she felt.

One corner of his mouth twitched. 'I suppose that calls for a penalty,' he said. 'You've no choice but to turn me over to *Kivi Kimmo*.'

She spoke without thinking. 'So you'll forget what happened?'

Ian half-smiled. 'I'll forget when you do.'

She knew his words were meant as a challenge, but she wasn't quite sure what about. To be honest? To let him know exactly what she wanted from him, or wanted with him? To reveal her feelings? In any case, she

46

didn't mean to take him up on it.

Though she was still certain Ian needed her, she was now clear-headed enough to ask herself if it was she, Sara, he needed, or if any woman would do. Even if she never forgot the damn kiss, she was afraid it was the latter.

'I think it's time for me to go home,' she told him.

5

When Ian picked Sara up for class the next week, neither of them made any allusion to their abortive luncheon date and what had happened afterward. Sara had decided she'd remain aloof and repel any advances he might make, only to discover he didn't make any. He confused her by being as uncommunicative as she. But she was very much aware of him. Too aware.

'I've decided to look for a job,' she said, when the silence stretched so taut between them that she felt she was going to snap.

As soon as the words were out, she regretted them. Telling someone else was, in a sense, committing herself to doing what she'd said.

'Oh?' His tone was neutral. 'I hope you're able to find something. Midterm isn't the peak time for hiring teachers.'

'I'm hoping there might be an opening in my specialty.' Sara paused, suddenly recalling what he'd told her about his son.

'And that is?'

She swallowed. 'Special ed.'

There was a short silence before he said.

'There's a field I've always felt would be depressing.'

Sara bristled. 'Not really. The kids are fun to work with. The slightest progress means so much to them. It's exciting to see them succeed in even a minor way.'

'Why bother when they'll never be normal?'

She stared at him. 'I can't believe you said that. Anything that improves the quality of life is surely worthwhile.'

He shrugged.

Remembering his dead wife and the mindless son lying in some nursing home, Sara told herself his callous words were only a protective shield. At the same time, what he'd said annoyed her. She believed in the work she did. Special ed kids deserved as much as any child.

In any case, she didn't want to worry about his problems with her own still unresolved. She wasn't ready for their tentative relationship to intensify. If she ever did become involved with a man again, she must make sure he wasn't as damaged as she. She needed stability, and she certainly wasn't going to find that in Ian.

He reached over and brushed her cheek with his fingers in a fleeting caress. 'Poor Sara.'

His touch made her remember the unequivocal demand when he'd kissed her at the beach. She was stirred both by the caress and the recollection. Watch it, she warned herself. Don't forget sex was the last part of the relationship to fade with C.W. Even when you knew the marriage was over. Even when you knew you hated him. Don't fall into that trap again.

You need a job, not a man.

★ ★ ★

In class, Ralph MacDuffy shook off his admirers to monopolize Sara during the break. Despite her realization of how deliberate his charm was, Sara found him overwhelming at close quarters. He really was the handsomest man she'd ever known. You could tell yourself handsome is as handsome does, but physical attractiveness was compelling, none the less. Especially at close range.

'I've borrowed a sitar,' he said. 'While I'm not an expert with it, I've played guitar long enough to sound fairly decent. I think we'll find the sitar better suited to the *Kalevala*. I'll bring both instruments to your house just to be sure. What night is best?'

Sara hadn't realized she'd committed herself to his proposal but saw no easy way out. 'How about tomorrow?' she suggested finally, hoping he'd have to refuse on such short notice.

'Fine. I'm looking foward to seeing you in your own surroundings, Sara. You have such an elusive personality. Eight-thirty?'

She nodded, hoping she wouldn't regret this.

As she got into Ian's car after class, she mentioned the appointment to Ian, as a way of putting distance between them. Distance she badly needed.

'Our Ralphie?' he exclaimed in disbelief as he pulled out of the parking lot.

'Yes. I don't know how the *Kalevala* will sound with my voice but — '

'I hope you realize he's got something else entirely in mind.'

'What?' she asked bluntly.

'Oh, come on, Sara. You may not be a woman of the world, but you're no innocent young girl.'

'Are you warning me that Ralph intends to jump me? I'm really quite capable of taking care of myself.'

'I know you're smart enough to figure he wants to get into bed with you — that's not what I mean, and it's your business anyway. But MacDuffy's a devious type. I wouldn't trust him one millimeter. His big aim in life is to promote himself, to come out ahead of the rest of us. At our expense, if possible.'

Ian might be right, but Sara couldn't think of how her taping of Finnish myths could possibly promote Ralph.

'I want to make the *Kalevala* better known,' she said. 'I had old-country grandparents who made the story very real to me. My mother never dared to tell grandpa what to do — she was afraid of him until the day he died. But I wasn't. He was a wonderful friend to me.

'Even after my grandmother died, he lived by himself out in the woods. He died the next winter . . . they found him in the farmhouse frozen. I remembered how he'd talk of *Pakkanen*, Jack Frost, and I tried to believe he'd gone away with *Pakkanen* to Pohjala, and I cried, but because I knew he loved the old stories, I could believe he wanted to go and was happy there.'

'Pohjala?'

'The dismal Northland. Not death or hell or anything like that. Just the ultimate north. A fantasy place where Louhi reigns supreme. She's a *noita*, a witch. Powerful and full of spite like all witches but funny, too. No one's infallible in Finnish mythology.'

'That sounds like real life.'

Should I tell him I know someone who

believes he's infallible? Sara wondered. C.W., the perfect.

'Okay,' Ian said, 'you've convinced me of what *you* want to do, but if you think our Ralphie's sole purpose is to tape you reading the *Kalevala* to his accompaniment, you're badly mistaken.'

'That's what we're going to do,' Sara said stubbornly. 'And, as far as I'm concerned, that's *all* we're going to do.'

'Even if he's the strangler?'

She glared at him. 'I don't think that's very funny.'

'I didn't mean it to be.'

'You don't seriously believe Ralph — '

'Maybe not, but be careful. I don't trust the man.'

Sara didn't need Ian's warning, she was already nervous enough about inviting Ralph into her home. She didn't like the feeling the invitation hadn't really been her choice, that he'd maneuvered her into it, but she certainly wasn't going to admit that to Ian.

When he stopped in front of her house, she was ready to fend off any embrace he might attempt. He smiled inwardly, as though reading her mind.

'I'll let myself out,' she said hastily, reaching for the handle.

Ian nodded. Without so much as taking a

hand off the steering wheel, he said, 'Good night, Sara.' He waited until she was safely inside her house, and then drove off.

The perfect gentleman, she thought peevishly, not quite certain why his exemplary behavior had annoyed her.

That night she dreamed she was trapped inside the rain forest aviary at the San Diego Zoo. The aviary was one of her favorite places at the zoo, with its exotic jungle plants and its colorful birds flying overhead. But in her dream, she'd inadvertently gotten off the path through the aviary and some unknown, unseen menace stalked her through the heavy growth, while birds twittered, chirped, and whistled all around her, oblivious to her danger.

She woke after midnight with her heart pounding and turned on the light to calm herself. Reassured by the cats' drowsy purring, she turned off the light and lay back down. But she was a long time relaxing enough to drift off to sleep again.

★   ★   ★

When Ralph rang her doorbell the next night at eight-ten, twenty minutes early, she let him in with careful casualness, trying to act as though she did this all the time. In reality, he

54

was the first man she'd ever invited to her house. True, C.W. had been there, but uninvited.

She wore an old pair of black pants with a long-sleeved loose top that showed nothing of her figure. All the lights were on. Namath and Friedan sprawled on the couch, although Violet had hidden herself behind the refrigerator at the first ring of the doorbell.

Ralph was dazzling in an open-necked white sport shirt, revealed when he shed the matching sweater. 'I've brought wine,' he announced.

'Oh. Thank you. I did make coffee.'

'I insist on opening this. Selfish of me I know, but I'd like your reaction. Where do you keep your wine-glasses?'

Before she could protest, Ralph was opening cupboards making himself at home. She felt invaded.

'Wonderful,' he said. 'This is lovely crystal. Austrian, I believe.'

Though C.W. had insisted on taking the sterling silver flatware when they split up, he hadn't wanted their wedding crystal, so she'd inherited it by default. She hadn't had any occasion to use the glasses since the divorce, and it annoyed her to see Ralph appropriate two of them without asking permission. As if it were his house, his crystal. He was as arrogant as C.W., she told herself, holding her tongue with difficulty.

Ralph opened the bottle with easy expertise, smelling the cork and giving it an approving nod before setting it aside. He poured the wine into two glasses and handed one to her. The wine was white and very dry. Also very good, Sara decided, her irritation easing a bit. C.W. had preferred sweet wines, which she loathed.

'Quite genuine,' Ralph said. Sara assumed he meant the wine, but he waved a hand to indicate the room.

'This tile has to be original,' he added.

He meant the house, not the wine. 'Yes. I was lucky enough to buy it from the builder who'd renovated it and lived here until he sold to me. He was a nut for authenticity and used everything he could salvage from the original house.'

'You live here alone. Never married?'

'I'm divorced.' Sara's words were clipped.

'I've never had the courage to commit myself to marriage,' Ralph said, smiling at her as though to suggest maybe she was the one who might change his mind. 'Perhaps someday . . . '

He's really a phony, she thought. At the same time his nearness made her so edgy she couldn't sit down. Damn, but the man was sexy. Why did she find herself reacting to a man she wasn't sure she liked?

Ralph glanced at the cats on the couch, eased to the floor, and opened one of the cases he'd brought.

'This is the sitar,' he explained, holding up a three-stringed instrument with a neck much broader than that of a guitar. 'Now, if you'll come over here, we'll get started.'

Sara picked up her copy of the *Kalevala* and perched on the edge of the chair nearest Ralph.

'No, no — on the floor.' He patted the rug. 'I'll need to glance over your shoulder until I find the rhythm.'

Sara sat next to Ralph, wondering why she was so reluctant to get close to him.

'I'll start chording,' he said. 'You begin when you like, and I'll try to pick up the beat.'

She'd never heard a sitar, and for a few minutes she just listened to the minor key chords. An Indian guitar, the dictionary had defined it, and the music definitely had an Eastern sound.

At the same time the sound was right for the Finns, she decided. Grandpa Saari would approve. He used to say he was half-Lapp and half-devil, and grandma would laugh and tell him one was as bad as the other.

Sara began reading at random:

'Sons of men, O never venture
In the course of all your lifetime
Wrong to work against the guiltless
Guilt to work against the sinless
Lest your just reward is paid you
In the dismal realms of Tuoni!'

Ralph's chording seemed to fit exactly with Vainamoinen's warning of the tortures awaiting evil-minded sinners in Tuoni, the Finnish realm of the dead. The eerie sound of the sitar wove in and out of her words about the everlasting fires and the loathsome snakes of hell.

After a time her throat became too dry to go on and she closed the book, ready to get up and offer Ralph some coffee. Before she could rise, he set the sitar aside and draped an arm over her shoulders.

'We make a good team,' he said, smiling.

If he'd tried to draw her closer she'd have been able to thrust him away, but he didn't, he just sat beside her, his arm around her loosely.

'Would you like some coffee?' she asked.

'Let's finish the wine, instead. No, don't move, I can reach it.' He picked up the bottle and refilled their glasses.

Sara drank hers too quickly.

'You're a very attractive woman,' he said.

Sara laughed and was surprised to hear the laugh come out as a giggle. 'Ian Wilson — he's one of your students, too — thinks I look like you.'

'He's the fellow with the assassin's face you're always talking to?'

She nodded, blinking. Assassin's face? Ian?

'The resemblance is the hair color, of course,' Ralph said. 'Like me, I'm sure you've been subjected to the mixed blessing of being a redhead.'

'I hated my hair when I was young,' she said. 'Even now, sometimes.'

'Afraid of the strangler?'

'Yes, but not only that. Redheads are never anonymous, we can't get lost, even in a crowd.'

He laughed. 'I've never wanted to be either anonymous or lost in the crowd.'

Sara could believe that. She glanced at him and found his bright blue eyes on her. They were sitting too close together. Ralph lifted his glass and touched hers in a toast.

'To us as a team,' he said.

She tried to edge away unobtrusively, but his arm tightened and prevented her from moving.

'The sitar's perfect with the *Kalevala*

verses,' he said. 'I'll bring my tape recorder next time.'

Next time. She really didn't want him here again, did she? Sara's head spun from too much wine. I need a cup of coffee, she told herself and reached up to move Ralph's arm. He caught her hand in his.

'Such a tiny thing,' he said. 'Bird bones.' He leaned toward her. 'Your eyes are as big as saucers. Afraid I'll gobble you up?'

Suddenly it seemed like C.W. was sitting next to her instead of Ralph, C.W. who used to say he could bring her around any time he chose, because she didn't know how to say no to a little loving. When Ralph bent his head to kiss her, the feeling intensified. He could almost be C.W., trying to humiliate her by making her want him even though she hated him.

Sara pulled her hand from Ralph's and sprang to her feet. 'I'll get the coffee,' she said firmly.

That night she slept poorly. Once she sat up in bed, certain she'd heard an alien noise in the backyard. She listened, her body tense, but whatever the sound had been, it wasn't repeated. The tree frogs were silent, though, something had disturbed them. A stray cat, she told herself, feeling along the quilt for the reassuring warm fur of her own cats.

Sara could tell she'd touched Namath because of his nicked ear, a relic of his frequent fights before she'd had him fixed.

'The word is castrated,' C.W. had said. 'You women make me sick with your 'fixing' and 'neutering.' Can't admit the old penis envy, can you?'

Useless to try to talk to C.W. about unwanted, starving kittens. He saw everything one way only. His.

Namath's head was up, she could feel his tense muscles under her fingers. Had he heard something, too? After a moment he yawned and curled himself back into a ball and began to purr. The frogs resumed their piping.

Go to sleep, Sara, she told herself. You're safe enough behind your locked doors. You even let a man inside the house and survived.

Ralph must be serious about taping the two of them doing the *Kalevala*. He'd hardly concoct such an elaborate scheme just to make it with her. Not with so many obviously willing women in the class. Pretty ones, too, most of them younger than she.

What would it be like to go to bed with Ralph? It annoyed her that she wondered, but she couldn't help being curious. He'd be smooth, she supposed. Unless he was kinky. Now why should she think that? A subconscious reaction? If so, she had no idea what had triggered it.

Ian would have no finesse at all. Sad-eyed Ian with his dead wife haunting him, as C.W. still haunted her. Only worse — Ian might never be free of Moira's ghost. But the day would soon come, she hoped, when she'd never be reminded of C.W. again. Former loves didn't linger forever in the mind, once the feeling was gone.

But what if death had claimed C.W. before she'd divorced him? She might be reacting quite differently, clinging to his memory as Ian clung to Moira's. Perhaps she'd have elevated C.W. to hero status in her own eyes, a position he hadn't held since the very early days of their marriage, never mind the praise the media heaped on him. Great football players weren't necessarily all that wonderful off the field.

C.W., she'd realized before the first year was out, had married her solely because he couldn't get her into bed any other way. It had taken her years to understand he hadn't really wanted her, Sara, his true need was to overcome the challenge she presented.

Do either Ralph or Ian want me? Sara wondered. Me, the person? Or would it just be sex, as it was with C.W.? C.W., who took his pleasure according to what he wanted at the moment, regardless of his partner's wishes.

Not so different from the rapist, really, except afterwards the rapist killed and mutilated.

Oh, God, why had she thought about him?

His last victim had been found in the park about a month ago, concealed, so the paper had said, among a thicket of pink oleander bushes. Raped, strangled, and mutilated like the others, though the paper gave no details of how she'd been mutilated. Strangling left no blood, but mutilation must. Blood on the pink oleander blossoms.

Sara shook her head and determinedly switched her thoughts. Was it oleander flowers or leaves that were poisonous if eaten? For all she knew, maybe the entire plant, roots and all, was. Like the South American upas tree. The street a block away was named Upas, after the tree.

From death to poison, she chided herself. Why can't you think of something more upbeat?

The only thing that came to her was the Finnish love charm Grandpa Saari had taught her long, long ago. Curious to see if she still remembered the Finnish words correctly, she murmured:

'*Kultani kallihin*
Minum Sydameni sinulle,
Sinum sydamesi minulle.'

Smiling a little, she repeated the words in English. 'Golden one, priceless one, my heart to you, yours to me.'

Another myth, charming enough, but no charm existed to make one person fall in love with another. It was just as well. Love was dangerous enough without being forced into it against your will.

The way Grandpa told the story, the Sea King uses the charm to make Juma's three daughters, one at a time, fall in love with him. It was a Bluebeard kind of story, in which the youngest daughter finally gets the better of the wily Sea King. So, in the end, the love charm brings him nothing but pain and loss.

Luckily Sara didn't believe in magic charms, because, while she'd recited the Finnish incantation, Ian's face had sprung unbidden to her mind. She had enough trouble without love. And she sure as hell didn't need any more pain or loss.

6

He walked Sheba through the park, glancing at the women who passed. Maybe she'd be here again today. He'd seen her twice in the park since she said hello to him. He'd watched her, keeping out of her sight. Was she the one?

The other redhead he'd noticed had bigger boobs. Both were small women, the kind he liked. He had another week or so before he had to make up his mind. It excited him to watch first one, then the other, debating his choice. There'd finally be a sign, he knew, that would show him which woman was right for him.

Once he was sure, it'd be goodbye, Sheba. With no regrets. He hated the damn dog, and he knew she hated him in return. He usually got on with dogs and it riled him that the shepherd wouldn't warm to him. It was almost as though she suspected what was coming.

She was a nuisance now and would be later. For one thing, he'd have to dig a damn big hole.

Forget Sheba. Pleasanter to think about the

women. The one with the big boobs worked in a clinic near the park. The other redhead lived nearby, he thought. If she was the one, he'd soon be following her home, getting to know what she did every day. And night.

He enjoyed that. Especially when he knew what he'd be planning for her final night.

Sheba tried to stop beside a child who obviously wanted to pet her, but he jerked on the leash, forcing her on. Even though she knew he was her master, the damn dog persisted in trying to have her own way. But he couldn't get rid of her, she was already irrevocably associated with the two redheads. To give up Sheba meant he'd have to give both of *them* up, too, and he had no intention of doing that.

Hank's Nam pup had been brown and white. Hank loved dogs. 'Unlike human hearts,' he'd said, 'the heart of a dog never forgets.' Probably quoting some poet, as usual.

He'd have remembered Hank's words, even if the truth Hank had spoken hadn't been forever etched in his memory by what happened. Some stinking Cong geek had stolen the pup, tied explosives to it, and turned the dog loose to find its way back to Hank.

His teeth clenched. Don't think about it,

you'll bring on a nightmare. Here, with people around. But the scene unrolled before him, despite all he could do to prevent it. In desperation, he turned off the walk and plunged into a thicket of oleanders, dragging Sheba with him.

She gave a short, irritated bark and he turned to glare at her. To his horror, he no longer saw a black German shepherd. A floppy-eared half-grown dog stared at him. A brown and white booby-trapped mongrel.

'No,' he whispered, dropping the leash and backing away.

The dog took a step toward him and he panicked, forcing his way through a green jungle tangle of branches. He slid down an embankment and ran along a trail winding through a brush-lined gully. He didn't dare look back, certain the dog was hot on his heels. When it reached him, he'd go up like a rocket, blown into bloody shreds along with the damn dog.

Just like Hank.

7

Because she'd spent half the night mulling over her differing feelings for Ralph and Ian and what her reactions might mean, if anything, Sara woke late to the irritated protests of the cats. She stumbled into the kitchen half-awake to fix their food, and promptly tripped over Violet who screamed and fled.

The roar of the lawnmower startled her, causing her to spill orange juice all over the tiled counter. A great way to begin the day.

The lawnmower meant Bobo was here. She'd have to remember to tell him to cut the back shrubbery.

'Yeah, I got tools,' he told her later, as she stood beside him in the small fenced backyard. Because he wore dark glasses with reflecting lenses, she'd never seen his eyes. Blue, she'd decided on the basis of the sunstreaked blond hair held back with a red bandanna across his forehead. It troubled her not to know for sure, but not enough to ask him.

'Don't take too much off,' Sara said. 'Just enough so that I can see where one bush ends and another begins.' She actually preferred the jungle look, but everything was so tangled it couldn't be healthy for the plants. Besides, she'd recently read a police warning that advised homeowners to keep the foliage next to their houses pruned, to discourage burglars from hiding in the overgrowth while they pried open windows for entry.

If a burglar could hide in her bushes, so could the strangler.

Bobo faced her. Was he staring? Maybe she should have put a bra on under her T-shirt. She hated sunglasses that showed only the onlooker's reflection, hiding any emotion of the wearer. He smiled, showing even white teeth.

The better to eat you with, my dear.

What was wrong with her? Bobo was merely the gardener. She'd hired him on the recommendation of the previous owner, and had never yet had any trouble with him.

But he knows I'm a woman living alone, she thought.

Stop it. He's only a kid, maybe twenty at the most.

She was getting worked up over nothing. He'd been cutting the lawn ever since she'd been in the house — four months now. He'd been unfailingly polite. Even thoughtful. Didn't he take care to leave his dog in the pickup so the cats wouldn't be frightened?

The phone rang and she hurried into the house. She half-expected to hear Ian's voice and, in her confusion when she realized she wanted it to be him, she was a moment or two recognizing the caller as C.W., of all people.

' . . . thought we'd have lunch.'

She stared at the phone.

'After all, we're not exactly strangers.'

What does he want? she wondered.

'I can't,' she managed to say finally. 'I'm busy. Busy looking for a job. What are you doing in San Diego?'

'I was up in LA making a few contracts for the old company, and thought since I was so close, I'd drop down here to see how you were getting along on your own. Just pop in for a friendly little visit.'

Her heart sank. Was the sporting goods company he sold for going to transfer him out here? She'd thought the Midwest was his permanent territory. Furthermore, she deeply mistrusted his apparent solicitude for her.

'Well, if you haven't got time for lunch, I'll just come by and say hello,' he went on.

'C.W., I don't — '

'In about an hour.' He hung up.

Just like him to cut her off before she had a chance to tell him to stay away. For reasons of his own, he might pretend he was concerned about her, but he actually had no consideration for anyone except himself. It wouldn't occur to C.W. that she didn't want to see him. Not in her house. Not anywhere. Not ever again. Whatever he wanted from her, she was damn well determined not to give him. Unless he could prove it was his by right.

Her mind scurried along the familiar grooves. The cats annoy him. Are they inside? No, thank God, I let them out. I'd better pick up the living room before I take these jeans off and put on a dress. He hates jeans.

Dustcloth in hand, she stopped abruptly. What was she doing? Still trying to please C.W.? The man she'd divorced once she finally learned she could *never* please him? Good grief! What was the matter with her?

All of a sudden the house seemed stifling, so she grabbed a sweatshirt, yanked it over her head, and rushed out, heading toward the park. She was barely aware of Bobo loading the power mower into the back of his truck. Two doors down a sprinkler sent a flurry of cool drops onto her as she hurried by.

She relaxed a little when she reached the line of palms marking the park boundary. There weren't too many people around this morning and, occupied by her own worries, she paid them scant attention as she passed

71

them. An old woman. A man with a black German shepherd. Another man with a tennis racket.

C.W. played a good game of tennis. C.W. was good at all games. Damn C.W. What was he up to now? What could he possibly want from her? And just why was she running away from him?

She slowed her flight as she realized what she was doing. Turning reluctantly, she retraced her steps. She'd have to see him, he'd persist until she did, so she might as well get it over with.

A dog emerged from a bunch of oleanders, its red leash dragging as it approached. A black German shepherd. Sara stopped, vaguely recalling passing a man walking a dog like this one. She looked around but no man was in sight. The dog loped toward her, tail wagging. Sara held out her hand for the shepherd to sniff, then patted the dog's head before stooping to gather up the leash. Where could the owner have gone? And what was she going to do with the dog?

Unlike some shepherds, this one — a female, she saw — was friendly. But even if she didn't have the cats, she couldn't bring her home, because this was no stray dog. No doubt she'd gotten away from her owner. He must be looking for her. Sara didn't intend to stand here holding the leash while she waited for the man to appear, and yet she hated to turn the shepherd loose. What if she ran into the street and a car hit her?

Glancing about, Sara's gaze fixed on a nearby park bench. She'd tie the leash to one of the bench legs; the dog would be safely immobilized and easily visible to the searching owner.

As she was testing the knot, a woman's voice said, 'What a handsome dog. I didn't know shepherds came in black.'

Sara swung around. A pretty young red-haired woman smiled at her.

'She's not mine,' Sara said, 'she's a runaway. I'm leaving her here for her owner.'

'Oh.' The woman frowned. 'But what if no one comes for her?'

'I don't live too far from the park,' Sara said. 'I'm sort of in a hurry now, but I'll come back and check.'

The woman glanced at her watch. 'I'd stay with her, but I'm already late for work.' She gestured toward a cluster of tall clinic buildings rising near the park. 'I suppose the dog'll be all right here.' She reached to pet the dog's head before hurrying off.

When Sara came to the edge of the park, she paused to look back at the dog and saw a stocky man approaching the bench. She waited, watching until he bent to untie the leash. Then she turned away, nodding in satisfaction, happy that dog and owner had been reunited.

Back in the house, her momentary lift of spirits vanished as she brushed her wind-blown hair. C.W. had insisted she leave it long and straight because he liked it that way, so one of the first things she'd done when they split up was to have her hair cut, permed, and styled very short.

But eventually it had grown to an awkward length, and the curl was only a memory. She needed to decide whether to go short again or have her hair restyled at this length. She made a face at her mirror image and tied her hair back with a blue scarf. She didn't change clothes.

When C.W. rang the doorbell, she was surprised to find his face looked vaguely unfamiliar. She'd thought she knew each nuance of his every expression, but this was a new C.W. standing in the doorway. A divorced, gone-away-for-good-thank-God C.W. The blond hair was as thick and curly, the eyes as blue, the cleft in his chin as charming as she remembered, his shoulders as broad, but the entire man was somehow diminished.

'How have you been?' she asked neutrally.

'No problems.' He looked her over. 'You

look rather bedraggled.'

'I'm fine.'

He glanced at the living room, went through the kitchen to the back door. The cats were back inside, and Namath came to rub against his ankles. Stupid cat, she thought, watching C.W. shove him aside roughly with his foot. Despite the many rebuffs, Namath never had been smart enough to steer clear of C.W..

'I see they're still around.'

'The cats? Yes.'

'Your yard looks good.' He sounded surprised.

Sara didn't mention that she'd just had Bobo prune the shrubbery.

'Why are you here, C.W.?' she asked. 'And don't give me that crap about being concerned about me.'

'God, you have a suspicious nature. I'd forgotten.'

I won't let him rile me, she told herself firmly. I'll stay calm, cool, and in command for once.

'I suppose you're pretty well settled in now and have been through all the boxes.' His tone was too casual, alerting her to the fact that he wanted something from those boxes.

'As a matter of fact, no, I haven't gotten

around to unpacking some of them.'

'Oh?'

'Are you still based in Chicago?' she asked, ignoring his raised eyebrows.

'Yes, of course.'

'Did you say you flew to LA on business? The West Coast isn't really your territory, is it?'

'Are you questioning what I told you?' Indignation laced his words. Too much indignation.

She folded her arms. 'I know when you're not telling me the truth. I should; I've had enough practice. But I really don't care why you went to LA. What does concern me is why you came to my house. What do you want?'

'You've changed,' he said. 'You used to be more hospitable.'

She refused to react, silently waiting for him to confess his real reason for being in San Diego. In her house.

'As a matter of fact, I came by to pick up something that must have gotten in with your things by mistake.' He smiled disarmingly.

She didn't smile back. 'What?'

'I'm sure you remember my coin collection.'

'No. I never knew you had a coin collection.'

'Well, the coins, then. You knew about them.'

'We saved silver coins. Is that what you're talking about?'

'They were mine!'

'Ours.'

'Oh, come on, Sara.' His voice was impatient.

'If you mean the sack of silver coins we both contributed to, yes, I did find that.'

'Good. Then I'll just pick them up and be off. I don't mean to distress you, Sara, I know this visit opens old wounds for both of us.'

'I sold them,' she said.

'God damn it!' he yelled. 'That money was mine.'

'Ours. So I'll be happy to give you half the proceeds, since we both did collect the coins.'

'What were you thinking of, you stupid bitch? I'll bet you were cheated on the deal, you never were any good at that kind of thing.'

'I'll give you half of what I got,' she repeated, refusing to be intimidated. 'That's fair.'

He clenched his fists, scowling at her, but she stood her ground, hardly believing she was actually asserting herself with C.W.

The phone rang. C.W. reached for it.

'Hello?' he growled. 'Sara. Yes.' He held out the phone to her.

Ian's voice came over the line. 'Sara?'

'Yes.'

'Are you free for a drink tonight? A drink and dinner? I owe you a meal.'

'Yes, of course, Ian. What time?' When she hung up, she smiled sweetly at C.W.

'Who was that?' he demanded.

She shrugged. 'I'll write you a check for the money.'

He grabbed her shoulders. 'Answer me!'

She pulled away. 'You have no right to ask me questions about my personal life. For that matter, you had no business answering my phone.'

He glared at her for a long moment, then whirled and stalked from the house.

Sara sank into a chair, temporarily exhausted. She'd done it — confronted C.W. without backing down, and actually come out the winner! A first.

I'll send him the check, she decided. It's only fair. It's a small price to pay for not having to see him again. I'm going to be damn careful how I commit myself to any man ever again. C.W. had seemed wonderful at first, she'd been too infatuated to notice any flaws. She'd been seven years younger, of course, and seven years dumber.

She'd accepted Ian's dinner invitation impulsively — at least partly because C.W. had answered the phone. Well, going to dinner with a man didn't commit her to anything but a thank you afterwards. She glanced at her watch and scrambled to her feet. Ian was certain to ask how her job hunt was coming. She'd make a start by going through the newspaper ads.

Somewhat to her consternation, she found two possibilities. Aware she had no choice but to make the attempt, she picked up the phone. Taking a deep breath, she dialed the first of the listed numbers.

When she hung up for the second time a few minutes later, she was shaking all over. They both wanted to interview her. She'd managed the calls, but how in hell was she ever going to make it through two interviews — one tomorrow and one next week?

Come on, she admonished herself, you handled C.W., didn't you? That's tougher than facing any interviewer. The worst they can do is turn you down.

She'd never been an aggressive type, but it seemed to her that before C.W., she used to have more self-confidence. Dr. Zimmer's words about self-made victims came to her and she grimaced.

Escaping into the backyard, she examined

the bushes Bobo had trimmed, aware that the cutting back had to be done, while mourning the loss of the yard's wild look. Children's voices drifted from one of the backyards across the alley, and even after all this time, an arrow of loss pierced her heart.

If her baby had lived, she'd still be tied to C.W. No matter how estranged they became, the child would always be a bond between them. She'd probably still be married to him. But not happily.

C.W. had been a mistake, one she'd refused to acknowledge for far too long. Sara sighed. She needed to practice standing up for herself. She'd have been wiser to choose a course in self-assertiveness training, rather than one in mythology.

Forget C.W. and his put-downs. What did *he* know? Both Ian and Ralph found her interesting, and neither of them called her a stupid bitch. Not that she wanted a close relationship with any man at the moment. If ever.

Hearing the unmistakable rattle and cough of Bobo's old truck starting up jarred Sara from her introspection. She still spent too much time thinking and not enough doing. Maybe it was just as well she'd agreed to have dinner with Ian.

Which reminded her that she hadn't

decided what to wear tonight. Her turquoise jersey? Ian had never seen her in a dress. Mentally running through her wardrobe, she let herself out through the gate, walking around to the front of the house, planning to sit on the front steps and bask in the sun for a while.

She stopped short, recoiling in horror. Blood spattered the cement of the front walk. Namath lay across the steps, literally torn to pieces.

8

Sara managed to control her nausea long enough to gather the cat's pitiful remains inside a plastic bag, but as she scrubbed her hands over and over in the bathroom, she began to gag, then vomited.

Bobo, she thought after she'd emptied her stomach and washed out her mouth. Bobo must have let his dog out of the truck. Poor Namath. Surely Bobo hadn't intended such a thing to happen. Had he?

From the back door she called the other two cats. After a few minutes Friedan, fur ruffled, dashed from the shrubbery and into the house. There was no sign of Violet. Sara walked into the backyard, calling, and heard a faint mew from above her head. Looking up, she spotted Violet high in the acacia tree. No amount of coaxing budged the cat. At last Sara left her there, hoping hunger would eventually bring Violet down.

Two hours later, when she'd begun to consider calling the fire department to rescue Violet, the cat finally started working her way down the tree. When she reached the ground, Violet streaked inside the house and hid behind the refrigerator. She was still there when Ian came by to pick Sara up for dinner. Once they were in his car, she told him about Namath.

'What a nasty shock for you,' he said. 'It's too bad. I feel sorry for the cat and for you, but dogs and cats are natural enemies. You really can't blame a dog for doing what his instinct tells him is right and proper.'

Sara didn't blame the dog, she blamed Bobo. 'I'm keeping Violet and Friedan in the house,' she said. 'I thought Violet would stay up the acacia forever. I don't see how I can ever let them outside again.'

'Of course, you will. Being shut up is hateful to cats. They'll drive you crazy.'

'You must have a cat of your own.'

'Moira had a Siamese. I gave the cat away after the accident.'

Sara wondered if he'd tell her more about his wife's death, but he didn't go on. A small uneasy silence fell.

'Who answered the phone this morning?' Ian asked abruptly.

'My ex.'

'I can feel the words you're not adding,' he said. 'Like it's none of my business.'

Sara shrugged. 'No big deal.'

'Okay, but tell me if you ever want my help. I feel sort of responsible for you.

Stupid, but there it is.'

'Responsible!' Sara's voice rose. 'I'm twenty-eight years old, and I've been married and divorced, for God's sake.'

'I said it was stupid. Maybe I react to your dreaminess. You don't seem to know what's going on around you half the time. I've watched you in class. You're in another world.'

Ian's right, I'm always rehashing the past, she thought. Why be annoyed with him? I do hold too many interior monologues.

'Besides, I'm almost ten years older than you,' Ian went on. 'Maybe no wiser, but ten years more disillusioned. Take our Ralphie for example. You don't seem to understand what kind of — '

'I don't care to discuss him,' she said crisply.

'How long were you married?' Ian asked after another silence.

'Seven years. Until I learned enough to know I'd better finish the marriage, before it finished me.'

'Yet you're friendly enough with your ex to have him visit you.'

'I didn't invite C.W. — he just showed up. And I don't care to talk about him, either.'

What was this sudden possessiveness? Sara asked herself. Ian had absolutely no claim on her. If he continued such an attitude, she'd have to stop seeing him. No way was she going to have her life directed again by a man.

⋆ ⋆ ⋆

Damn it, Ian thought, I'm messing up. He didn't want to be involved with Sara, with anyone, but when he wasn't with her, he remembered every movement she made, the way her hands fluttered as she tried to explain some point, the way she ducked her head and turned away when she was out-argued or embarrassed.

I can't afford to get obsessed with her, he warned himself, knowing at the same time he couldn't keep away from her. He had no right to be jealous of her ex or of that ass MacDuffy. But he was.

'I don't belong to you,' Moira had warned him. 'One person can't own another. Let me loose. If you don't, I'll smother.'

Long-limbed Moira with her high breasts, her sly green eyes. So different from small-boned Sara, whose eyes revealed her every thought. Why did she attract him?

'Would you come with me the next time I go to see Jamie?' he asked impulsively.

'Jamie? Oh, your son.'

'Yes, I try to visit him once a month. Not that he knows I'm there.'

'You can't be sure of that.' She leaned toward him, peering into his face. 'He may sense your presence, but be unable to show it. Tell me more about Jamie. Does he see? Hear?'

'They think he sees and hears, but that his brain can't — as their lingo goes — process the input. Like he's a computer with malfunctioning chips.' Ian's face twisted. 'No one seems to remember he's my son.'

She put her hand over his. 'It's hard for you, I know.'

He jerked his hand away. 'How can you know when you've never had a child?'

Sara clutched her hands together. 'But I did. She died before she was born. They told me she was dead, and I had to carry my dead baby around inside me for two weeks until they decided to induce labor. It messed me up for a while — my head, I mean. The doctor lost patience with me. He was a man, and no man can know how it feels to have a dead baby inside.' She turned her face from him so he couldn't see her expression.

'I'm sorry,' he said. 'Are you all right?'

'Yes.' Her voice was choked and husky.

He pulled the car over to the curb, put his arm around her, and held her.

She clung to him momentarily, then cleared her throat, and sat back. 'I thought I was over that.'

'Grief is always there, waiting for your defenses to go down.'

This time the silence lasted until they reached Pirate's Cove, overlooking the bay. In the restaurant he ordered vodka martinis for both of them, hoping alcohol would drive away the demon of melancholy that had settled in him, but instead he found himself superimposing Moira's face over Sara's.

'We're a cheery pair,' Sara said finally.

'I was remembering the past,' he admitted. 'An exercise in futility.'

'How long had you been married?'

'Ten years. Jamie is eight. I've always felt the accident was my fault.'

'I thought you weren't with them.'

'I wasn't. But Moira — I — we argued, and she was angry when she left the house.'

He could see her clearly, Moira standing by the door, eager to be away, furious with him, tossing her head so her long black hair swirled over her shoulders.

'Good God, Ian, can't I go out the door without you conjuring up imaginary lovers?'

'All I said was I couldn't see why you don't pick up Jamie after his swimming lesson, instead of having me go after him,' he'd protested.

Moira shut her eyes and gave an exaggerated sigh. 'Because I'm dropping him off and then going to Fashion Valley to shop, that's why. You know very well the pool's miles from Fashion Valley. What's the matter with you, Ian? I'm taking him, it's only fair you pick him up — you aren't all that busy. Besides, it wouldn't hurt you to spend more time with your son.'

He suspected her of having an affair, that's what was wrong with him. His beautiful Moira, so lovely men turned to watch her. Had she been meeting other men all along? An occasional Saturday afternoon shopping trip had always been her thing, but now it was every Saturday, and when she came home she looked — different. Had he been too naive to notice before?

His stomach churned in distress, at the same time he felt a fierce desire for her. Moira had never looked more lovely, her face flushed with annoyance, her eyes bright with anger. He reached for her, but she glared at him, spun around, and called to Jamie to hurry up, she was waiting.

Ian thought of grabbing her, ripping her clothes off, and taking her right there in the living room, but his son came in and Ian turned away. He'd never seen Moira alive again.

He shook his head to dispel the memory and found Sara's grave amber eyes staring into his. As he watched, her pupils dilated and, suddenly aroused, he leaned over to kiss her.

Sara pulled back after a lingering moment, her breathing quickened. What was the matter with her, that she could respond so easily to two men? Maybe it was normal, but her upbringing allowed for only one at a time. Warmth suffused her body from Ian's kiss, just as when Ralph had held her. Before, only C.W. affected her. Casual kisses from other men had been just that. Casual. Now . . .

She stared into her drink, not wanting to look at Ian. A relationship with him would be difficult. He was moody, morose, and in love with a dead woman. Yet she felt he was capable of more genuine feeling than Ralph. There'd be no complications in going to bed with Ralph, that's all he wanted from her, wasn't it?

Then why didn't she? She certainly wasn't ready for another possessive man like Ian showed symptoms of being. She'd be better off not going out with Ian again. Yet the thought of him going alone to see his brain-damaged son tugged at her heart.

89

One more time, that's all.

After they'd eaten, Sara asked for a doggie bag so the cats could have her leftover fish. Her throat tightened when she remembered there were only the two females left.

'Are you afraid of me, Sara?' Ian asked, when she tried to say goodbye to him on her steps before unlocking her front door. 'After all, our Ralphie's visited you at home. He can't be less of a threat than I.'

'I don't mind you coming in,' she said. 'But I'm not — I don't — '

'Are you afraid of sex?'

'No! But I'm afraid of mistakes. My marriage was a disaster I'm still recovering from. It was wrong for C.W., too.'

He smiled wryly. 'I'm not proposing.'

'Sex isn't that casual for me,' Sara said. 'I need time.'

'I won't come in tonight,' Ian said, 'but you can't keep me out forever.'

After he'd left and Sara was alone in the house, she began to wish she'd at least had Ian walk through the rooms with her — their dark emptiness made her uneasy. What if it hadn't been Bobo's dog that killed Namath? What if the strangler waited for her behind one of these closed doors?

Stop it! she warned herself. But she couldn't relax until she turned on all the lights and examined every room in it, closets included.

I ought to get a dog myself, she thought. One that would get along with Friedan and Violet.

The phone rang.

'Hello?' she said.

Silence.

'Hello!'

Was someone breathing on the other end of the line? She'd heard about breathers. But how could one call her, when her number was unlisted?

Sara slammed down the phone, only to have it ring again. She lifted it cautiously.

'Hello?'

Breathing.

This time she hung up, then unplugged the phone.

Who knew her number? Ian, of course. And Ralph. And C.W. She didn't have it printed on her checks, so no one could acquire it easily.

Ian or Ralph wouldn't do such a thing. Would they? A chill crawled along her spine. What did she really know of either of them?

She did know C.W. Definitely not his style.

The sound of breathing ought to be asexual, but she was sure the breathing she'd heard was a man's. A man waiting on the other end of the phone. Did he gloat at her fright and distaste?

I won't think about it, she told herself. He can't call me again tonight. Never mind that I can't call out, either. I won't need to.

As she settled herself into bed with the two cats, it occurred to her that the breather could come to her house instead of calling. If he knew her phone number, wouldn't he also know where she lived? She lay rigid in bed, unable to close her eyes.

Wasn't he most likely a stranger who'd punched buttons at random and gotten her number by sheer accident? He wouldn't know where she lived or who she was.

But what if he was the strangler? What if he'd followed her because she had red hair, and watched to see which house she entered? Sara forced herself to take in a deep breath and let it out slowly. He couldn't know her phone number from following her. Anyway, no one *had* followed her, she was being silly.

Suddenly she sat up in bed, frightening Violet. Bobo. Had she ever given Bobo her number? She couldn't recall. She pictured Bobo's face, his dark glasses hiding God-knows-what. Madness? Lust?

She sighed wearily. This was stupid. She'd read to distract herself from these dark notions, read until she got sleepy. The bedside lamp was still on. Sara eased from the bed and padded over to the small bookcase against the wall. Many of the books had been gifts to C.W. that he hadn't bothered to take when they split up. C.W. wasn't a great reader. Some of the books had never even been opened.

One entitled *The Short History of Decay* caught her eye. The author was unfamiliar to her — E.M. Cioran — but the title was intriguing. Anything was better than lying in bed frightening herself.

She opened the book at random and a sentence sprang up at her. 'Once man loses his faculty of indifference, he becomes a potential murderer . . . '

Then again, 'The devil pales beside the man who owns a truth, his truth.'

Sara shivered at this reminder that men with obsessions are dangerous. Even if a man spoke the truth about his ideas or convictions, how could you tell the reasonable men from the fanatics?

Ian?

Ralph?

Bobo?

She laid the book aside and went into the kitchen to make coffee. If she couldn't sleep anyway, she might as well drink coffee. The cats joined her, blinking in the light. Friedan decided she needed food if Sara was going to have something, but Violet crouched unhappily under the table, suspicious of this unusual activity in the middle of the night.

I can't continue like this, Sara told herself. The cliché woman, terrorized without a man in the house. I'll have the phone number changed, surely the breather is a stranger who dialed mine by accident. A new number will stop him. There's nothing to be afraid of, nothing but my own emotions.

Bobo is merely a guy earning a living doing yard work. Naturally he wears dark glasses, since he works in the sun. Hardly sinister.

Ralph's a handsome man on the make, used to getting his own way, of not having women refuse him. He *is* hard to refuse, but he's no more frightening than any Don Juan.

And Ian. Still mourning his wife but reaching out for — what? Sex? Love? Understanding?

Well, who doesn't want those things? She did, didn't she?

Violet spat suddenly and shot out of the kitchen, disappearing into the living room. Friedan stopped eating and shifted to face the back door. Sara looked, too, and froze as she heard the unmistakable sound of a key being inserted in the lock.

9

Before Sara could force herself to move, the back door opened and a man stood framed there.

'C.W.!' Relief washed over her, to be replaced almost immediately with anger at his presumption. Her gaze left him to check the hook over the counter where she hung the extra key. Missing. He'd lifted it when he was here earlier. Damn him!

He came into the kitchen.

'What are you doing here?' she demanded.

Yet despite her anger, she couldn't help but be glad that she was no longer alone in the house. Even though she didn't want C.W. here.

C.W. swayed on his feet. 'No money,' he said, the words slurred.

'You're drunk.'

'Yo. And broke.'

'You can't spend the night here. You must have a hotel room.'

He shook his head. 'Bet the plane ticket, too,' he mumbled. 'Friendly l'il game.'

Gambling again. God only knew how many

times he'd promised her he'd stop. He was hopeless.

'What about credit cards?' Sara asked, as he slumped into a kitchen chair.

'Accountant's got 'em locked up. Cut expenses down, he tol' me.'

She sighed. 'I'll make you some coffee.'

'Good ole Sara.'

From where she stood she could see the back of his head, where the hair was thinning. Inexplicably a lump came into her throat. She wanted no part of C.W. anymore, and yet she'd loved him once. He was growing older but no wiser. She felt a hundred years wiser than C.W.

'I'll fix you a place to sleep in the living room,' she said.

He looked at her owlishly. 'Wanna sleep with Sara.'

'No way. I only have one bed, so you're going to sleep on the couch.'

He reached for her as she passed him but she evaded him easily. Friedan came out from under the table and eyed him cautiously. There was no sign of Violet.

'Damn cats.' He looked around. 'Where're the others?'

'There are only two now. Namath is — he was killed.'

'The hell you say.' He reached down and

picked up the startled Friedan. When she realized he didn't mean her any harm, she settled into his lap and began purring.

'Don't mind this one,' he said, 'it's that slinking one I can't stand. Too bad it wasn't her.'

I'll have to make sure Violet isn't hiding in the living room, Sara thought.

'Here's your coffee,' she told C.W. 'Drink it while I get the sheets.'

When she led C.W. to the living room, he collapsed onto the couch and began to snore. She pulled off his shoes and covered him with a sheet. Sara expected to be wakeful, but once she crawled into her bed, she fell asleep quickly. In the morning C.W. was grouchy.

'Don't snap at me,' she said. 'I didn't invite you here.'

'I'm not even welcome in my own house,' he complained.

'It isn't your house, this never was your house. It's mine. I traded you my half of the equity in the Western Springs house for the down payment on this one, as you well know. This is my house, C.W., and I want the key you used last night. You had no right to take it.'

He fumbled in his pocket and slammed a key on the table between them, making the coffee in his mug slop over.

'Do you have any money at all?' she asked.

He shook his head. 'God damn poker game last night.'

'All right, I'll look up the receipt for the silver coins. You can have your half. I'll have to write a check, though.'

She paused on her way out of the room. 'I don't want you coming here again without asking first,' she said coldly. 'Just like the house isn't your property, neither am I, and my time belongs to me.'

'You've changed,' he said. 'You've gotten hard.'

'I'm not hard. But I certainly hope I've changed.'

He stood up and lunged, grabbing her so suddenly she couldn't escape. His lips were warm and familiar on hers, but his kiss no longer stirred her.

'I can still make you want me,' he told her.

'No.' She struggled to get away. 'That's all over, C.W., let me go.'

'Little Sara,' he said, lifting her off her feet and carrying her toward her bedroom.

Panic rose in her and she pounded him with her fists. 'No, put me down. Stop it!'

She fought him as he threw her onto the bed. 'You can't, C.W., damn you, let me go!'

Only when she realized he wasn't going to stop did she begin to cry in angry frustration, because she wasn't strong enough to prevent him from undressing her. He yanked off her panties and forced her legs apart, lying across her heavily. Her rage left no room for any other emotion.

She was still sobbing when he finished. When he rolled off her, she slid from the bed and fled into the bathroom, where she locked the door and flung herself into the shower.

Even after a thorough scrubbing, she felt defiled. Raped. Horrible, even when the man was once your husband. Horrible because it's against your will, terrible to be so helpless. Whoever first said 'relax and enjoy the inevitable' had to be a man. A woman would know better.

She didn't want to unlock the bathroom door. Having to look at him would make her sick. Wrapped in an old terry-cloth bathrobe she kept hanging on the inside of the door, she sat on the floor cross-legged.

If I'd had a knife, I would have killed him, she thought. She started to tremble and hugged her arms across her chest. I really would have killed him. I hate him. You can't trust any man.

'When you're through in there, Sara, I'd like the money,' C.W. called through the door.

She was speechless.

After awhile he began to coax her to come out and finally, getting angry, threatened to break down the door. Knowing him capable of that, she unlocked it and pushed past him to get her checkbook. With shaking fingers she wrote out a check for four hundred dollars.

'That's close enough,' she said. 'Take it and leave. If you ever try to come here again, I'll call the police.'

'Those coins were worth more than eight hundred,' he complained.

'Damn you!' she screamed. 'Get out of my house or I'll call the cops *now*.'

He laughed in disbelief and all control left her. She picked up the nearest object, the metal coffeepot, and threw it at him. He ducked. Coffee spewed over the floor and across the wall. She flung a cup, a plate, silverware. C.W. retreated from her attack and she ran after him, shouting incoherently. He grabbed his jacket from a chair in the living room and fled through the front door.

She locked the door and leaned against it, spent, while tears rolled down her face and dripped onto her neck. At last she pulled herself together and went into the bedroom to get dressed. She rolled the sheets C.W. had used together with her bed linen and the clothes he'd torn off her and threw them in the washer, wishing she could cleanse herself as easily.

She picked up the broken dishes and scrubbed the kitchen wall and floor. The coffee pot was dented but seemed useable, so she made more coffee, then sat staring into the mug. It was too late to call the police, she'd already showered. Besides, she didn't want to notify them. C.W. might not be playing pro ball anymore, but his name and fame hadn't yet been forgotten. The media would have a field day if his ex-wife accused him of rape. Even if the police didn't release her name, some scandal sheet was sure to dig around and discover who she was.

Sara shuddered, imagining being badgered by newspaper and TV reporters. Facing them would be as bad or worse than the actual court appearance. And even then she might lose the case, who could tell? She couldn't go through all that and survive.

Something nudged her ankle gently, and she looked down at Violet. She'd forgotten to feed the cats.

Violet buried her nose in the can of cat food, but Friedan didn't appear. Sara walked from room to room calling her. The cat wasn't in the house. Had she gone out with C.W.?

Sara opened the back door. 'Kitty, kitty,'

she called, fear gripping her when Friedan didn't come. She searched the yard and along the street. No cat. Reluctantly, she locked Violet in the house and left for her interview, hoping Friedan would be waiting for her when she came home.

Some impression she'd make at the interview. Maybe she should postpone it. She smiled bitterly, thinking she could call and say that due to being raped she couldn't make it today. But she needed to go, needed to get away from what had happened.

Someone spoke to her as she crossed the park but she didn't answer, she was in no mood to greet strange men. Only after she'd gone by did she realize he was the man with the black shepherd.

It was after three when Sara got home, certain she'd botched the interview and made the worst impression of her life. Anxiously she circled the house, calling Friedan. When she saw the dark mound humped on the cement by the garbage cans, she stopped and leaned against the side of the garage.

I can't face anything more, she thought. I can't. Please don't let Friedan be dead.

But she was.

Not torn apart as Namath had been, but contorted, her face in a rictus of death. She lay in a pool of vomit. Had she been poisoned? Sara glanced about. Was someone watching, someone who gloated over her reactions when she found her dead pet?

She shook her head, gagging, and stumbled inside to find a plastic bag.

Later, locked in her house, she curled on the bed with Violet clutched to her. Her throat ached but she couldn't cry.

The phone rang. She started up, then put her hand to her mouth. What if it was the breather? She couldn't bear to find him on the line. She listened to the rings, counting to ten. There was silence for a few moments, then the phone began to ring again.

Sara forced herself to her feet.

'Hello?'

'Sara — what's the matter?'

'Oh, Ralph. I — nothing's the matter.'

'Your voice sounds odd. I've been thinking about what you've told me about your grandfather's stories. Do you think you might have enough material to put a book of folk tales together? I'd be willing to help with the editing and, of course, I do know publishers interested in that sort of thing.'

Sara struggled to focus on what he was saying. 'I don't know. I'm no writer, Ralph.'

'You don't have to be. Tell the stories into the tape recorder, and I'll have them transcribed, then I'll edit them.'

'I'll have to think about it.'

'Until Thursday, then. We can discuss it after class. I thought we might go out for a drink. See you then.' He hung up before she could accept or refuse.

Like C.W.

She stared at the phone, her annoyance at Ralph fading as she wondered if a book of Finnish folk tales really could be published. What if she didn't get chosen for either special ed job? She had to earn some money soon, she couldn't live off capital forever. C.W.'s alimony payments stopped in a few months, the judge had felt she could work, could support herself, and she could hardly disagree. Though she wasn't extravagant, she was already spending more than his monthly checks because of the house payments.

She wished she didn't have to take another cent of his money. She'd like to deposit C.W.'s last few checks in the bank and donate them to charity. If she got a job, she would. If.

'Work is good therapy,' Dr. Zimmer had advised. 'Think of the interviews as challenges.'

Obviously he'd never interviewed for a job after being raped. For all she knew he'd *never* gone through the miserable uncertainty of an interview. Much less the horror of being raped.

Could she really make money from her childhood memories? Sara thought of Grandpa Saari's tales of magic grist mills and bewitched maidens and the casting of spells. The woods of Finland once were full of *noitas*, wizards who dealt with the supernatural as an everyday routine, thinking nothing of slipping out of a noose totally unharmed, after being hanged for some escapade or vanishing altogether from a locked dungeon.

There was *Terhen Neiti*, the Fog Maiden, who might aid the traveler lost in an unfriendly mist, might aid him and expect nothing. But one never knew. She might decide to exact a price for her assistance by bearing the traveler away in her damp embrace to *Kivi Kimmo*.

I've changed my mind, Sara thought. I'd gladly give away my memories. *Kivi Kimmo* is welcome to everything I've ever known of C.W.

As far as she was concerned, life would be better if she had a little magic of her own, a few spells to use against the world's dangers.

The thud of the evening *Tribune* against her front door startled her. She brought it in and headed for the kitchen, to fix a sandwich to eat while she read the paper.

The lead story featured a letter received by the newspaper purporting to be from a woman who'd managed to escape from the rapist-strangler and had fled the city. Now she wrote to warn possible victims.

'I don't know how else to let people know,' the letter read. 'He said he'd watched me for over a month, getting ready. He said he liked to know about the women he took. It was dark, but I could see he was a white man, and later I saw a tattoo of something with wings on his upper arm. It might have been a bird.'

Sara picked up Violet who was nudging her ankles and stroked the cat automatically while reading on.

'I left San Diego because I was afraid he'd get me again — and I'm not coming back. He knows me, but I don't know him. He started to choke me and something happened to make him stop. I think it was a light, I remember a light flashing. All of a sudden he let me go and I sprang up and ran, and there was this bunch of kids in an old van and they gave me a ride. I got away and I'm never coming back. But I had to tell, maybe someone will know who he is and stop him. He needs to be put away where he can't ever get out. Or shot. I'd like to shoot him myself.

'It was because of my red hair, he said. That's why he picked me. He said I had a sexy walk. He said awful things like you hear if you've ever had an obscene phone call. Like that.

'I was afraid to go to the police because I'd have to stay in town, I'd have to live where he could get me again, and anyway I can't really describe him. I'm five four and he was bigger than me. Stronger, too. I didn't have a chance to kick him or anything, because he grabbed me so I couldn't move. Besides, he had a knife.

'I don't even like to write about him, it was and it is a nightmare turned real. I'm afraid every moment, but even worse when it's dark or foggy. I got away before he killed me, but I didn't get away before he forced me. He said nasty things all the time he was doing it, some didn't make sense. Like how he hated cats, they were like women.'

Sara stopped reading and tightened her hold on Violet, squeezing the cat so hard she yowled.

Two of her cats were dead. Who had killed them?

What if it was the strangler?

She eased her grip on Violet, telling herself she had to stop this nonsense. If she wasn't careful, soon she'd work herself into a state where she'd be too afraid to leave the house.

It was foolish to panic when, with the new

107

information from the woman who'd escaped the strangler, it was likely the police might be able to find him before he claimed another victim. And even if they didn't, she had no reason to believe she was the strangler's chosen victim. No reason at all.

Other than her red hair.

And her two dead cats.

10

He read the newspaper, frowning. Annoyance, then anger boiled inside him. That bitch! He'd wasted a perfectly good dog on her. When he finished with his latest one he'd find her. It wouldn't be too hard, people left trails behind them wherever they fled. He hadn't worked two years for a collection agency without learning how to track those who skipped.

He flexed his fingers, then rubbed the owl lightly and smiled, thinking of her reaction when she'd realize he'd found her. Excitement gripped him. He'd hold her in the darkness and tell her he'd read her letter and this was his answer. The white flesh under his hands, the hair tangling in his fingers, burning them with fire.

Not yet. Something to savor for the future. He'd never let an account go untraced when he was collecting, he was a man to finish what he started. And he'd started with this other. The letter-writing bitch could wait, could stay frightened, worrying and wondering if he'd find her someday. As he would.

Besides, Sheba belonged to this other.

There'd be no dog when he trailed the one who'd written the letter — he'd used up her dog. Hers had been the black spaniel, a cowering beast, but one who'd bitten him at the last. He should have known something would go wrong.

He picked up the paper again. A van of kids had given her a ride, interfered with what was his. Punks. The boys were bad enough, but the girls were vermin, immoral, letting anyone screw them. If time wasn't so important, he'd track them down, figure out a way to punish them.

He couldn't deviate from the schedule. He checked the small black notebook to be sure he'd carried out every requirement.

Choose dog. Check.

Find bitch. He'd found two.

Follow to learn address. He knew where they lived.

Speak to her. He'd done that. He'd spoken to both of them, but now he'd made a choice.

Cut hair. He hadn't gotten close enough yet to snip a lock of hair. He had to do it undetected, of course, and that was hard in the daylight. But he'd never yet failed.

Until he had the strand of red hair in his possession, he couldn't go any further.

He glanced at Sheba. Though she was lying down, her head resting on her paws, her eyes were open, watching him. He hadn't punished her for running off; punishment wouldn't be fair when it had been his fault, not hers. And she hadn't gone far before someone had found her and tied her to a park bench.

Damn those waking nightmares. Luckily he'd managed to get off by himself, so this last one hadn't landed him in deep shit. No way was he going to be locked in a psycho unit again.

He wasn't crazy, he could think as clearly as the next guy. Unless he was caught in a nightmare. And he came out of those a lot quicker than he used to — the planning for the hunt helped. And the hunt itself kept him sane.

Sheba raised her head, and he realized he'd begun clenching and unclenching his hands. He stopped and grinned at her.

'Your turn will come soon enough, old girl. Till then you'll just have to put up with me.'

11

Sara sat huddled in the kitchen chair, Violet clutched to her, the paper spread before her on the table. The cat struggled to get away, her heart thudding against Sara's fingers.

I'm frightening her, Sara thought. Scaring myself, too. What good does that do either of us? When Sara forced herself to let the cat go, Violet fled into the living room. Sara rose to pour a cup of coffee and noticed her hands were trembling. From the window she saw the long shadows of late afternoon across the backyard and realized night was coming. Soon.

The strangler had a tattoo on his upper arm. Sara didn't know anyone with a tattoo. Wait, what about the men in class? Had she seen their bare arms? She had impressions of curling black hair, blond down over tanned skin. Ian? That's silly, Ian wouldn't —

But she'd never seen his upper arms bare. Or Ralph's either, for that matter.

Bobo worked in T-shirts. With a small flick of fright, she wondered if he had a tattoo. She'd never paid much attention, because Bobo's dark glasses made her uneasy and so she tried not to look at him unless she had to.

It didn't have to be someone she knew. There were men in the park all the time, men in the stores where she shopped, men on the street. Was one of them following her? A man with a tattoo on his upper arm?

Stop it, no one is following you.

She did have red hair, though, and two of her cats were dead. He hated cats.

Night was coming. She was alone.

Better alone than with C.W. C.W. didn't have a tattoo on his arm, no, C.W.'s method of destroying her wasn't by strangulation.

The strangler's victims had always been found in the park. He didn't go into homes and attack women there. She was safe as long as she didn't venture out at night. Surely she was safe enough in the daytime. She didn't go anywhere at night, except to class, and then she was with Ian.

Ian?

'Unless I'm the strangler,' he'd said the second time he walked her to her car. Of course, he'd been joking. Hadn't he?

What turned a man into a killer? Were all men potential killers, just as they were potential rapists? Like C.W.

Ralph wanted her to go out with him after class Thursday night. What did she know about Ralph? Even less than she knew of Ian.

He was handsome, women were obviously interested in him.

The woman who wrote the letter to the paper had been raped. He raped first, then killed. Sara turned back to the newspaper.

' . . . such men are murder-prone due to their unstable ego defense and the surcharge of aggressive energy they carry.'

The paper had found a psychiatrist to evaluate the strangler. Sara read on.

'The victim is perceived as one who played a key role in some past trauma. The murder temporarily releases the tension, but the relief never lasts, because the man is forced to kill his phantom again and again.

'There is often a history of parental violence in childhood, and the child is frequently exposed to early sexual encounters. He comes to equate sex with violence. There is a tremendous sense of release following the act of rape and murder. Unfortunately, the pattern must be repeated over and over.'

The psychiatrist gives reasons, Sara thought. He's trying to make me believe the man is just a traumatized human being. I don't. I won't. Only a monster would be able to plan such a grisly routine, following a woman he doesn't even know, stalking her, planning how and when he'll brutalize and murder her.

' . . . as for the red hair, I can only surmise it links the victims in some way to the key figure in whatever early experience forced the man into deviant behavior. Often there is a memory of the idealized all-giving mother, who in some way is lost or rejected.'

Sara went on to read a review of the four murders attributed to the strangler. Four women dead in less than two years. How many others were near misses like the letter writer? Stay out of the park at night, the police warned. She certainly didn't intend to be there at night. There was no way the police could effectively patrol the area — it must be over a thousand acres of land, with many isolated ravines and wooded hills.

She was safe enough inside her house with the doors locked, and no one locked inside with her. Suddenly Sara looked at her watch.

'Damn,' she said aloud. She'd forgotten about calling the phone company to have her number changed, and now it was too late to notify them today. Who called her and breathed into the phone? The strangler? But how could he have her phone number? Unless he was someone she knew. How was she ever going to sleep tonight, with these fears circling in her mind?

She could take a sleeping pill. She had a few left, ugly red and beige capsules that made her feel equally ugly when she awoke the next day, logy and slow of thought. What if she took one and fell asleep, as she would, sleeping so soundly she couldn't hear the stealthy forced entry, the footsteps creeping down the hall . . .

Stop it!

She didn't take a pill; she read most of the night, dozing off with the lights on, when the birds started chirping at dawn. The phone woke her near noon and she answered it, still groggy.

'Yes, this is Sara Henderson. Who? Mr. Putnam? Oh, yes, yes, I did have an interview with you yesterday.'

She listened with mounting incredulity as Mr. Putnam offered her not the six-week summer position she'd interviewed for, but a job substituting for a special ed teacher in the system who was taking an eighteen-month maternity leave, beginning in March.

'Of course, if you do want to work during the summer,' he added, 'we'd be pleased to have you then, too.'

Pulling herself together, Sara said, 'I wasn't expecting your offer, so I'm a bit over-whelmed.' She took a deep breath and let it out slowly. 'The substitute position sounds fine; I accept. I'll let you know about this summer by the end of the week, if that's all right.'

After assuring her that would present no problems, and arranging for a time when she could come in and fill out the necessary forms, Mr. Putnam said goodbye.

Sara put down the phone and stared at it, unable to make herself believe she'd been offered and had accepted the teaching position. She'd felt like a zombie during the interview, and had been certain she'd made a terrible impression. Apparently she hadn't. Thank God she had a couple of months to brush up on advances in special ed before beginning to teach.

*   *   *

Thursday evening was damp and cold, a fog bank already hovered over the downtown area, and would soon slither across the park. But the gloomy December weather didn't dampen Sara's spirits. When Ian stopped to pick her up, she smiled at him as she got into his car.

'I start teaching in Chula Vista in March,' she told him proudly. 'It's substitute work, but lasts for a year and a half.'

'That's good news. I'm glad you found

something so quickly.'

'I'm not so sure I'm glad. Actually I'm scared to death, because it's been so long since I worked with disabled kids.'

'You'll do fine.' He glanced at her. 'Maybe we should stop somewhere after class and have a drink to celebrate.'

Sara bit her lip. 'I won't be riding back with you after class.'

'Oh?'

'We're — that is, Ralph's bringing me home.'

Ian said nothing for a time. Sara glanced at him, her gaze drawn despite herself to his arms, covered by the sleeves of a gray sweater.

'I'm going Saturday,' he said at last.

'Saturday?'

'You said you'd come with me to visit Jamie.'

'Oh. Yes, I did.'

'I'll pick you up around two.'

Since it was so near Christmas, she wanted to ask him what she might bring Jamie as a present, but she held her tongue, realizing she'd know better after she saw the boy for herself. That would mean she'd have to visit again to bring the present, though. Perhaps she'd better forget about it, Christmas or not.

'Ralph has an idea my grandfather's tales

might make a book,' Sara said after another silence.

'With our Ralphie as co-author, I expect.'

'Well, it *is* his idea.'

'But *your* stories.'

'I can't write, Ian. I'm going to tell them into a tape recorder.'

'A recording that anyone can transcribe from.'

'Ralph knows a publisher who — '

'Our Ralphie *needs* to be published, you mean. Haven't you heard the dictum, publish or perish? It's a must in the academic world.'

She stared at Ian. Was he jealous because she was doing this with Ralph, or might what he said be true? Still, even if Ralph needed the stories for his own ends, she'd never do anything with them on her own. Didn't he deserve some credit?

Ian's words stayed with her as she listened to Ralph's lecture on how Beowulf overcame the monster Grendel. In the past, monsters lurked in every fable and in every mythology, but heroes always arose to finish them off. There were still monsters today — but where were the heroes?

★　★　★

Ian sat in class and watched Sara. She's nothing but a tease, he told himself. Teasing me. MacDuffy. Even her ex, for all I know. Does she nestle in their arms, too, then flee from the final commitment?

Moira had enjoyed sex, wanting it sometimes when he didn't. Is that why she'd taken a lover? Or had she really? Had he angered her with ill-founded assumptions, or was it the fury of guilt that made her hurry from the house and drive so recklessly she caused the accident? Blackness rushed toward him and he closed his eyes, forcing it away with an effort of will.

No. Don't think of Moira. Listen to that ginger-haired bastard, MacDuffy.

' . . . a certain amount of brutality is demonstrated in the Germanic imagination. If you compare the English Beowulf epic to the *Nibelungenlied*, you soon see the latter hasn't a single character who is in any way attractive. Treachery, cruelty, a kind of cosmic destructiveness . . . '

Who cared? Ian thought. The legends of heroes were old. Passé. There were no more heroes. Charisma was punished today. Be different, stand out, and someone will kill you. Besides, didn't a hero presuppose a heroine? A maiden for the knight to rescue? Today women preferred equality to being rescued. Whatever equality meant.

Cosmic destructiveness. Yes, the Germans had certainly demonstrated their capability at that in the forties. But destructiveness wasn't limited to German myths or to the German people.

Sara insisted the *Kalevala* wasn't destructive. Were the Finns so different? Sara was different. A bright butterfly flitting from one to another, fluttering away before she could be grasped. Had it been her husband who made her so wary of men? Or was it something within Sara herself?

I don't trust MacDuffy, he thought. That blonde in the front row is more his style, he likes them under twenty, I've heard. What's he want from Sara? A chance to publish? Or that and something more?

He shook his head unhappily, knowing it was none of his business. But he hated to see Sara get hurt.

★ ★ ★

The blonde pouted at Ralph from the front row. He avoided her eyes to give Sara a quick sideways grin. Damn it, her stories might actually be worth publishing, if she could tell them decently. Quite a bonus. He'd be careful not to frighten her tonight. All business, with maybe the odd pat here and there. A touch of romance. No sex. He liked the feel of her fragile bones under his hands. She'd be so easy to crush.

No good came of rushing things. She was a wary little bitch.

'Now the Minnesingers were a different proposition,' Ralph said, picking up the strands of his lecture. 'Chivalric tales spread from France into Germany and these talented poets . . . '

★　★　★

Chivalry sounded wonderful in the abstract, but Sara knew she'd find it tiresome to be serenaded so worshipfully, on and on. It made the woman an object, no matter how admiringly the poet sang her praises.

She noticed Ralph smile at her. Was Ian right? Was Ralph's only interest in her what she might be able to do for him with her stories? She remembered how he'd held her when he was at her house. There'd be none of that tonight. She didn't know if she could ever stand to have a man touch her again. Damn C.W.

Ralph wore a long-sleeved shirt. Many of the men in class didn't, and had taken off sweaters or jackets. She saw not a single tattoo. But, then, the rapist's tattoo was on his upper arm.

Wings, the woman's letter had said. A bird? Maybe an eagle. Or could the tattoo be of an angel? Not all angels were on God's side — there was always Lucifer, a fallen Angel.

Was it safe to be with any man until the killer was caught? But she didn't really believe Ian was the strangler. Or Ralph. And she couldn't hide in the house all the time. Though she'd be on her guard, she'd go out with Ralph after class.

★   ★   ★

Ralph chose a piano bar in Mission Valley. Sara blinked at the noise and the people, having vaguely expected a dark, nearly deserted lounge.

'I like the Copper King,' Ralph said. 'They always have a pretty girl at the piano.'

A young woman with brown curly hair sat there now, smiling dreamily over the customers' heads as she played a minor-keyed melody. A man's voice began to sing the words.

'I walk upon
The dead leaves of the past . . .

'He has a fair tenor,' Ralph said. 'Anyone can sing here if they choose. Some who do are really lousy.'

'I've never heard this song before.'

'It's French.' He smiled and, looking at her, began to sing softly.

'*Même dans cert ans la hantise*
De votre visage
Continuera a me poursuivre . . . '

'You have a better tenor than he does,' Sara told him, trying to shake off the intimacy he seemed to be striving for. 'The problem is, my French is nonexistent.'

'I told you that your face would haunt me a hundred years from now.'

'Romantic but impossible.'

'Nothing's impossible to a poet,' Ralph said. 'Why shouldn't good things last? That's why I want to keep your grandfather's folk tales from being lost. I'll come over this weekend.'

'I'm busy Saturday,' she said.

'Sunday's fine. I'll bring my tape recorder and leave it with you, so you can tell a tale whenever the urge strikes you.'

Sara pushed away her irritation at his assuming her time was his. Wasn't Ralph doing this for a good cause? 'Come for lunch,' she said. 'Around one.'

On the way home in his car, Sara realized she shouldn't have had the third drink, but she'd hated to leave. The bar had been so warm and bright, the people all having a good time. Nothing waited for her at home except fear and emptiness.

'I envy you a house close to the park,' Ralph said.

She controlled a shiver. 'I don't know about that — at least not lately.'

'Oh yes — that letter in the *Tribune*. The woman's obviously a publicity seeker.'

Sara stared at him. The letter had been so real to her, she'd never considered it might be a fake. 'She didn't give her name, so the publicity wouldn't do her much good.'

'I'm not saying she couldn't be genuine,' Ralph said. 'There's also the possibility one of the reporters concocted the letter.'

Sara shook her head. 'The description of what happened, the tattoo, and the other details were too real.'

'Who can check them? Only the murderer would know for sure, and I doubt if he'll comment one way or the other.'

'I'm afraid,' Sara said.

'I could come in with you,' Ralph offered.

'Not only tonight. I'm always afraid these days. I think maybe he — ' Sara broke off.

Ralph reached over and caressed her thigh gently and quickly, moving his hand before she could react. 'I'll come in with you,' he repeated.

Sara pulled herself together. 'Thank you, no,' she said stiffly. 'I'm quite safe inside my house. I'm just a bit nervous.'

When they started up her walk, Sara saw a dark blotch on her front steps and stopped, putting her hand to her mouth to hold back a cry. Violet! But she'd left the cat in the house, she knew she had.

The cat on the steps plunged past Sara, and she smelled the acrid odor of tomcat urine even as she called Violet's name.

'What's the matter?' Ralph asked.

'I thought my cat had gotten out, but that was just a stray tom.'

'Would you like me to come in with you and look around?'

She inserted her key before answering and saw Violet jump off the living room couch, startled by the door opening. If Violet had been sleeping there until now, the house was safe. Violet was as efficient as an early warning system.

'Thanks, Ralph, but I'm all right now.'

He stroked her cheek, slowly, deliberately, his eyes half-closed, then dropped his hand, smiled, and turned away.

She chided herself for wanting more of what seemed to be a staged performance. Was a performance. If his emotion had been real, she'd have felt it. There hadn't been any. Why did Ralph pretend? No doubt to impress little fools. Which she'd be, if she fell for any of his practiced seduction.

When she'd locked the door, she felt the emptiness of the house. Coaxing Violet into the kitchen with a chicken leg, she fixed herself a cup of coffee.

What's the matter with you? she asked herself. You're in good health, young. Why can't you relax and enjoy living alone? You don't need a man to share with; he'll only try to dominate you like C.W. Besides, invite a man into your house, and he might be the rapist, the murderer. All *he'll* share with you is violence and death.

Sara defied fate and took a sleeping pill, waking as she knew she would, feeling heavy and out of sorts. Her eyelids were puffy and her mouth tasted like moldy lettuce. The day was overcast and gloomy. She crouched over the kitchen table drinking coffee, until she couldn't stand being inside any longer.

Dressing in her faded blue sweats, she jogged the two blocks to the park, where she usually ran or walked. She'd stay away from the place at night, but there was no reason not to go there during the day when it was perfectly safe. The wind was chill and mist blew in her face, not a true rain but miserable. The park was almost deserted, and there was no one on the benches.

A man with a German shepherd passed her once, then later approached again. She glanced at the black dog and found its brown eyes meeting hers, as if in recognition. This had to be the lost dog she'd rescued, there weren't too many black shepherds around. She recalled that the man had spoken to her the other day, when she was too distracted to reply. Sara tried to examine him without being obvious.

He looked normal, an average-sized man in a khaki windbreaker, who walked his dog in the park. Not old but not young, either. Just a man. His cool gray eyes caught hers briefly, he nodded a greeting and was gone. Was it possible he mistreated the shepherd? Sara wondered. She'd never seen such a mournful-eyed dog.

The man had been harmless enough, but she was glad he hadn't spoken to her today with so few people in the park. The mist combined with the nearly empty park made her uneasy.

She didn't have to walk in the park. In fact,

she didn't have to live in San Diego. She could sell her house and leave. Get away like the woman who wrote the letter to the paper. If she left Ralph and Ian behind, she wouldn't have to worry whether one of them might be a psychopath.

On the other hand, did she actually think one of them might be the strangler? An easy way to find out was to ask Ian to push up his sleeves and take a look at his arms tomorrow. She could do the same with Ralph on Sunday. Chances were she wouldn't find a single tattoo, and then she could stop this foolishness.

But what if she did find one? What if a winged creature flew on an upper arm? Sara shook her head and realized she was trembling.

If I were still seeing Dr. Zimmer, she thought, he'd tell me I'm paranoid. He'd say face my fears, do something about them. Why am I so afraid? There must be thousands of red-haired women in San Diego. Namath could have been killed by Bobo's dog.

Why couldn't she remember if Bobo had a tattoo? He often peeled off his T-shirt when he mowed.

Friedan could have been poisoned by the people across the alley, who liked to feed the birds. They'd complained several times about her cats going into their yard and scaring the birds.

Was she imagining a campaign of terror directed at her?

Still, the woman in the paper had said the rapist hated cats.

Sara hugged herself against the chill, deciding she might be getting a cold. Her throat felt raspy and she had the beginning of a headache. If she were still a little girl, Grandma Saari would say, 'Into the sauna with you!'

On her grandparents' farm the sauna was a wooden building behind the house, not one of today's fancy hot tubs or steam baths. Just a wooden shed where stones were heated over a wood fire, and steam was created by pouring water onto the hot stones. Primitive, but the extra work made the stifling steam yours, the heat your own doing.

Evergreen branches stimulated the skin, though she'd never whacked herself with them like the older people did, since a light slap here and there was enough to release the fragrance of the spruce boughs. Afterwards, Grandma always had to push her out — into the snow if it was winter, the icy white fluff tingling her flesh. Into the cold lake in the summer. Once was usually enough for her, and she'd rush into the house to dress. The older people, though, would alternate heat and cold until they felt completely cleansed.

Would the sauna cleanse her now of all the debris accumulated in her twenty-eight years. Would the steam banish the chill of her spirit?

Grandma Saari had often told her how the saunas were communal in Finland in the old days — large buildings where village women gathered. Babies were born in the sauna. There was the story about the virgin, Marjatta, who became pregnant by swallowing a talking cranberry and who was refused admittance to the village sauna when her time came to deliver.

The cranberry story was hard for the villagers to swallow, so poor Marjatta, like the other Virgin Mary, found a stable in the woods and had her child among the horses. A lively boy, healthy, though fatherless.

Not like my baby, my little girl who didn't even live to be born. The child I carried dead within me and whom I never saw. The doctor wouldn't let me see her. I had everything for her — a father, a doctor, a hospital, a home — but she didn't wait.

Sara put her hand to her throbbing forehead, feeling worse with every step she took. She turned and headed home, where she stretched out on the couch and fell asleep.

The jangle of the phone woke her. She sat up, confused, answering on the sixth ring. It was the phone company with her new number. Unlisted. She scribbled it on a pad near the phone. Now no one could reach her, not even C.W. Instead of relief she felt a tremor of fear, as though she'd further isolated herself.

Don't be foolish, she thought. You can call out, but he can't call in. The breather. The murderer. Were they one and the same?

Realizing she felt a little better, Sara fixed toast and tea, collected the *Tribune* from outside the front door and prepared to read it while she ate.

'For almost two years,' she read, 'San Diego has been plagued by a series of murders. A letter printed yesterday from an intended victim has given police a new lead in their hunt for the rapist-strangler. The *Tribune* has cooperated in every way with the police department, and now we ask that any other women who may have escaped from this man to come forward with information. Don't be afraid of reprisal. We've been assured all names will be kept secret, and the police will do everything possible to protect anyone furnishing information. Remember, what you know may save another woman's life.'

Sara read on with morbid fascination, while the article reviewed each murder in detail — four in all — and then quoted a psychiatrist who felt the strangler had a set pattern he was incapable of deviating from.

'If we speculate that there may have been at least one other failure besides the letter writer,' the doctor said, 'then the man seems to operate on approximately an eight-week schedule. This would put the date of his next attempt about a week from tomorrow, or perhaps two weeks, if we regard the time schedule loosely.'

Should I go to the police? Sara wondered. What can I say? I've got red hair, two of my cats are dead, I've been getting peculiar phone calls. Not really information of value. It'll mean nothing to them if I say I'm afraid. How many other women reading this article are afraid, too?

A week from tomorrow. Maybe two. Is he scanning the paper right now, the murderer, looking for articles about himself? How does he feel reading about the crimes he's committed? I wonder if he relives his emotions, gloating, even getting sexually excited.

She grimaced. He couldn't be anyone she knew, she didn't know any monsters. Sara's mind jerked back to the other morning, C.W.

forcing her onto the bed, making her accept him even though she did her best to fight him off. Raping her. C.W., a man she'd lived with for seven years. Someone she thought she knew. Inconsiderate, selfish, chauvinistic, and belittling, but never brutal until then. How could she trust any man?

A dog barked outside and Violet, who'd been sleeping on Sara's feet, sprang up wild-eyed and streaked into the living room.

I'm getting as bad as Violet, she thought. Afraid of everything, cowering, timorous. Someone who shrinks away from life. I can't be like that; I must resolve my fears. Ask Ian and Ralph about tattoos. Check Bobo out when he shows up next week. I'll find none of my fears has any basis in reality. They haven't. Ian or Ralph couldn't be this deranged strangler. Probably not Bobo either. The reason I don't remember a tattoo on Bobo's arm, must be because he doesn't have one.

I've changed my telephone number so the calls will stop. Violet is safe in the house. So am I. I still have red hair, but so do other women.

Sara got up to pull the curtain across the kitchen window, where the gray drizzle had been blotted out by winter dusk. I won't take any more sleeping pills, she told herself firmly.

The doorbell rang.

12

He'd never had trouble choosing before, never had two at once to choose from. He'd been following them both, and he had to stop. Pick one. One only. The other could wait, would wait until he needed her.

He scowled. It was bad luck to plan too far ahead. Stick to the schedule, don't think about the next time. He jerked Sheba's lead and the big dog resisted, lifting her lip in a snarl before she gave in to his command. He'd really enjoy getting rid of this dog. She watched him with those knowing eyes, as if she were aware of what was in store for her and for the human bitch, too.

The fog clung about the trees and bushes and the park lights wore halos. A solitary walker approached and Sheba growled. The man made a slight detour to pass them. Afraid of her. Big dogs had their uses, but he didn't care much for this one.

Bitch, he thought. A bitch like all women. Only let them get in heat, and they wanted any male they met. Every male. They might pretend different, but they were all bitches in the end.

What the hell did those fancy head-shrinkers know? Talking in the paper about sex and violence. Sex *was* violent, hadn't anyone told those doctors in their ivory towers? Maybe they were all gay. He wasn't, by God, he knew how to be a man.

He fingered the chain around his neck, making sure the heart was tucked under his shirt.

The dog watched him with her knowing eyes, and he swore at her.

The miniature poodle's eyes had been bright and friendly. Minx had been his friend. His only friend. Or at least he'd thought she was a friend. Hank had been so damned sure the heart of a dog never forgot. Maybe not. Minx might never have bitten him, if that bastard who was screwing his sister hadn't gone after him. In the scuffle Minx got so excited and confused she didn't know what she was doing. Maybe.

He'd never really know. It was years too late to speculate. Years too late to tell himself that if he'd been certain Minx loved him, he never would have strangled her. He always wished he could have seen his sister's face the next morning, when she found the present he'd left her.

The fog fluttered about him, soft and feathery as wings. A good night if he'd been ready. But he needed to know more about each of them. His final decision might well rest on which one would be easier to get to at night.

She might have to be the last he'd do in the park. Those articles in the paper were meant to harry him. He could ridicule them as much as he wanted, but he couldn't ignore them. He wasn't a fool, he wasn't crazy. Too much attention added to the risk, and he had no intention of getting caught. Much as he hated to leave San Diego with its wonderful fog, he might have to. For a while. Come back when the fuss died down.

If he left, he'd hunt down that bitch who wrote to the paper. He'd find her all right, but it'd take some time. Time well spent. To simplify his life, he wouldn't bother with another dog until he located her.

Now, though, he was still in San Diego, where the fog was his friend. And he had other prey to stalk.

13

Sara eased the front door ajar and peered through the narrow opening allowed by the chain. Ian stood on her doorstep, his hair damp with drizzle.

'It's only me, Sara,' he said.

She hesitated as his soft brown eyes stared into hers. Finally she unhooked the chain. Ian stepped inside.

'What's the matter with your phone?' he demanded.

'Nothing. I had my number changed.'

'I've been trying to call you for hours. What's the new number?'

'I — it's unlisted,' she said. 'I was getting weird calls. A man who breathed.'

'One of those sickos.' He shook his head. 'I don't blame you for changing your number. What's the new one?'

'I don't know it yet,' she lied.

'I wanted to tell you we have to visit Jamie in the morning,' Ian said. 'Something came up and I can't go tomorrow afternoon. Is the morning all right?'

'Why, yes.' Suddenly she was ashamed by her suspicions. Ian, with his brain-damaged son, his dead wife, Ian a murderer? As a substitute for the apology she could hardly make, she offered him a cup of coffee.

He smiled at her. 'I thought you'd never ask.'

In the kitchen he took off his jacket. His dark blue polo shirt hid his upper arms. Sara busied herself with the coffee, knowing she had to find out, so she could stop upsetting herself over the tattoo business.

'Were you ever in the service, Ian?' she asked, hoping her voice wasn't as tense as she felt.

'Navy. A three-year hitch.'

'Oh. Well, if you were a sailor, you must have a tattoo. Right?'

He grinned. 'How'd you guess? Here I thought the old sophisticated act had taken you in, but all the time you saw through to the callow swabbie underneath.' He reached for his right sleeve.

Sara held her breath, the coffeepot clutched in her hand like a weapon. Ian shoved up the sleeve.

'Glorious, isn't it?' he said. 'Also trite. But what else would you expect of a nineteen-year-old sailor?'

The tattoo was an anchor, blue with red lettering below. USN. A chain twisted up the side.

'That's all?' Sara asked.

Ian pushed up his other sleeve to show a bare arm. 'I'm perfectly willing to strip for you, but if you care to take my word, that's it.'

Sara smiled at him, relief warming her. 'Why don't you come for breakfast tomorrow?'

'Better still, we'll have breakfast out, since I won't have time to take you to lunch. Is eight-thirty too early?'

'No, it's fine. Nobody's bought me breakfast in ages.'

★ ★ ★

Go home without making a pass at her, Ian urged himself. She's relaxed and friendly, after that initial freeze she gave you at the door. Take your time, be careful.

How could he simply walk away when his body ached with the need for her? The way she moved, the quick butterfly motions of her hands, made him edgy with desire. When she got up to get more milk from the refrigerator, he rose and followed her, and when she turned, startled, he put his arms around her.

'Sara,' he murmured. He caught her close, kissing her.

He tried to go slow, but when he felt her response, he lost control. His hands slid along the curves of her body, gathering her hard against him. His lips grew urgent, demanding. She began to struggle, protesting, and he tried not to listen. If he persisted, she'd be his.

'Ian, please, Ian, you know I feel something for you, but not now, not tonight, please, Ian.'

Reluctantly he dropped his hands, let her go. 'I'll see you in the morning.'

He pulled from the curb with a screech of tires, skidding on the wet street. I should have forced her, he thought. She'd have given in, she wanted to. That's what all women really wanted, wasn't it, a man who made them do what they both wanted? A man who threw them on the bed and took them. Would Moira have stayed home, if he'd been more aggressive?

He'd never managed to play the brute, at some point it went against the grain. What was wrong with him anyway? Christ, he was edging up on forty. Hadn't he learned anything in all this time?

He couldn't survive another Moira, another involvement with a woman he loved so much he wanted to die after she did. Yet he'd hated her, too. Talking to the doctor, vomiting all those emotions, had made him realize his deep resentment of Moira's refusal to let him be everything to her, as she was to him. Jamie had gotten in the way and the shopping and — other men? He'd never know for sure.

Now Jamie was paying for his father's mistakes. The sins of the father —

No. Stop thinking about the past. It's gone beyond anyone's control, there's never any way to change what's already happened. Don't get so worked up you'll need the reds and the whiskey to sleep. You know better. Death lies in the pills and the bottle. Dr. Thomas made that thoroughly clear.

Suicide.

You don't want to die, Ian, old buddy, nor do you want more blackouts. The reds lead to blackouts. Think of red-haired Sara instead, with her hangups and her sexy little body and her frightened eyes. Does salvation lie in Sara? She's the first woman since Moira who hasn't been just someone to bed as quickly as possible. Not that you wouldn't like to get Sara in bed, too.

It had been her eyes tonight, pupils dilated in panic as they stared into his, that stopped him. Why was she so afraid? And of what? Of him? Of sex?

She's seeing MacDuffy. Is she sleeping with him? A muscle in Ian's cheek began to twitch.

She's a tease, he told himself. A common, garden variety tease. Don't make her into an exotic flower, another Moira. Get her out of your system, flip her into bed, screw the hell out of her. MacDuffy probably has already, why not you?

When Ian got home he tried to read, gave it up, tried to sleep, and when he couldn't stand being awake with his thoughts any longer, he took three of the red capsules and poured himself a shot. So they didn't go with whiskey. So what the hell?

The next morning Ian was late. Sara had been ready for forty-five minutes, when he finally pulled up to the curb in front of her house. She hurried to the car.

'Sorry,' he said.

He looked terrible. Ill.

'That's all right,' she said. 'If we don't have much time, just coffee's fine with me.'

'Oh, there's time. Jamie doesn't care when we get there.'

Sara glanced at him, then away, uneasy about the sardonic undertone to his voice. 'Is there anything wrong?' she ventured.

'With me? No. I won't pass out in the restaurant again, if that's what you're afraid of. I'm actually quite healthy, believe it or not.'

He took her to a Denny's near Jamie's nursing home, Palo Oro, a facility within walking distance of the park. Ian ordered eggs and sausage, eating with a good appetite. She studied him while she nibbled her toast.

He had dark circles under his eyes, eyes that didn't meet hers this morning. Had he slept at all last night? A strand of hair lay on the wrong side of his part, as though he'd combed his dark hair hastily. Without thinking she reached across the table and moved the strand to where it belonged.

He started, then smiled at her. 'I'm a mess today. Sorry. My barber says if I'd learn blow-drying, he'd style my hair so I could give up the part. What do you think?'

His sad eyes didn't smile. Sara had a fleeting impulse to hold him as she would a child, cradling his head against her breasts, telling him everything would be all right, the hurt would pass.

How could one person ever tell another things would be all right? How could *she* when she couldn't even get her own life right?

'Somehow I don't see you as the blow-dry type,' she told him.

'I'm not sure if that's a compliment or a put-down.'

'Maybe this will help — Ralph's the blow-dry type.'

He grinned at her. 'Okay, then I thank you for your kind words. The part stays.'

At the entrance to Palo Oro, she realized she didn't want to go in. Why had she agreed to come? The building reminded her of the hospital where she'd delivered her dead baby. Other babies cried in the nursery, but hers would never cry.

Ian took her arm. 'What's the matter?'

Sara bit her lip. 'Nothing.'

The lobby, entrance, foyer, whatever, contained brightly colored plastic furniture and dark simulated-wood tables holding pseudo-Spanish lamps. No magazines or any homely clutter. Unused. Sterile. They passed through the emptiness and came to the nurses' station. A gray-haired woman wearing a white cap with a black band lifted her head to look at them.

'May I help you? Oh, Mr. Wilson, I didn't recognize you for a moment.' Her eyes flicked to Sara, then away.

Mrs. F. Hodges, R.N., her name pin read. Supervisor.

'Jamie's still in bed,' she went on. 'The aides haven't had a chance to get him into the chair; you're earlier than usual this Saturday.'

'I don't mind if he's in bed.' Ian's voice was low, he didn't look directly at Mrs. Hodges.

He turned away and Sara followed him down a corridor. Though she tried not to stare into the rooms as they passed, she caught glimpses of old faces, blank eyes, and, in one room, in a crib, a child with a grossly enlarged head.

The hall smelled faintly of urine with an overlay of a scented disinfectant. Sara swallowed uneasily. They passed a teenager in a wheel chair who was drooling. He grinned widely at them. Reminded of some of the kids she'd taught, she smiled back.

Ian entered a room and she went in behind him.

'This is Jamie,' he said.

Sara found herself looking at tousled brown curls, a pale, pointed face, and green eyes with the longest lashes she'd ever seen. A beautiful child. His eyes stared straight ahead at nothing. Jamie's arms, frail and sticklike, lay atop the covers.

Sara leaned over the bedrail until her face was within Jamie's field of vision. She thought something flickered in his glass-green eyes. 'Jamie,' she said softly, 'I'm Sara.'

The eyes focused on her and she smiled at him. 'I'm a friend of your father's. He's here, too.' Jamie's gaze seemed fixed on her face. She turned and motioned to Ian to come closer.

He didn't move.

'Jamie's looking at me,' she said. 'Lean over the bed, so he can see you, too.'

'He doesn't know what he sees,' Ian said.

Sara stared again into the green eyes. She was sure they were focused on her face. Slowly she straightened, and the eyes tracked her until she left Jamie's field of vision. She turned to Ian and grasped his arm, urging him next to the bed.

'Lean over,' she ordered. 'Get close enough so he can focus on you.'

Ian's arm was rigid under her fingers. He shook his head.

'Jamie,' she said, glaring fiercely at Ian, 'your father's going to lean over so you can see him.'

Slowly, reluctantly, Ian bent over the bedrail.

'Talk to him,' Sara said.

'Hi, Jamie.' Ian's voice broke; he cleared his throat.

Sara leaned over far enough to see the boy's eyes. They were fixed on his father's face. A corner of Jamie's mouth twitched.

'He's trying to smile at you,' she said to Ian.

Ian straightened, turned, and left the room. Sara stared after him, knowing he wouldn't return. What should she do? She couldn't walk away and leave Jamie without any kind of goodbye.

Several moments passed before she decided what to do. Bending over Jamie, she smoothed his hair back from his forehead and said, 'Your father and I have to go now, Jamie.'

A sound she couldn't interpret broke from the boy's throat. Acting on instinct, she eased down the bedrail, put her arms around his frail body, and pressed her cheek to his. She kissed him on the forehead before she let him go.

'That's a goodbye kiss,' she told him as she slid the rail back up, 'but I'll be back to see you again. So will your father.'

Ian wasn't in sight when she stepped into the corridor, but Mrs. Hodges was coming toward her. Sara stopped and introduced herself. 'Does Jamie ever say anything?' she asked.

The nurse eyed her for a moment, then said, 'Not words. He rarely makes any sound at all.' She hesitated, finally adding, 'Several of the nurse assistants think he recognizes them, when they take care of him. I can't be sure.'

'Can he move by himself at all?'

'His fingers, a little, sometimes. We do range-of-motion exercises every day, so he won't lose his muscle tone.'

'I know he saw me and heard me.'

The nurse nodded. 'His doctor says he sees and hears. Whether he can interpret what comes to his eyes and ears, no one knows.'

'Thank you for answering my questions,' Sara said. 'I'm a teacher of disabled children, and I'd like to try to help Jamie.' Until she said the words, she hadn't realized she'd made up her mind.

Mrs. Hodges smiled for the first time. 'We could use a few volunteers around here. I never have enough help.'

Sara found Ian pacing up and down outside.

'I didn't mean to upset you,' she said.

He took a deep breath, let it out. 'Jamie was such an active boy, a bundle of energy, always into something. I can't bear seeing him like this, and knowing it's my fault.'

'I thought your wife was driving.'

Ian ran his hands through his hair. 'I fought with her before they left, I made her so angry she had the accident. In a way, I'm to blame.'

'That's sick.' Sara's voice shook. 'You want to punish yourself.'

He glared at her, wheeled around, and strode toward the car. She ran after him. 'Okay, but don't punish Jamie,' she cried. 'None of it was *his* fault.'

He didn't answer, but when they were both in the car, he turned a cold face to her. 'You don't understand.'

Sara twisted in the seat to look him in the eye. 'You think I don't know what guilt is?' Her voice rose. 'I used to tell myself if I hadn't had those drinks at the party, or if I hadn't gone on that boat ride and got so sick, maybe my baby wouldn't have died. I believed I'd done something to kill her, that it was my fault.' She clasped her hands together tightly, fingers trembling. 'Nothing the psychiartist said made me think differently, until one day he told me that whatever I believed I'd done, I certainly hadn't meant to kill her, had I? I'd wanted a live baby, hadn't I?

'Then I realized I had to free myself from the guilt. That's when I was able to see what drove me to blame myself. I still grieve for her, but I've conquered the guilt.'

Ian turned away from her and started the car.

How can I explain so he'll understand? she wondered.

'C.W. didn't want a child, and I went off the pill without telling him,' she began, forcing the words from her tightening throat. 'That was dishonest and I expected to be punished. For a long time, I saw my baby's death as my punishment.' Tears stung her eyes but she blinked them back.

'Jamie can see and hear you,' she said. 'I kissed him goodbye, but it should have been his father kissing him, not a stranger. The child you used to have is still inside him, he still needs your love. Why go to see him, if you don't touch him?'

Sara could see the cords in his throat working, but Ian said nothing. She sighed and gave up. They drove in silence until they got to her house. Ian spoke as she reached for the door handle.

'Wait, Sara.' He grasped the steering wheel, staring straight ahead. 'Maybe we'd better not see each other again. We don't seem to — ' His words trailed off and he shrugged.

'If that's how you feel.' Sara held her body rigid, her words brittle and cold as slivers of ice.

He started to turn to her, then checked. 'Yes, that's how I feel.'

'It's just as well. We could never have much of a relationship.' She spoke the truth, didn't she? Then why did she feel so shattered? She opened the door, started to get out, then turned back to him.

'I'd like to visit Jamie again, if you don't object,' she said.

'Why in hell — ?' Ian broke off and

shrugged. 'Go ahead.'

He still didn't look at her, and she was determined to make him meet her gaze before she left the car. 'Goodbye, Ian,' she said.

'Goodbye,' he muttered.

'Damn it, look at me!'

When he faced her, the haunted eyes staring from his grim face tugged at her heart.

'I'd rather make it *au revoir*,' she told him.

He swallowed and she thought he gave a slight nod, but he said nothing. She eased from the car and strode up the walk to her door, not once looking back.

Inside, she leaned against the door, fighting tears, damned if she'd cry over Ian. What did she care if he never wanted to see her again?

Her half-formed plan to work with Jamie crystallized as she struggled not to cry about his father. The boy could see, she was sure of it, and she thought he could hear, as well. Furthermore, based on the visit today, she believed there was a good chance he understood what he saw and heard. She intended to build on what meager abilities Jamie had shown, to work with him in the hope that she could develop a method of communication between the two of them, and then go on from there.

'Jamie is *not* a vegetable,' she muttered. 'Never.'

★ ★ ★

Jamie lay in the dark, with only the light from the hall slanting in through the door the night nurses left ajar. He was glad they did, because the dark frightened him. Worse than the dreams he sometimes had at night. But the worst dreams of all came in the daytime, because those were true dreams.

They weren't really dreams, more like pictures inside his head. Almost like watching TV. Only real. That's when he wished the most that he could talk. If he could, he would've warned his favorite nurse, the one who used to come in the afternoons, not to go on that boat, because she'd get drowned.

Tears came to his eyes as he thought about her. He missed her a lot.

He'd liked the red-haired lady who came with his dad today, especially after she kissed him goodbye. He didn't get kissed much. Sara was her name, and he hoped she'd come back like she said she would, and maybe kiss him again. Most of all he hoped he never, ever had a true dream about her. 'Cause true dreams were always bad ones, and he didn't want anything bad to happen to her.

Ian cursed and slammed on the brakes, almost running a red light. He had to slow down. Where was he going in such a hurry anyway? He didn't want to go home. Even less did he want to meet the friend who'd invited him to lunch.

Jake was always so damn cheerful. Too damn cheerful. He refused to admit disaster existed. If Jake was on his way to the Silver Strand beach and his car went out of control on the Coronado Bridge, smashed through the rail, and plunged off the bridge into the bay, Jake would tell himself how lucky he was to be wearing his bathing suit.

He knew Jake would bug him about this fall, insist on him signing the contract he'd been offered. He also knew he had to sign it, because he'd need the extra money to provide for Jamie. A year ago he'd have jumped at the chance to be an administrator in the San Diego school district. Why else had he gotten his degree?

'You're an excellent administrator,' Jake would assure him, because he'd been saying the same thing for months now. 'And you're innovative without antagonizing people — a rare combination. We need you in the district.'

That might or might not have been true once, but he wasn't sure how much was left of the old Ian. If anything. But for Jamie's sake, he did have to go back to work in September, whether he wanted to or not.

What Ian really wanted to do was — what? He had nothing to do, nothing to look forward to.

Sara's interference at the nursing home had infuriated him. How he behaved with Jamie was none of her business. Didn't she realize it was almost more than he could bear to show up there every Saturday?

True, she'd lost a baby, but that child was dead and buried. Naturally she grieved for her, but it wasn't the same as having to visit the living dead once a week.

Sara wouldn't let him go his own way, she was forever pointing out new paths, paths he didn't want to take. She was a compulsive interferer. He was right in cutting their relationship short.

Unfortunately, being right didn't stop him from wanting her. Knowing he was better off without her did nothing to diminish his need for her.

Okay, so he did know what he really wanted to do. Be with Sara. But when he was with her, things never seemed to work for them. Sometimes it was her fault, and sometimes his. Theirs was obviously an ill-fated relationship, why get any further into it?

Because he couldn't keep away from her.

Maybe so, but he'd damn well try.

14

Sara spent a restless night, rousing often from dreams of formless terror, to the reality of being frightened and alone in her house. When she saw her bedroom window show light behind the drawn drapes, she rose thankfully to shower and dress.

Fog hung in the backyard, and she wondered if the day would clear or be like the last two, gray and misty. I'll clean the house, she decided, before I fix lunch for Ralph.

He'd expect her to have a few Finnish folk tales ready to tell. She thought of the time Vainamoinen had gone to hell, to Tuonela, and the ugly daughters of Tuoni trapped him there. Tuoni was the ruler of the underworld, but fallible, like all Finnish myth characters, not godlike in the sense of the heroes of Greek and Roman myths.

Grandpa Saari used to tell her the tales as though they'd happened to friends of his, neighbors who lived down the road. Old Vaino might be powerful, but he could behave as stupidly as any human or act as childish. When caught out he'd say:

'True it is I lied a little —
And again I spoke a falsehood . . . '

She'd never thought of Vaino as being godlike.

Ralph, now, if Ralph had hair a little less red and a trifle more golden, he'd be a perfect Apollo. As he'd probably be the first to admit. He was certainly a handsome man, even better-looking than C.W. She couldn't help being somewhat flattered he'd chosen to pursue her.

But did she like *him?* Was she looking forward to Ralph coming today because she wanted to see him, or because it filled the emptiness when someone was in the house with her. Oh, what difference did it make? What did matter was while he was here, she'd have to find a way to check for a tattoo.

Ian's was an anchor, nothing with wings — but she meant to put Ian from her mind completely. Who did he think he was, telling her they shouldn't see each other again?

Actually they'd have to, they were in the same class. Unless he didn't plan to attend any more. Sara stood with the dust cloth in her hand, her throat tightening, as she realized Ian might not come to class and she might never see him again.

After a moment she shook her head and

bent to polish the coffee table. C.W. would label Ian a loser. According to C.W., some guys were winners, some weren't, it was as simple as that. C.W. never thought of himself as a loser, the worst he'd admit to was being a winner in a slump. Winners could make comebacks, but once a loser, always a loser.

Sara grimaced at her dredging up of C.W.'s instant philosophy. She preferred no reminders of him. Still . . . there was something in it. There *were* losers. In fact, she'd begun to wonder if she wasn't one, until the job offer came. Dr. Zimmer, though, would undoubtedly insist losers were made, not born.

She made soup and sandwiches for lunch, with sugar cookies for dessert. Afterwards, she and Ralph brought their coffee into the living room where Ralph had set up the tape recorder. He slipped off the beige shirt-jacket he was wearing over a sleeveless yellow knit shirt, and she stared at his bare arms. The left had no tattoo, but the right was covered by an elastic bandage that wound over the elbow and up the armpit.

'Hurt it playing handball,' he said. 'The doctor thinks it's just a strained tendon, but he advised the support.'

Sara couldn't think of a casual way to introduce the subject of tattoos, so she began to talk into the microphone, telling about why

Vainamoinen went to Tuonela and how he had to outwit Tuoni and all his tribe to return to his home in Kalevala.

' . . . then the wife of Tuoni offered him beer, but the crafty Vaino looked inside the mug and saw frogs and worms swimming in the dark liquid and refused to drink . . . '

As she spoke, she was once again a little girl in her grandparent's large farm kitchen, where the coffeepot always simmered on the back of the old wood range her grandmother wouldn't part with. Grandma always let little Sara have coffee, even though at home Mama didn't.

On the farm she was safe, nothing could happen to her. Grandma and Grandpa wouldn't go away and never come back like daddy had done and, though they were busy with farm chores, they didn't go off to work every day like Mama had to. At the farm Sara was never alone.

'Fine, Sara,' Ralph said when she finished. 'I'll have very little editing to do on that before I have it typed up. You have a way with a story.'

'I just told it like Grandpa Saari did. I remember one more — is there room on the tape?'

'Yes.'

She told about Marjatta's baby born in a

woodland stable and how, when he grew up, he displaced the aging Vainamoinen who, offended, sailed off in a copper boat to a land between heaven and earth.

'That's a familiar myth,' Ralph said. 'Though I admit the Finns add twists of their own to any story. A talking cranberry, for instance. No wonder the poor girl couldn't get anyone to believe her tale. The Holy Ghost sounds so much more impressive. The virgin birth is a big thing in mythology. A mother but no father.'

They were seated side by side on the couch, with Violet peering suspiciously from behind the lounge chair. Ralph draped an arm over Sara's shoulders.

'Are all women in Finland ugly hags or else virgins?' he asked. 'I hear about Fog Maidens and Marjatta or Louhi, the Pohjala witch, who's as repellent as any of Tuoni's daughters.'

'Old Louhi had several very beautiful daughters. Men were constantly getting into trouble trying to seduce one or another of them. Not only Vaino but also Ilmarinen, the smith. There's a story about how Ilmarinen wins the Maiden of Pohjala, acing out Vaino.'

Sara told the tale briefly, and also one about Lemminkainen, another wooer of Louhi's daughters, who wound up chopped into little pieces for his trouble. His mother had to rake him out of the river of Tuonela and put him back together by magic. Then he wasn't satisfied to be merely alive again, he wanted revenge, and so went to the maiden's wedding and created such an uproar he had to flee to another land.

'... and so the lively Lemminkainen enjoyed the women of his land of refuge, while the men were off fighting ...'

'Those old Finns were real swingers,' Ralph said when she finished.

His arm tightened around her, and he turned her face with his other hand. The bandage on his arm brushed against her and she stiffened, pulling away.

'Ralph,' she said, speaking quickly so she wouldn't lose her nerve, 'do you have a tattoo?'

'A what?'

'On your arm. A tattoo.'

'What the hell would I be doing with a tattoo? Of course not.' He stared at her.

'Will you let me undo the bandage and see?' Let him think her mad, she was tired of suspecting every man she knew.

His eyebrows shot up, but all he said was, 'If you want to, go ahead.'

She unhooked the fastener near his shoulder and unrolled the elastic bandage.

There was no tattoo. In silence she rewound the dressing.

Ralph leaned back on the couch. 'Want to tell me what that was all about?'

Embarrassment flooded her cheeks with color. 'The paper,' she managed to say. 'That woman who wrote the letter, the one who escaped the strangler — she said he had a tattoo. Something with wings. On his upper arm.'

Ralph began to laugh. He threw back his head and roared. Sara clasped her hands together in her lap and looked at them, feeling totally ridiculous.

Ralph wiped his eyes with a handkerchief. 'You really thought I — ?' He shook his head. 'Why me?'

'Well, not only you. Any man. I had to know, that's all.'

'The rapist-strangler? That kook who's got a thing for redheads? I've got red hair myself, for God's sake. You thought I might be — ?' Ralph shook his head again.

'I guess I've gotten too worked up to be reasonable about the killer,' Sara said. 'I didn't *really* think you were. The psychiatrist in the paper says he's a lonely man, a reject. While you must have . . . ' Her words trailed off.

Ralph captured her hands. 'I *am* lonesome,

Sara. More than you realize.'

She looked at him, wondering if there was any truth to his words. He leaned over and kissed her, gently at first. Slowly he drew her closer, tightening his embrace until she began to respond. It was warm and pleasant in Ralph's arms, she felt safe. Soon, though, his random caresses became more specific, and his fingers touched her breast. She knew if she didn't move soon he'd try to maneuver her into the bedroom. She wasn't sure she was ready for that. Or that she ever wanted Ralph in her bed.

The doorbell rang.

Sara sat up and smoothed her hair, relieved at the interruption.

'Ignore it,' Ralph advised.

She paid no attention to him, standing and straightening her clothes before she walked to the front door.

To her shock Ian stood on the steps.

'Damn it,' he said, 'I want your phone number. I came to get it, and I won't leave until you tell me.' His words were slurred, his hair disheveled.

He's been drinking, she thought, although she couldn't smell alcohol on his breath.

'I don't know — ' she began, uncertain whether she should let him in or not. On the one hand, he wasn't himself, but on the other hand, his presence would discourage Ralph. At the moment she didn't want anymore of Ralph's company.

Ian solved her problem by pushing past her into the house, into the living room where Ralph still lounged on the couch.

'Hello, Wilson.' Ralph's voice was cool.

'Well, if it isn't the heroic MacDuffy. Been taping Sara's stories, I see.' Ian gestured at the recorder. 'Funny people, the Finns. Mystic.' He sat on the lounge chair. Violet had long since fled the room.

'Is that coffee you're drinking?' he asked.

'Would you like some?' Sara said.

'Why not?'

She went into the kitchen to get him a cup.

' . . . changed her phone number,' Ian was telling Ralph when she returned. They both watched Sara set the cup of coffee on the end table next to Ian.

'I was getting unwelcome calls,' she said. 'A man who breathed.'

'She wouldn't give me the number,' Ian went on. 'Didn't like my tattoo.' He tried to push up his sweater sleeve, finally struggled out of the sweater. Unbuttoning his cuff, he rolled up his shirtsleeve. 'Little old anchor, see?'

Ralph glanced at Sara, smiling wryly. 'Drink the coffee,' he told Ian.

'You think I need it?'

'Frankly, yes.'

Ian mumbled something Sara couldn't make out. He picked up the cup. 'Chug-a-lug,' he said, gulping the coffee all down at once.

'Get him some more,' Ralph told her. 'He's not drunk, he's taken something, I think. Some kind of downer.'

'Talking about me,' Ian said. 'Don't like that.'

· 'What did you take?' Ralph asked.

'Little red pills to sleep, couldn't sleep, I'll never sleep again.'

As Sara went into the kitchen for the coffeepot, she told herself what she really wanted was to get rid of both of them, before their hostility toward one another got out of bounds. She returned to the living room trying to think of a polite way to say, 'Get lost, you two.'

'Wouldn't call you up and breathe at you,' Ian said as she filled his cup again. 'Not my style. Even MacDuffy wouldn't.' He frowned at Ralph. 'I could be wrong about that.'

Ian drank two more cups of coffee and then fell asleep in the lounge chair, his head hanging loose on his neck like a rag doll's. Ralph tried to rouse him but couldn't.

'I don't like to leave him here,' Ralph said,

glancing at his watch. 'I'd stay until he came out of it if I could, but I have an appointment.'

'I'm not afraid of Ian,' Sara said.

'No, of course not.' Ralph's face creased with faint distaste. 'Hardly a sight to strike terror in a feminine breast. Disgust, perhaps. Poor Sara. Obviously the man's fallen for you. I assume you've been trying to dump him, giving you more than one reason for a new phone number.' He checked his watch again.

'Don't worry about me. I'll send him home when he wakes up.'

'Until next week, then.' Ralph smiled at her. 'We'll resume where we . . . left off. You keep the recorder, so it'll be easily available whenever you remember a story.'

Sara let him out, wondering what would have happened if Ian hadn't interrupted. She'd felt no real desire for Ralph, but she'd enjoyed the security of his arms. Would she have bartered herself for safety? Sara made a face, refusing to believe she'd ever become that desperate. Never!

She fixed herself cottage cheese and black currant jam for supper. Ian slept on, oblivious. She checked him several times but he seemed all right. Violet gained enough confidence from his immobility to come back into the living room and jump on the couch next to Sara.

Tenderness for the sleeping Ian crept up on Sara, surprising her. Why should she feel anything for this man, who was tied to a dead wife and a damaged son? He had no room for anyone else.

She got up and knelt beside his chair, stroking the tangled hair from his forehead. She brought a blanket to cover him and kissed his cheek before she went to her room.

I'm sorry for him, she argued in defense of her behavior. I want to soothe him, to comfort him as I would a child.

Once in bed, she fell asleep almost immediately and slept soundly, until a crash aroused her in the middle of the night. She sat up in bed, her heart pounding, until she realized Ian had probably awakened. She thought of the three cups of coffee and wondered if he was looking for the bathroom.

She went into the hall and found him walking unsteadily toward her, silhouetted against the light from the lamp she'd left on in the living room.

'How the hell did I get here?' he asked. Without waiting for an answer, he fumbled his way into the bathroom and closed the door.

She waited, but when she heard the shower

she went back to her room, thinking she ought to get dressed, ought to make him eat something, drink some more coffee before he drove home.

She sat on the edge of her bed in the thigh length T-shirt she slept in, her heart beating faster and faster, her breath catching in her chest. Put on your robe, she urged herself, while she sat and waited as if mesmerized.

At last she heard the bathroom door open. Ian came into her bedroom with only his pants on, carrying the rest of his clothes.

'Sara?' he said.

She rose and went to him. He dropped his clothes as his arms came around her, and she held him to her as their lips clung together. Desire flared through her until her skin burned. Maybe it wasn't wise to let Ian make love to her, but she knew she'd waited for him to come to her, fully aware of what might happen. She also knew she wasn't going to stop him.

He broke the kiss to murmur, 'I want you, Sara, want you so much, feel like I'll die with wanting you.'

Soft as his words were, they jolted through her like an electric current, increasing her own need, making her realize just how much she wanted him.

His caresses weren't smooth and practiced

like Ralph's, they were wild and urgent. His lips were hot, not warm, his kisses didn't coax, they demanded. As he stroked her breast, his hands trembled with the need surging through him. His obvious, desperate desire added fuel to the fire of her own, flaming away the last of her doubts.

They shed their clothes in a flurry of motion, and tumbled onto the bed locked in each other's arms. Sara couldn't remember ever wanting any other man with such intensity. When he rose over her she opened to him with eager abandon, so close to the edge that his first few thrusts sent her soaring up and over.

★　★　★

Sara woke from a nightmare where the strangler had captured her and, his terrible task over, was burying her. Only she wasn't dead. She tried to scream but couldn't. There was a roaring in her ears as the weight of the earth he threw over her made her arms numb. Soon he'd cover her face and she'd die more horribly than even he'd intended . . .

Her eyes opened and the bedroom was light, with sun glinting through a tiny slit where the drapes met. The whir of a power mower came from outside. Her left arm was asleep, Ian's head was lying on it.

His arm was flung across her, the arm with the red and blue anchor. She grimaced. But then she turned her head and saw his unshaven face, relaxed and young in sleep, and began to smile. His brown hair curled over his head. Like Jamie's, she thought. The boy's green eyes might come from Moira, but the hair was Ian's.

She lifted her free hand and stroked his shoulder. His eyes opened and his pupils dilated as he saw her.

'My God, Sara! What happened?'

'Oh, come on, Ian.' She leaned over and kissed him.

His arm tightened around her, and he buried his face in her neck, pulling her close. In no time at all she wanted him again as much as she had earlier.

He made love to her as though there'd never be another time, as though touching her, caressing her, giving her pleasure, was all he'd ever wanted. He still held her when it was over, unlike C.W. who always turned away.

'You're so lovely, Sara,' he murmured.

She felt a faint thrust of disappointment. Not 'I love you, Sara.' But if he didn't, she was glad he hadn't lied. She'd been ready to say the words to him, she was soft with love.

Or was it only the aftermath of lovemaking

'I don't remember coming here,' he said. 'As ungallant as that may sound.'

'You came to the house yesterday afternoon.' Sara eased away from him. 'You acted drunk, but I think it was drugs, sleeping pills, or something.'

'The reds,' he muttered.

'Well, anyway, Ralph and I tried to bring you around with coffee, but you passed out in my lounge chair.'

★ ★ ★

Jesus, that bastard MacDuffy was here, Ian thought. I don't remember one damn thing. Since I was naked here in bed with Sara, we must have made love sometime in the night.

He had no memory of it. For him this morning had been the first time. God, it was good with her, better than he ever could have imagined. She was so responsive, as eager for him as he was for her. Damn the reds for cheating him out of the first time.

He shook his head. No, not the reds. They hadn't leaped down his throat on their own. He had only himself to blame. It was hell to come awake and not know what you'd done for the last ten hours.

Don't remember any of it. Got to get rid of

the reds. Must have taken a bunch of them. A thin snake of fear coiled in his chest. Don't recall taking any. Am I blacking out without knowing it now? Walking around, driving in a blackout?

A roar from outside pounded through his skull, and he clutched his head with his hands. 'What's the racket?' he demanded.

'Bobo — he's my yard man — is cutting the lawn. I'll get you some aspirin, if your head hurts.' She eased from the bed. 'How about food? You like your eggs scrambled or how?'

Ian's stomach churned at the thought of food, but he knew he'd better eat. 'Soft-boiled, three and a half minutes.'

Sara smiled at him. 'Picky, aren't you?'

He stared at her as she slipped into a robe. She *was* lovely. Small pointed breasts, slim, but with an enticing curve to her hips. He wanted to touch her, to hold her, and never let her go.

'There's another bathroom down the hall,' she told him. 'I have a disposable razor you can use, but no shaving cream.'

'Great.' He was reluctant to climb from the bed in front of her. Not because he was ashamed of his body — he hadn't gone to flab yet — but because he'd already exposed too much of his life to Sara. He waited until she disappeared into the master bedroom before he got up.

All through his shower he probed his mind for any shreds of the day before. Sunday. He'd gotten up late, hadn't slept well after taking Sara to see Jamie on Saturday, disturbed by what she'd done at the nursing home and by the argument they'd had afterwards.

He'd gotten so damn mad at her, mad enough to tell her they'd better stop seeing one another. Before it was too late, he'd meant. Before he couldn't give her up.

She'd been hurt, acting all stiff and formal. Love brought hurt. Love was a killer. No one knew that better than he did.

He'd read the paper and lounged around the house. Finally he'd taken the ten speed and ridden to the beach. Cold, foggy, he'd been alone on the sand, thinking of how Sara had walked on the beach in the fog with him. Depressing to be alone. Rode the bike back. House was unbearable, smelled stale. Decided to get drunk, like he'd done the night before. No whiskey. Sleep, take some pills and sleep, blot out the house, the gray weather, the stale life. Sara.

Jesus.

Had he tried to kill himself? How many had he taken? And how in hell had he managed to drive his car over here?

MacDuffy. Had his arrival interrupted something with that ginger-haired fake? No, MacDuffy would have gotten rid of him if he'd had anything going with Sara.

She'd shooed out MacDuffy. Because she preferred him? Maybe, because somehow he'd wound up in her bed. He knew now she wasn't the tease he'd mentally accused her of being.

He thought of Sara's slender body in his arms this morning, passion arching her against him, and desire clobbered him. He wanted her again. Now.

★ ★ ★

Regret clawed at him because he couldn't remember how it had been with her last night. This morning had been wonderful, pure joy, but he'd cheated himself out of last night. Had she invited him to bed? Had he gone to her room uninvited? What had happened? Much as he'd like to know, he didn't dare ask her.

What of his plan not to see her again? His need for her throbbed in every pulse. It was too late to cut off the relationship. Way too late. Too late after the first time he kissed her. Yet, what did he have to offer her? To offer any woman?

He looked at himself in the mirror over the sink, noticing every crease in his face. A few gray hairs threaded through at each temple. He glanced down at his body. Skin as white as a shark's belly, except for the tan on his upper arms, face, and neck. He didn't have a spare tire, but he was out of shape; he was getting older with nothing to show for the years. Nothing to hold.

He was afraid to remarry. Another child would be another hostage to fortune. He shuddered.

In the kitchen, Sara was waiting. What he wanted to do was sweep her off her feet, carry her back to bed, and stay there with her forever. He shook his head, telling himself to get real.

Much as he'd enjoy making love to her, it would solve nothing. He wasn't ready for an on-going relationship with Sara; he had to set himself straight before he'd let himself touch her again.

But in the meantime, supposing he could take control of his life, how could he bring himself to stay away from her? And what in God's name was he going to tell her?

15

'Coffee?' Sara asked Ian when he came into the kitchen.

'Half a cup, thanks.'

'This is the second time we've had breakfast together,' she said.

He agreed, avoiding her eyes. What was the matter? she wondered. She longed to reach over and brush back the strand of hair that fell to the wrong side of his part. She wanted to kiss him, wanted him to hold her. Didn't he feel the same?

There was a knock at the door.

'Who's that?' Ian asked.

'Probably the guy who cuts my grass.' She went to the door. It was Bobo.

'Anything more you want done?' he asked.

'Could you do something about the bougainvillea at the side of the house?' Sara asked. 'It's beginning to take over everything.'

Belatedly, she realized he could see into the kitchen, see Ian seated at the table. Her face reddened and she straightened her back. What business was it of Bobo's if she ate breakfast with a man?

'Did you let your dog out the last time you

177

worked in this block?' she asked, her voice clipped.

Bobo shook his head.

'One of my cats was killed.'

'Wasn't old Royal, no way, not him. He was in the truck the whole time.' Bobo's voice was sullen.

Was he telling the truth? He wore a no-sleeve knit shirt and she checked his bare arms, the sun turning the hair on the backs to gold. No tattoos.

'I'll pay you when you've finished,' she said abruptly, closing the door.

Should she let Bobo go? The money wasn't going to hold out forever, she had to economize. Even after she began working. Still, the lawn needed regular cutting, the shrubs needed pruning, watering, fertilizing.

Couldn't *she* do it?

Sara took a deep breath. This morning she felt equal to anything. A burst of energy shot through her, making her want to whirl in a dance of happiness at being alive.

Violet crept into the kitchen, her eyes on Ian.

'That's the slinkingest cat I ever saw,' he observed. 'What's the matter with her?'

'She lives in chronic fear of just about everything,' Sara said. 'She must have had a terrible time as a kitten. I found her when she was a half-grown stray.'

'Ugly little thing, too.'

'I like her.' Sara's tone was defensive. 'Poor kitty.'

'Apparently you have a talent for rescuing unfortunate strays.'

Something in his voice caught her attention and she glanced at him, seeing something flicker in his eyes — fear, she thought in confusion. But that didn't make sense. Why would he be afraid?

'I'd better be going,' he said without looking at her. 'God knows whether I left my house unlocked or whatever. I'm sorry you had to put up with me in such a state.'

'Sorry?'

His eyes met hers. 'Not for everything.' He rose and walked away from the table.

Dismay nibbled at her. After last night, how could he simply walk away?

'Ian.'

He looked over his shoulder.

She didn't know what to say. 'You ought to take care of yourself,' she finally told him. 'Sleeping pills are a one-way street.'

'I know.' His voice was harsh. 'Don't you think I know?'

'Then why do you take them?'

He shook his head and left the kitchen. She followed him into the living room, where he picked up his sweater from a chair.

Was he actually going to leave without anything more? A word? A touch?

She put her hand on his arm. 'Ian?'

With an abrupt movement he gathered her close, and held her so tightly she couldn't catch her breath. Just as suddenly he released her, thrust himself through the door, and was gone.

Maybe he was the kind of man who had trouble finding the right words, Sara thought, finding small consolation in the idea. Don't brood about what he might or might not have said or done, she warned herself. Accept him as he is.

She cleaned the kitchen, made the bed, and thought about vacuuming. But the sun shining through the windows coaxed her to embrace the bright day, to leave grayness behind and enjoy the outdoors.

'This enough?' Bobo asked as she came down the front steps.

She eyed the pile of prunings at the side of the house, the violet flowerlets of the vine brilliant against the grass.

'Yes, it seems to be.'

Why did Bobo make her so uneasy? He'd never said anything insolent or tried to touch her. Was it those sunglasses he habitually wore?

'Anything else I can do for you today?'

Was there a tinge of mockery in his voice, or was she reading more into his words because she knew he'd seen Ian at breakfast? Sara took a deep breath. Why worry about Bobo? With no tattoo, he could be eliminated as the strangler.

'I'm going to start doing my own yard work,' she informed him briskly. 'You've done a fine job, but I need to cut down on expenses. I'm sorry.'

'Me, too.' He shrugged and took the money she handed him.

Sara walked toward the park, her mind filled with Ian. He hadn't spoken of love, of anything permanent. Or even of seeing her again. She didn't know how he felt, but she warmed herself with the memory of last night, or this morning. A small boy toddled across the sidewalk in front of her, and her heart contracted.

We could have a child, Ian and I, a baby to make up for the loss of mine. Another child might ease his anguish over Jamie . . .

Stop it! Stop creating your own myths from your own wishes. You live in reality, so accept reality.

She walked faster, deliberately focusing her attention on the people strolling in the park. There were more of them than usual for a weekday. The morning, though sunny, was not really warm — maybe they were all as glad to see the sun as she was.

She smiled at a pregnant woman, at an old man with a cane, and a couple in identical red sweatsuits who jogged past her.

'Nice day.'

Sara turned her head to see who'd spoken and saw the man with the black shepherd.

'Yes,' she said, looking at the dog's mournful eyes.

As they passed the dog paused and turned her head to watch Sara, only to have the man jerk roughly on the lead, forcing the dog on.

Sara felt a spurt of anger. He's cruel, she thought. Is he put out because I seemed more interested in the dog than in him? She stopped, sat on a bench, and observed him walking away from her.

Quite ordinary-looking — brown hair, not long, thinning over the crown. Khaki jacket. An average man. She shrugged. His dog was more distinctive than he was.

She leaned back on the bench and thought of Ian. He wasn't ordinary at all, there'd been nothing ordinary in the way they'd come together last night. She hadn't realized how much she wanted Ian until then. Now that she knew, what could she do about it?

Since she didn't want to think about

whether they might have a future together, she forced herself to watch the passersby. Young mothers with babies and toddlers. Old people. Lovers. Dog walkers of both sexes. No young women alone on a Monday morning with nothing to do.

But in a couple of months she'd be busy. Be gainfully employed. She stood up, feeling confident, able to accomplish anything — as though the lovemaking with Ian had triggered a hidden switch to stored energy.

Would it have been the same with Ralph? she wondered, as she rose from the bench. She shook her head. No. With Ian it wasn't only sex. She felt a tenderness for him she was too wary to call love, but wanted to believe might be the beginning of love. The tenderness spilled over to include Jamie. Hadn't she promised to try to help Jamie?

Christmas is less than two weeks away, Sara reminded herself. I haven't so much as thought about presents, but I must get something for Jamie. And how about Ian?

She frowned, uncertain. There was no one else to shop for. Her mother, an only child, was dead, and Sara had never known what became of her father after he left them when she was six.

No, not Ian, she decided. Just Jamie. As she wondered what an eight-year-old boy as physically limited as Jamie might enjoy, she made up her mind to buy him a small present for every day from now until Christmas, visit him every day and bring one each time. She'd seen a wheelchair in the room, perhaps she might be allowed to push Jamie outside when the weather was good. Like today.

★ ★ ★

Mrs. Hodges seemed pleased to see her. In answer to Sara's question, she said, 'Jamie's in his chair. I'm sure he'd enjoy a little fresh air.'

Jamie sat on a pad of foam rubber covered with sheepskin. A vest restraint held him upright in the chair. His legs, Sara noted, were almost as thin as his arms.

'Hello, Jamie,' she said from the doorway, 'it's Sara. Remember me?' She deliberately paused a moment before entering and coming into his line of vision, in order to gauge his reaction.

Did his head turn toward her just a fraction? She couldn't be sure, but she knew she'd seen him blink, making her positive he'd heard her.

She approached the wheelchair, pulled up a chair in front of it, and sat down, so he could see her easily. 'I brought you a present,' she said, leaning over to lay the gaily wrapped box onto his lap.

His gaze shifted from her face to the box and back, convincing her he'd understood what she'd said. His lips twitched in what she chose to regard as a smile.

'That smile is enough of a thank you,' she told him. 'Shall I open the package for you?' She waited and was rewarded when his right hand moved slightly.

'Great! If you wiggle the fingers of your right hand for yes and your left hand for no, we'll be able to talk to each other.' She smiled encouragingly as she lifted the package and peeled off the paper. Opening the box lid, she showed him the contents.

'I brought you a ball,' she said, easing the small red and yellow ball free. She started to reach for his right hand and paused. Ian was left-handed. 'Are you a lefty like your father?' she asked.

Jamie wiggled the fingers of his right hand and she beamed at him. She gathered his left hand into hers and placed the ball into his palm, pleased to see the ball was the right size to fit his hand. Curling his fingers around the ball, she said, 'Now you can remember how a ball feels when you hold it. It's a good feeling.'

Doing most of the work, she helped him

transfer the ball from his left to his right hand and back. Then, slowly and carefully, she let go of his fingers. He watched what she did, blinking when his fingers stayed curled around the ball.

I've surprised him, she thought. He didn't know he could hold a ball all by himself. She hadn't been sure, either, and found herself elated at his small victory.

When he finally transferred his gaze from the ball to her face, she said, 'The sun is shining and it's so warm today, that I believe we may be in for Santa Ana weather soon. Cold weather, right?'

He opened his left hand and wiggled the fingers, losing his grip on the ball. It rolled off the wheelchair and bounced along the floor.

'Chasing after that ball's my penalty for teasing you,' she said, after retrieving the ball and handing it back to him. She was secretly pleased that he'd understood her directions for yes and no and was able to carry them out appropriately.

'I know you couldn't forget how easy it is to melt in one of our hot Santa Anas,' she added, 'but we won't melt today, so I'll push your chair outside and we can sit in the sun awhile.'

In back of the facility, an old man sat on a

bench tossing crumbs to the tamest ground squirrels Sara had ever seen. Noticing how intently Jamie watched the antics of the little animals when they crossed his field of vision, she stood behind him and gently turned his head to the right, so he could see the squirrels pop in and out of their holes. When she tried to turn his head to the left he resisted, so she didn't persist.

I'll bet he'd enjoy the zoo, she thought. I wonder if it's possible to take him there.

Casting her mind back to when she'd taught, she tried to recall stories she'd read to her special ed class, hoping to remember one that Jamie might like to hear. All that came to her were Grandpa Saari's Finnish tales, so she told him the one about the boy who couldn't win his true love unless he hid in a place where she couldn't find him. First he hid in the heart of a gray rabbit, then in the heart of a bear, choosing animal after animal. She found him each time, until he fooled her by hiding in her very own heart.

'And so they lived together happily ever after,' she finished.

'Now that was a pretty damn good story,' the old man said. 'Kind of short, but better'n that crap on TV.'

Sara laughed and, looking at Jamie, saw his

upper lip twitch into a definite curl of amusement.

I don't believe there's much if anything wrong with his mind, she thought. He shouldn't be here, where no one has the time or knowledge to work with him. She couldn't do anything about where he was, but she certainly could and she damn well *would* volunteer her time and expertise to help Jamie.

After returning him to his room, she pressed her cheek to his and kissed his forehead before saying goodbye. 'I'll come again tomorrow,' she told him. 'I've heard San Diego always gets a Santa Ana for Christmas. Let's hope it holds off until then.' As she went out, she saw he was still clutching the ball.

On Tuesday she brought him a jack-in-the-box that popped open at the push of a button. It took Jamie some time to exert enough pressure with his finger to make jack pop out. When he finally managed it, his sparkling eyes brought a lump to Sara's throat.

Sara had gotten permission ahead of time, so when she came in on Wednesday she pushed a hook into the wall and hung her present, a battery operated clock, on the wall where Jamie could see it. At each hour, a panel on the clock's lighted face slid open and a different picture appeared, twenty-four in all.

'We're going to try something new today,' she told him. 'Did you ever hear the story of a girl named Helen Keller?' When he wriggled his left hand for no, she went on. 'Helen was blind and deaf from the time she was a tiny girl. So she couldn't learn to talk like little children usually do, by imitating what they hear. Nor could she learn to read, because she couldn't see. But, through her teacher, Helen learned that the things she could touch had names. I won't go into everything the teacher taught her, just the one you and I are going to try together.'

Sara took Jamie's left hand in hers and, with her forefinger, traced a printed capital *A* on his palm. 'Do you recognize that letter?'

He wriggled his right hand.

'Is it a *B*?'

He wriggled the fingers of his left hand.

Sara smiled at him. 'An *A*?'

He gestured a yes.

'Great. Now I'll give you my palm, and you try to trace the letter *A* on it with your left forefinger, okay?'

★ ★ ★

Jamie knew what an *A* was. He could read words when he saw ones he recognized. He could even picture the letter *A* in his head. But when he tried to trace it on Sara's palm, the picture wouldn't go from his head to his finger, no matter how hard he tried. He curled his left hand into a fist, angry and frustrated.

'Never mind, Jamie,' Sara said. 'It's my fault for pushing you too fast. Forget about letters. But think about it — is there anything you can trace on my palm? A triangle? A number?'

As he thought, his fingers uncurled. A few moments later, with great effort, he touched her palm with his forefinger and drew a shaky heart.

Sara beamed at him. 'Wonderful! One of the best hearts I ever saw.' She closed her hand carefully. 'I'll keep the heart to remind me of you when I'm home.'

He wished she didn't have to go home, wished she'd stay with him all the time. He liked the presents she brought him, but her company was better than any present in the whole, entire world.

'I talked to Mrs. Hodges about taking you to the zoo,' Sara said. 'She's going to ask your doctor. If he says it's all right, we'll go. If not, why we'll find something else to do.'

The zoo sounded great, but he guessed she didn't understand that anywhere was okay with him if she was along.

'I have a cat named Violet,' Sara said. 'Maybe I can take you to see her sometime. Poor Violet, she's afraid of everyone but me. Every noise scares her. I like her, though, and maybe you will, too.'

If Sara was going to take him to see Violet someday, that meant she'd bring him home with her. Excitement coursed through him at the thought of being in Sara's house.

'Do you like cats?' she asked.

As he gestured yes, he remembered how he'd played with Kiki, the Siamese cat they used to have. Maybe they still did. He didn't know. He smiled as he recalled how she used to chase Ping-Pong balls all over their house. Would Violet play with him, or would she be too scared? He wouldn't mind if she hid from him. He'd been scared lots of times himself, and he knew how terrible it felt.

Sara told him a story before she left, like she always did. This one was a story about Vaino, a Finnish wizard who was always getting into trouble. This time the girl Vaino wanted to marry turned into a salmon. He caught her in a net, but didn't recognize her in fish shape, so she got away from him forever.

Just as Sara was different, the stories were, too. Different from those he was used to, and nothing like TV. That old man had said they were better than TV, and Jamie agreed. Partly 'cause Sara was real, she was right here with him, and not just a picture on a screen.

He tried not to mind when she left, fixing his attention on the clock and trying to figure how many hours it would be before he saw her again.

Jamie liked the clock. He didn't want to fall asleep that night, because he'd miss some of the pictures. Also, its light brightened the darkness, and he liked that, too. Most of all, though, he liked Sara.

She must like him, he thought, or she wouldn't come to see him. Before she left today, she'd asked him if he wanted to kiss her goodbye, and he'd almost been too shy to signal yes. Boy, was he glad he found the nerve to tell her he did.

Before he tried to kiss her cheek, he didn't even know if he *could*. Like holding the ball. And popping open the jack-in-the-box. And tracing the heart. When he really, truly tried, he could do all those things. Sometime, maybe, he'd even be able to trace an *A*.

Today Sara said she thought he could learn to turn his head a little bit. If she thought he could, he knew he'd try his darndest. He'd try anything for Sara. He'd even practice now. Not to the left, though. He knew he couldn't turn his head to the left. Ever.

After a struggle, Jamie wasn't sure whether his head had turned slightly to the right or not, but he knew the effort tired him. He focused on the clock, fighting sleep until he finally couldn't keep his eyes open. Just as he started to drift helplessly into the deep darkness he mistrusted and feared, he saw his father lying on a bed. Not in his pajamas, but all dressed except for his shoes. Daddy's face looked dirty, like it did when he forgot to shave.

It wasn't Daddy's big bed, but the one in the guest room. The bed covers were all mussed and a pillow lay on the floor. Daddy wasn't awake, but he wasn't asleep either. A stab of fear struck Jamie. He didn't know what was wrong with his father, but something bad was. Something awful.

Inside daddy's head was darkness as bad as any nightmare. Jamie's fear mushroomed into terror.

Daddy! he thought desperately. *Wake up, daddy!*

And then he wasn't with his father anymore, he was somewhere else, in a place he'd never been. A strange man was sitting in a chair reading a newspaper, and a big black dog lay on the floor by the door. She was watching the man, and Jamie understood she didn't like him. She couldn't go to sleep, because she didn't trust him.

Jamie watched the man. Though the man's face wasn't one he knew, he had the feeling he'd seen him before, but he didn't know where. Pretty soon the man put down the paper and scowled. His hand pushed up the sleeve of his T-shirt and rubbed a picture on his upper arm. The tattoo of an owl.

The yellow eyes of the flying owl seemed to look directly at Jamie. It was like the man and the dog didn't know he was there, but the owl did. Its yellow eyes grew bigger and bigger, shining and bright as it swooped toward him.

Then Jamie heard the sirens begin, the owl disappeared, and a flashing red light came and went, came and went, along with the moaning. Men shouted. Jamie couldn't scream, he couldn't move. He was locked into the dreadful nightmare again.

16

She asked for it, he thought, wriggling her ass around in those tight pants, why didn't she write a letter to the newspaper about how she didn't wear anything under them — he'd found that out — and how her nipples showed through her shirt. She'd wanted him to take her, wanted any man to take her. Even Sheba wasn't in heat continuously, like these human bitches.

The ones with red hair were the worst, he'd watched most of his life and he knew. Always pushing up against a man and asking for it. He gave it to them all right. A smile curved his lips.

He ran a finger along the tawny wings of the owl. When he was a kid, one of his teachers read 'Hiawatha' to his class in school. He still remembered the part where old Nokomis sings the baby Hiawatha to sleep: *Ewa-yea, my little owlet . . .*

Sometimes, like an incantation, he'd whisper the words to himself at night when he couldn't sleep, pretending he had an old grandmother who took care of him, instead of no one at all.

When he got older, he'd sometimes imagine Koko-koho, Hiawatha's spirit owl, was at his beck and call. Because it was a magic bird, the owl could be any size. He'd ride on the owl's back and it would do everything he said, stab his enemies to death with its sharp talons, crush them in its giant beak. It would kill and eat his slut of a sister that he had to live with, kill and eat her and those slobs who came to screw her.

He'd had to barricade himself in his room after that time the fat guy went for him, wanting him instead of his sister. Had his bitch of a sister helped him? No chance. She'd laughed when he screamed in pain and terror and, twisting a strand of her stringy red hair around her finger, got her kicks while she watched, urging the bastard on.

He spat to remove the taste of bile from his mouth. When he was a kid, no magic owl had come to save him, but once he got his owl talisman, he'd discovered how to save himself. He'd learned how to deal with bitches.

It was time to get the hair of the new one, to have her hair with him at night, to feel it between his fingers in anticipation. Soft, silky, hiding the true meaning until afterwards, when he burned it. Then the smell was acrid, nasty, revealing the corruption.

He crumpled the newspaper in his hands. Damn that letter-writing whore, she didn't deserve to live. If the cops had tracked her down, he sure as hell could. If they could find her, it wouldn't be too hard for him.

Not yet, though. He'd finish his schedule with the other, the new one, then there'd be time. He wouldn't need to wait between them, because there'd be no schedule to follow. No dog, either, he'd already used that dog.

Excitement gripped him. Two. He'd never had two. But the second would be permissible, wouldn't really count. She'd already been processed.

17

After shopping, Sara decided to treat herself to a guacamole tostada at one of the Mexican fast food takeouts. Dusk was weaving its long shadows by the time she arrived home. Because she thought she heard her phone ringing, she rushed up the steps and fumbled with the key.

By the time the door opened, the ringing had stopped. She sighed and flipped on the lights. Violet slunk into the living room to meet her. She fed the cat, then opened the food container, and set her tostada on a plate.

Had she missed a call from Ian? He hadn't phoned since he left on Monday morning. Should she call him? Sara shook her head. The last mythology class before Christmas was tomorrow night. She'd see him then.

She looked around for the evening paper to read while she ate, and realized she'd been in such a hurry to open the door that she hadn't picked it up from the front walk.

As she pushed open the screen door, she made a mental note to tighten the door, because its latch wasn't catching. As she turned to go back after retrieving the *Tribune* from the walk, she gasped in dismay. Violet was peering around the open screen. Before Sara could move, the cat slid around the door and out.

Sara lunged at her. Violet leaped off the steps in alarm and disappeared into the shadows between the shrubs. Sara called and called, but Violet didn't reappear. She rushed into the house, grabbed her jacket, and rummaged in her bag for the house key. Locking the door behind her, she went outside and began to circle the house, calling for Violet.

The backyard was in almost complete darkness. Sara hesitated, thinking she should have turned on the back light. But the backyard was fenced and it was only seven o'clock — not late.

She took two steps and stopped to listen. What had she heard? Her spine prickled with uneasiness, and the hair bristled along her nape, as though she were a cat herself. It had been a snuffling sound, not exactly a growl. No person would make such a weird noise — would they?

Something appeared in the darkness, a whitish blur coming toward her, far too big to be Violet. A dog? It didn't behave like any dog she'd ever seen. Sara backed away as the animal headed straight at her. What on earth was it? She gave ground as the thing shuffled past, snarling, and watched it go into the street. Bare skin — or was that fur? — a naked, skinny tail, a pointed muzzle. It certainly was the ugliest beast she'd ever set eyes on.

Possum? Yes, it must be. But right here in the city? Would it hurt a cat?

Inside the house the phone began ringing. Ian! Sara ran back to the front door to let herself in. She dashed for the phone.

'Hello? Hello?'

Silence on the other end. Then breathing. Sara held the phone away from her ear and stared at it in disbelief mingled with fear, before slamming it down. Shivering, she sank into a chair and hugged herself. After a few moments she stiffened. Had she remembered to lock the front door behind her?

After checking, she hurried to the back door and flicked on the outside light. Peering through the kitchen window, she saw no one in the yard, so she opened the door and called to Violet, called over and over. She was about to give up when a streak of white dashed from the darkness into the circle of light, into the house, and behind the refrigerator.

She couldn't coax the cat out, but Sara decided not to worry. If Violet could run that fast, she must be all right.

Sara had lost her appetite, but she made an effort not to give in to her fears by sitting at the table, opening the paper, and forcing herself to start eating her tostada.

'Rapist Victim Located,' the headline said.

Sara dropped her fork, pulling the paper closer. Though they'd found the victim who'd written to the newspaper, she read, for the woman's protection the police were keeping her name and whereabouts secret.

' . . . I got to thinking about that tattoo,' the woman was quoted as saying. 'Because of the wings, I thought maybe it was an eagle, because I've seen other eagle tattoos. Then I seemed to remember big eyes, too, like owls have. What with owls being associated with death, you'd think a monster like him'd be more likely to have an owl tattoo. But I don't really know for sure what I saw. It was just a glimpse, and I was scared out of my wits . . . '

An owl, Sara thought. The bird of ill omen. Yes, it fit the killer.

Was he the breather?

Her glance shifted to the window. Had there been someone in her backyard earlier? Someone who'd frightened the possum away? If there had been, that person would have been in the yard when the phone rang. So it couldn't have been the breather.

But it could have been the strangler.

Sara shook her head, telling herself to be logical. That possum had looked to be the least scared animal she'd ever seen, so probably no one had been in her yard.

Whoever called her had her new unlisted number. She'd given no one that number. Wait — both Ralph and Ian had been in the house since the number was changed. She'd jotted it on the pad by the phone. One or both of them could have seen the new number.

Was one of them the breather?

The shrill ring of the phone made her jump. She stared at it in horror. Finally, on the seventh ring, she made herself pick it up.

'Hello?'

'Sara? Are you all right? Your voice sounds strange.'

'Ralph! Oh, Ralph, I'm so frightened.' Words tumbled from her — the noise in the backyard, the possum, the breather phone call, the strangler.

'Wait a minute, Sara. You really are upset, aren't you? I'll come right over, you shouldn't be alone in a state like that. Hold on, I'll be there as soon as I can.'

Sara gripped the phone after she hung up. Ralph was coming, she wouldn't be alone, nothing would happen with him here, she'd be safe.

He arrived within a half-hour. 'Have you eaten?' he demanded.

Sara recalled the almost untouched tostado. 'I wasn't hungry.'

'No wonder you look so peaked. Come on, we'll go out and have a drink and some food. What's all this about a possum?'

She told him.

'The beast probably lives in the park and forages in all the garbage cans around here,' he said. 'Possums are harmless. Better put on a jacket before we go, it's cool tonight. Oh, wait, before we leave — have you gotten any more stories on the tape?'

'I finished both sides,' she said.

'Great. I'll leave this blank tape with you and take your completed one. I've decided to retape what you've done, adding appropriate comments, and send it directly to the publisher I think is most likely to be interested. Your singsong style may be just the right gimmick to hook an editor. Besides, it'll save time.'

Sara shrugged. She knew nothing about the publishing business and, at the moment, didn't care what Ralph did with the tape.

The Copper King was crowded. With people and with Christmas decorations. Sara, sitting at the bar with her third drink while they waited for a table, thought she'd never felt less Christmasy in her life.

'I need to eat,' she said. 'I'm getting light-headed.'

'That's better than shivering like a frightened rabbit.' He put his arm around her, and she leaned toward his warmth and security.

'Do you really want to wait around to eat?' His voice was husky. 'I'd like to take you home.'

Sara's mind was fuzzy, but she knew she needed food. 'I think I'd better eat,' she told him.

'We'll pick up some hamburgers on the way.' Ralph eased her off the bar stool without waiting for her to agree.

She needed his arm around her to help her walk from the restaurant to his car.

'You're drunk,' he said, smiling. 'Admit it.'

Distaste flared briefly in her fuddled mind. For him. For herself. It took all her concentration to get in the car without his support, but she managed.

'I don't get drunk,' she said huffily, as she fumbled with the seat belt.

He laughed as he buckled it for her.

She leaned back against the seat and closed her eyes, while her head whirled. Sometime later she was groggily aware of him leading her to her own door, which he unlocked. When had she given him her key?

'Where's my hamburger?' she asked.

'Sara, you can't eat now, you'll be sick. We'd better get you to bed.' He began to pull her along the hall.

She resisted, trying to focus clearly. 'Ralph . . . no . . . '

He stopped. 'Do you want me to stay or go? The choice is yours. If you'd rather be alone, just say so.'

Alone. Panic penetrated her alcoholic haze, and she grabbed at his arm. 'No, no, please not alone.'

His lips were warm and comforting. In the bedroom she let him undress her, since he was doing a better job than she could. His arms were warm, too.

But when he started to pull her onto the bed, she was reminded of C.W. and what he'd done to her. Did she want Ralph in her bed? The way she felt now, she was in no condition to resist anyone. Yet she knew going to bed with Ralph wasn't really her choice.

'Wait a minute,' she said, vaguely aware how slurred the words were.

Ralph's hold tightened and alarm tingled through her. Like C.W., he wasn't going to stop.

'I don't want — ' she began.

'You don't know what you want,' he murmured, tumbling her onto the bed. 'Let me show you.'

She did know, and it wasn't anything he could show her. But he wouldn't listen. If only she could think clearly.

'Bathroom,' she mumbled.

He let her go. She rolled off the bed and staggered into the bathroom. After locking the door, she wrapped the terry robe around her. Too dizzy to do anything else, she lay prone on the bath rug, her cheek on the cold tile floor, closed her eyes, and dropped into oblivion.

Sara woke, shivering, in the gray light of predawn with a pounding headache. She pushed herself to her feet. What was she doing in the bathroom? Had she fainted? Her mouth tasted like used kitty litter smelled.

Hangover, she had a hangover. She'd gone out for a drink with Ralph. Bits and pieces of the evening dropped into place. Ralph had tried to manipulate her into bed with him. He never did buy her a hamburger. Wouldn't let her eat. He knew she was scared, and offered to stay the night if she slept with him. Bastard. But it wasn't entirely his fault; she should have had more sense than to drink so much.

Surely he wasn't still around. She swallowed two aspirins before unlocking the bathroom door. When she saw Violet sitting in the hall looking reproachfully at her, she was positive Ralph was long gone.

Had he knocked on the bathroom door? Called to her? If he had, she hadn't heard him. She checked the front door and grimaced when she found he'd left it unlocked. What a cruel thing to do. He knew how frightened she was; if he cared about her at all, he would have locked the door on his way out.

She stared at the blank tape he'd left. After last night, did he really expect her to continue with the stories? One thing for sure, she was *not* going to his damn class again.

The day was sunny, without clouds. After she drank two cups of coffee and forced down a piece of toast, Sara sat in the backyard, nursing her headache and watching Violet slink in and out of the shrubbery. It was already hot, a Santa Ana must be building.

She never could remember if Santa Anas caused positive or negative ions, but whichever they were, they set most people on edge. Perhaps this would be a good day to take Jamie to the zoo, though; he wouldn't get chilled.

She'd waited and waited for Ian to call her.

Now she had an excuse to call him. Two, really. First, to tell him she wouldn't be going to class tonight, and also to ask him if he minded if she took his son to the zoo.

Sara smiled despite her headache. Maybe Ian would decide to come along.

Not wanting to disturb his sleep, she waited impatiently until ten before looking up the number and making the call. As she listened to the rings, her heart began to pound so loud in her ears she could scarcely hear the voice that answered.

'Ian? Is Ian there?' she asked.

'Ian?' the voice repeated, and Sara realized it was unmistakably female. 'Just a minute.'

Sara couldn't seem to breathe while she waited.

'He can't talk to you right now,' the female voice said.

Sara bit her lip. Can't or didn't want to? Who was the woman? Without another word, she banged down the phone. Staring at it, she pictured the woman in bed with Ian — another Moira with green eyes, lithe and lovely.

Her stomach roiled, and she blinked back angry tears. No wonder he hadn't bothered to call her. She was a fool. Would she ever learn? With Ralph last night, because she'd been afraid to be alone, she'd come close to bartering sex for the security of a man in the house. At least she'd never make that mistake again.

But with Ian, it had been different. Or at least she'd thought so at the time. Apparently he hadn't shared her feeling. Damn him, anyway. He'd been another mistake she wouldn't make twice.

She'd forget both of them. Lead her own life. Starting now.

But there was still Jamie. Jamie needed her; she couldn't desert him. Wouldn't desert him. They'd go to the zoo today, as she'd planned. First, though, she needed to settle her nerves.

Settling nerves was an expression she'd learned from Grandma Saari. Hard work was a great settler in Grandma's opinion. Work and strong, hot coffee. She'd had the coffee. A walk in the park would be her substitute for work.

In the park, the sun shone hot and strong, the temperature already edging into the nineties. Seeking shade, Sara left the sidewalks for a trail that wound under the trees along the rim of a gorge. On the steep slope, dirt and rocks superseded grass, and the growth was mostly wild native plants rather than the prettier, lusher imports.

A man appeared suddenly in front of her, as though he'd materialized between bushes.

She stopped, startled and wary. Before she could retreat, he unzipped his jeans and began to stroke his rigid penis, never taking his eyes from her face.

Sara gasped and he smiled. After a moment of agonizing paralysis, she turned and ran into the open, glancing over her shoulder to make certain he didn't follow. When she came to a sidewalk with people walking along it, she paused to catch her breath.

It happens to everyone, she told herself. All too often she'd listened to women complain about men exposing themselves in public places. What was wrong with men? Rapists at heart, all of them. C.W. Even Ralph.

No, not all of them, not her Grandpa Saari. She couldn't lump all men together, some must be different. Ian, for example. Angry as she was at him, she didn't see him as a rapist.

How about the breather? A mind-raper, certainly.

'Hello,' a woman's voice said.

Sara started at the greeting. She looked up and saw a red-haired young woman.

'Remember me?' the woman asked. 'From when you found the lost dog?'

'Oh, yes. Yes.'

'What happened to the dog?'

'Her master came for her,' Sara said.

'Good. I was hoping I'd see you again, so I

could ask.' She held out her hand. 'I'm Najla Kajian.'

'Sara Henderson.'

As they shook hands, Najla said, 'We have something in common. But with that weirdo running loose, I'm thinking of going blond. How about you?'

'It's crossed my mind. Do you live around here?'

Najla shook her head. 'Can't afford it. I've got a one bedroom near Old Town.'

'That's right, I remember you telling me you worked in one of the clinics near the park.'

'Yeah. Today's my day off, 'cause I have to work Saturday. We take turns. But it was so hot in my apartment, I came to the park. Only it's not much cooler here. Maybe I'll try the beach.' Her gaze traveled over Sara. 'You married?'

Sara shook her head.

'Me neither. I was wondering — would you like to go out with me some evening? Maybe a movie or something. It's no fun alone.' She grimaced. 'And I'm alone at present. By choice. Aren't men a pain in the you-know-where?'

'Mostly, yes.' Thinking that Najla must have had a recent bad experience with a man, Sara warmed to her.

Najla smiled and dug in her bag. 'Here's my phone number. Give me a ring, if you want to go out sometime. Okay?' She looked expectantly at Sara.

Sara hesitated, then returned Najla's smile as she took the card and rattled off her own phone number, as Najla scribbled it onto the back of a used envelope. Why not accept this woman's tentative offer of friendship? A movie wasn't much of a commitment, after all.

'I *will* call you,' she said. 'It sounds like fun.'

'Hey, great. Glad I ran into you. Bye-bye for now.'

Sara watched Najla walk away, warmed by the contact. It'd been years since she'd had a woman friend who was more than an acquaintance. True, Najla was only an acquaintance, but her guileless friendliness appealed to Sara.

★   ★   ★

Since Mrs. Hodges took it for granted that Sara had Ian's permission to take Jamie off the premises, it was simple enough to sign him out of the facility for their trip to the zoo. He weighed so little that Sara had no trouble lifting him in and out of the car, and because of her teaching experience, she was used to managing wheelchairs.

On the drive to the zoo, she learned by asking questions he could answer by wriggling his fingers, that Jamie had been there before. Twice. The monkeys were his favorites, and he liked the elephants next best.

Since this was Jamie's first trip away from the facility, Sara didn't want to exhaust him. Pushing the wheelchair, she commented on what they passed, from the scurrying bantam chickens that roamed free on the zoo grounds, to a tiny green-throated humming-bird sipping from a red hibiscus blossom.

When they reached the monkey exhibit, she watched Jamie's eyes sparkle as he followed the monkeys' antics, and came to the realization that she'd have to see Ian again whether she wanted to or not. Jamie's father must be made to understand that his son didn't belong to an institution. Jamie needed to be with Ian, needed to be at home.

After a time, seeing that Jamie's attention was wandering, she pushed his chair on toward the elephant pit. As they passed the raptors' cages, she was startled to see Jamie's head turn abruptly to the right. A strangled cry burst from his throat as he stared up at a Great Horned Owl, blinking sleepily down at them with its huge yellow eyes.

Sara locked the chair and dropped to her knees in front of Jamie. 'Don't be afraid,' she said, taking his hands in hers. 'The owl can't hurt you.'

His head turned slowly until he faced her.

'All right now?' she asked, opening her hands so she could see his.

He wriggled the fingers of his right hand.

'Still want to see the elephants?'

He gestured his yes.

She rose and they went on. As they approached the elephant pit, she said as casually as she could, 'You turned your head all by yourself, Jamie. That's good news.'

He'd made a noise, too, which meant he wasn't mute. But she didn't mention that. It was best to concentrate on one thing at a time.

After seeing the elephants, she bought Jamie an ice cream cone. Rather than holding it for him to lick, she put the cone into his left hand. After his fingers closed around it, she bent his elbow and raised his hand until his tongue could reach the ice cream, then propped her shoulder bag under his elbow, and took her hand away.

She was gratified when he was able to eat half the ice cream, before his hand became too shaky to hold the cone.

'We'll have to work on building up your muscles,' she told him, as she held the cone for him to finish. 'They've gotten weak from lack of use. But just think how much you did for yourself, even with weak muscles.' She hugged him. 'I like someone who keeps trying — you're my kind of guy, Jamie.'

He smiled at her, obviously pleased with himself. She wished she knew what had upset him at the owl's cage, but didn't want to ask questions that might distress him all over again. She knew she must move slowly, because Jamie needed to experience a series of successes to build up his confidence.

She really needed access to his medical records, but she wasn't likely to get that unless Ian got involved.

As he damn well should be! Jamie was his son; Jamie needed his father.

Once the cone was eaten and she'd wiped Jamie's sticky face, they left the zoo. She was pushing the wheelchair toward the parking lot, when Jamie gave another choking cry. She stopped and moved around to look at him. His gaze went past her, and she turned to see what he saw.

Coming toward them on the sidewalk was a woman holding a small boy's hand, a man in shorts carrying a tennis racket, and a man walking a black dog. Nothing unusual. Since

Jamie appeared to be all right, she walked on. The man with the dog cut across the street to her left, and she realized she'd seen them before — he was the man with the black shepherd.

Jamie didn't turn his head to the left to watch, so she concluded it was one of the others who'd caught his attention. Perhaps the mother and child had reminded him of his own mother and himself.

She *must* speak to Ian. The poor boy had already lost his mother, it wasn't fair that Jamie should be deprived of his father, too.

★   ★   ★

Jamie settled into his hospital bed with relief. He was really tired. But he'd enjoyed the day more than anything he could remember. Not only the zoo, but Sara. She'd bought him a toy monkey that fastened onto the arm of his wheelchair, and he liked the monkey a whole lot. But he'd like Sara even if she never bought him anything or took him anywhere.

Just her coming to see him every day was the best present of all.

When he was with her, it seemed he always learned to do something new. Like eating the ice cream cone. And turning his head. That'd really been the owl, though. He'd caught a glimpse of those round yellow eyes staring at him, and got really scared for a moment. Without even thinking about it, he'd swung his head around for a better look.

'Course it was only an owl. A real one, shut up in a cage. After that bad dream he didn't much like owls, but he felt sort of sorry for that one at the zoo. He was kind of locked in a cage, too, so he knew about cages. It was worse for the owl, 'cause owls could fly. But not in cages.

He tried to go back to thinking about Sara, but he couldn't shut away the other thing that had happened. He'd met the bad man with the dog. He'd known right away it was the man and the dog he'd seen in the dream that wasn't a dream. And he thought maybe the dog recognized him, from the way she'd looked at him with her dark eyes. He didn't see how that was possible, but then he didn't understand why he had the dreams that came true, either. He never used to. Before.

He'd tried to turn his head to watch the dog, but it was to the left and he couldn't. He'd never be able to. Not to the left. Because then he'd see something more horrible than the worst nightmare he could ever imagine.

★   ★   ★

Ian sat on the edge of his disordered bed. He rubbed a shaky hand over a heavy growth of beard. Christ. The room stank. He stank. How long this time?

There wasn't supposed to have been another time. Had he meant to kill himself? The dream came back to him and he shuddered.

He lay on his back in the bed. Dying. Then somehow Jamie floated into the room, stared down at him with frightened green eyes, and begged him not to die.

That's when he'd staggered up and into the bathroom, where he puked his guts out. Which was probably why he was still alive.

He shook his head. Getting up, he stumbled into the bathroom and slammed open the medicine cabinet. He grabbed the bottle of reds, opened it, dumped the remaining caplets in the toilet, and flushed. No more. Damn it, he'd never been a copout, and what else was killing yourself? Even if he hadn't meant to.

The doctor said he had a guilt complex over the accident, and that guilt sometimes triggered a death wish. Damn it, no! No more reds. No next time.

He wandered into the living room. Velma, his cleaning woman, had been here — he could tell by the spotless living room and kitchen. She knew enough not to bother him. Newspapers were piled neatly on the kitchen table along with the mail. He picked up the top paper. Thursday. My God, four days.

Ian showered and shaved, then made coffee, all the time wondering what he hadn't done that he should have during the missing days. He drank a cup of coffee as he scrambled three eggs. At least he hadn't missed his weekly Saturday visit to Jamie. Not that Jamie would know the difference.

Or would he? Could Sara be right about his son? Did Jamie recognize his father?

Sara. Sunday night came back to him in bits and pieces.

Ian took a deep breath. The reds hadn't solved the problem of Sara for him, just like they'd never solved any of his other problems. He'd been stupid to think they might.

Sara was something he'd have to solve on his own. Either take her or leave her.

He wished to hell he knew how he was going to be able to do either one.

18

By late afternoon the heat drove Sara to sit on the floor in front of the fan. She had no air conditioner — who needed one in San Diego? Except, of course, during a Santa Ana.

She'd thought it over and decided, much as she loathed him, she'd honor the commitment she'd made to tape the Finnish stories for Ralph. Once she mailed the completed tape and his recorder to him, that would be the end of Ralph as far as she was concerned. Beginning in March she had a job, so she didn't need to count on the tapes bringing her any income.

She knew better than to depend on any man. Which reminded her of one of her grandfather's stories about pretty but independent Kyllikkikki, who lived in Saari. Saari was also Grandpa's last name, meaning island in Finn. Kyllikkikki lived on Saari alone, and when handsome Lemminkainen wanted her as his wife, she refused him.

Sara began telling the story to the machine.

' . . . and so he abducted her in his sled. Poor Kyllikkikki was then forced to marry him. But their union was stormy . . . '

After Sara finished and shut off the recorder, she sat musing over the table. Finn heroes were always kidnapping maidens into their sleighs. Apparently that was tantamount to rape — or at least seduction.

One of the saddest seduction stories of all was about Kullervo, who enticed a maiden into his sled and seduced her, only to discover she was his long-lost sister. In horror she drowned herself, and Kullervo later fell deliberately on his own sword.

There were so many Finnish tales of treachery, greed, and vengeance. Stories pitting brother against brother, friend against friend. Yet the same was true of myths from other peoples. Why should the Finns be immune?

Sara shook her head. Why did she persist in remembering the tragedies, when her grandfather had also told her funny stories?

Violet, who'd been stretched out on the floor beside her, raised her head. A moment later the cat gathered herself and dashed for the bedroom. At the same time, through the locked screen door, Sara heard footsteps coming up her walk. Tensing, she rose. It better not be Ralph.

Her heart slammed into her ribs, when she saw Ian on the other side of the screen. He looked haggard, but his eyes were clear.

'Sara?'

She scowled at him.

'You're angry,' he said. 'I don't blame you. But please let me in.'

Reminding herself that she wanted to talk to him about Jamie, Sara unlocked the screen.

He entered, stopping beside her to lay his hand on her arm. Ian's touch made her entire body react, warming her, softening her, unsettling her. She hung onto her anger with grim determination.

'Please let me explain,' Ian said.

Never explain, never apologize, was what C.W., with his plastic philosophy, used to say. He had a point — explanations were often lies, so why bother?

Hoping she didn't look as shaken as she felt, Sara retreated to the kitchen, where she could put a table between herself and Ian.

'I'll make coffee,' she offered. 'Would you like a sandwich?'

'If you're having something.'

She wasn't hungry, but she toasted English muffins and put them on the table with cream cheese and blackberry jelly. By then the coffee had dripped enough and she set out mugs and spoons, postponing the moment she'd have to sit down and face Ian.

As she poured his coffee, Ian said, 'Sara, the first thing I thought about when I came out of it this time was how you'd feel, what you'd think.'

She stared at him. 'Came out of what?'

'I lost four days. After drinking. And taking sleeping pills. I was completely zonked.' Ian slapped cream cheese onto a muffin half. 'I thought I was over that stupidity, but I was wrong. It won't happen again, because I threw the damn pills away.' He ate the muffin in three bites and fixed another.

Sara said nothing.

'I tried to find your phone number,' he said. 'Did you ever give me the new one?'

She shook her head.

'It's just as well; you probably wouldn't have talked to me if I'd called you. This way you can't avoid me.' He smiled lopsidedly.

'So what do you want to say?' She aimed for an indifferent tone and was surprised at how well she succeeded.

'You know damn well we started something. There's more between us than one night in bed. The truth is, Sara, you scare the hell out of me. I don't know if I'm ready to give again. Maybe I'll never be. Maybe I can't. But you make me want to.'

Sara met his gaze, finding his eyes so desperately sad that she had to glance away.

'I'm not proud of what I did,' he went on, 'hitting the bottle along with the reds. Not wanting to think about you — about us — is no excuse.'

Who was the woman? she wanted to ask, but pride held the words back. He didn't know she'd called him.

Ian finished a third muffin. 'I missed a few meals,' he apologized.

In silence, Sara poured him another cup of coffee.

'Can you understand?' he asked. 'Will you try?'

'I don't know. Perhaps you were right when you said you wanted to end any contact between us.'

Ian shook his head. 'Too late. You know damn well I want you, Sara. Right now. Tomorrow. Next week. Next year. But there's more to it . . . that's the problem. Sex is easy. Loving isn't.'

Was the other woman only for sex? she wondered. Or did he speak of love to her?

Ian wore a short-sleeved, blue knit shirt, the sleeves riding up so she could see the lower part of the anchor on his arm, the colors garish. Why did people disfigure themselves with tattoos?

'Something's wrong, Sara. What is it?'

'Nothing.' She shook her head. 'No, that's

not true. You're what's wrong. You bother me. I feel you wanted to die after your wife did. You couldn't. But you're still trying. I'm afraid of getting any closer to you, Ian. I have no intention of involving myself in another doomed relationship.'

She heard her own voice, low, monotonous, speaking the words without emotion, almost as if she were reading sentences from a book. She felt closed-in, shut away from Ian. Nothing seemed to matter, not the present nor the future, nor whether she lived or died.

* * *

Sara's fixed expression alarmed Ian. She wasn't as he remembered her — quick butterfly movements, fluttering now toward him, now away. She spoke as though she'd memorized the words.

'Christ, what's wrong with you?' he demanded. 'Are you sick?'

They stared at one another across the table. Abruptly he rose and jerked her to her feet. Something flared in her eyes. Anger? Whatever it was, any emotion was better than none.

He held her face in his hands and tried to kiss her gently, but desire made him clumsy, he wanted her so much he couldn't think.

225

Hold her close, try to show her —

'No, Ian, please.'

He paid no attention, scooping her up and carrying her down the hall to her bedroom, where a flash of movement startled him, but he saw it was only that crazy cat leaping from the bed.

'Sara,' he murmured, setting her on her feet. 'My lovely Sara.'

She jerked free, half-falling, her face turned away from him. 'No!'

He tried to hold her again, kiss her, but she wriggled from his grasp and fell onto the bed. The sight of her sprawled there, hair disordered, eyes wide, was intensely provocative. He flung himself beside her and slid his hand under her shirt.

She fought him wildly, exciting him more. They rolled all over the bed, until at last he had her trapped beneath him. Suddenly she went limp, and he unbuttoned her shirt and unzipped her jeans. She murmured something, her voice so low he couldn't hear.

'Sara?'

'Go ahead,' she muttered. 'Rape me. Get it over with.'

Her voice was toneless, and her face had the same masklike look he'd disliked earlier.

'Sara, what's wrong?'

Her eyes were fixed, not on his face but on

his hands. He rolled away from her and sat up. She lay as he'd left her, making no effort to reclothe herself, her face blank.

'You look like a damned zombie,' he told her, irritated and frustrated. Frightened.

She said nothing.

Sudden rage drove him to his feet. He'd tried his damnedest to be honest with her, and all she could do was play games. He rearranged his clothing and ran a hand through his hair.

'I'm not addicted to rape,' he said coldly. 'If that's what you want, find another playmate.'

Turning his back, Ian stalked from the room and left the house.

* * *

Sara heard the screen door slam as though from miles away. She lay unmoving until a warm touch on her bare abdomen startled her. It was only Violet, who'd crept back onto the bed. Sara clutched the cat to her and burst into tears.

When her sobbing stopped, she asked herself if she was going crazy. Even at the worst of her marriage to C.W., she hadn't had such a strange feeling of dissociation, as though a sheet of glass separated her from what was happening. She remembered Sylvia

Plath's notion of living under a bell jar, and shuddered. Anger, jealousy, terror — anything was better than this absence of feeling.

Zombie. The dead reanimated. Bodies without souls. The gold and silver bride Ilmarinen forged for himself in his smithy. The beautiful bride he found cold to his touch and had to discard. Even Louhi's daughter, the witch maiden, was preferable to a bride with no warmth. With no heart. No soul.

What had happened to her? She'd retreated into herself in the kitchen, determined not to be beguiled by the lost look in Ian's eyes, and she couldn't help responding, until she realized what she was doing.

How could she let him make love to her, after his four days in bed with someone else? She'd struggled against him until his tattoo flashed in front of her, the swirl of rope at the top seeming to reach out to coil numbness around her. Sex. Death.

The hunting owl.

She couldn't win. Give up. Retreat. Feel nothing.

Sara shook her head and began to put her clothes in order. The shrill buzz of the doorbell made her freeze. The front screen was unlocked!

Once she was buttoned and zipped up, she

made herself go to see who was there. Bobo stood on the doorstep, with his circles of dark glass facing her.

She stared at him.

'I, uh, came to tell you about Royal,' he said.

'Royal?' What was Bobo talking about?

'I told you I never let him out of the truck, but he got out once in a while, and there wasn't nothing I could do.'

Did he mean his dog? Sara couldn't seem to clear her mind.

'So, uh, yeah, I'm afraid he did get that cat of yours. I was working down the street and I tried to catch him, but I was too late. I didn't mean to lie to you, but when I saw what happened, I sort of panicked and threw old Royal back in the truck and took off.'

'Your dog killed Namath?'

'That the big black and white one? Yeah, he did.' Bobo chewed on his lower lip. 'Been wanting to tell you. I sure am sorry.'

Sorry didn't bring back Namath, but there was no point in saying so. Sara sighed. 'Well, it's over now. I appreciate your coming to tell me.'

Bobo nodded and began backing down the stairs.

She locked the screen and turned away. What was the matter with her lately? Bobo's dog *had* killed Namath, exactly as she'd thought at first. Likely that weird neighbor across the alley had poisoned Friedan, as he'd threatened. Why had she terrorized herself, with visions of the strangler creeping into her yard and murdering her cats one by one as a prelude to killing her? Why was she examining men's arms for tattoos?

As a grand finale, there'd been that scene with Ian a little while ago. She was getting a bit weird herself.

The phone rang. She hesitated, then picked it up with grim determination.

'Hi, it's Najla. Want to go out tonight?'

Since she'd been half-expecting to find the breather on the other end, Sara took a moment to recall who Najla was.

'If I've called at a bad time,' Najla said, 'just say so.'

Najla Kajian. The red-haired woman in the park. She'd given Najla her phone number.

'No, it's all right,' Sara said. 'You took me by surprise.'

Najla laughed. 'Yeah, I get accused of being impulsive a lot. Well, you want to or not?'

On the verge of saying she couldn't make it, Sara paused. Why not go to a movie with Najla? Hadn't she just convinced herself the strangler wasn't stalking her? She couldn't hide in the house all her life. If she didn't

230

accept Najla's invitation, she'd spend the evening holed up here alone, because she was damned if she was going to Ralph's class.

'Fine,' she said. 'Where should we meet?'

'I thought we'd grab a sandwich at Poll's and discuss what to do, okay?'

'Where is Poll's?'

Najla told her, giving precise directions. 'See you about seven, then,' she finished.

* * *

Even before she left, Sara was having second thoughts. When she found the place, she almost drove past without stopping. The red neon lights of the sign spelling out Poll's Cage, alternating with the flashing of a gold neon cage, identified it as more of a nightclub than the restaurant she'd expected.

Deciding that leaving wouldn't be fair to Najla, she reluctantly pulled into the parking lot and found Najla already waiting for her.

Najla's glance skimmed over her gold shift and tan sandals. 'You're really cute, you know? And all of a piece. I wish I didn't have these big boobs — they don't fit the rest of me.'

Sara tried to think of something to say. Najla wore a purple shirt that hung from a yoke, a garment designed to make her bosom as inconspicuous as possible, but, even so, her generous breasts were obvious. Otherwise she was fairly slim.

'Just once I'd like to meet a guy that didn't notice my tits first,' Najla went on. 'I've been thinking about reduction surgery, but it costs a fortune.'

Sara decided to come directly to the point. 'What is this place?' she asked.

'Hey, Poll's makes the best hoagies in the county. Good chimichangas, too. Come on, I'm starved.' Najla took Sara's arm.

Since I'm here, I might as well go in and eat, Sara told herself.

As they stepped inside, a raucous voice called, 'Hiya, honey.'

Sara found herself face to face with a brilliant green parrot chained to a perch. Cocking its head at her, the parrot repeated, 'Hiya, honey.'

'Hello, Poll,' Najla said.

'Pretty Poll,' the parrot answered. 'Pretty Poll.'

The small room beyond the entrance had a bar, with tables around a cleared space in the middle of the floor.

'For dancing,' Najla explained, walking quickly to sit at the only unoccupied table.

Sara followed. The bartender waved at Najla, calling her by name, then glanced assessingly at Sara.

The truth dawned on Sara. This was a singles bar. 'I thought we were going to a movie,' she protested.

Najla shrugged. 'If nothing good turns up by the time we finish eating, maybe we will. Anyway, don't you think real life beats make-believe, hands down?'

'I suppose it depends on what the real life is,' Sara said, trying to find a way to tell Najla that she didn't care for singles bars. She didn't want to hurt Najla's feelings. Nothing occurred to her other than, 'Sometimes I prefer make-believe.'

'What can I get you?' The fortyish waitress wore a miniskirt with a sleeveless tunic down to the skirt's hem, making her look as though the tunic was all she had on.

'Hoagie and a beer,' Najla said.

'Um . . . a vegetable chimichanga and tonic water,' Sara told the waitress.

'You don't drink?' Najla said.

'Sometimes,' Sara admitted. But not tonight. Not in this place. She'd eat and find a polite way to leave.

'I get the idea you don't like Poll's,' Najla said, reaching to pat her arm. 'Relax. It can be fun. I've met some real hunks here. And even if you don't run across anyone you like, you still get to dance and have fun.'

'Don't you ever worry about — ' Sara glanced around and lowered her voice, 'the guys you meet here? For all you know, one of them could be the strangler.'

Najla grinned. 'Hey, I thought you were going to warn me about AIDS or syphilis or something, and I was going to tell you I don't sleep with every guy I meet, and besides, there's always condoms.' Her smile faded and she shook her head. 'I don't think the strangler hangs out at Poll's. I worry about him a lot less here than I do when I'm home alone. I wish the cops would catch him.'

'Catch who, honey chile?' a man's voice asked.

Startled, Sara looked up at a wannabe Kevin Costner somewhere in his twenties. He was staring at Najla's breasts.

'I'm Dave,' he said, without being asked, slid into the seat between her and Najla. Ignoring Sara, he leaned toward Najla and began talking.

The waitress brought the drinks and Sara sipped her tonic water, thinking that as soon as she caught Najla's eye, she was going to tell her she was leaving.

'Drowning your sorrows?' another male voice asked. A bearded fiftyish man, with lank gray hair framing his tanned face, slid into the remaining seat. His predatory gaze unnerved her. 'My name's Adrien,' he added. 'What's yours?'

'Uh — Violet,' she told him, watching a trio of musicians file in and begin setting up at one end of the room.

'Violet's an old-fashioned name,' he said. 'Are you an old-fashioned girl?'

What was she supposed to say to that? What's a nice old-fashioned girl like me doing in a place like this? Except she certainly wasn't old-fashioned, she wasn't a girl, and she wasn't so sure she was nice.

Adrien touched her hair, his long fingers twisting a strand. 'Whether real or unreal, I like red hair.'

What *am* I doing here? she asked herself. The next she knew, he'd ask her to dance.

'Excuse me,' she said, rising to her feet.

'It's that way.' Adrien nodded toward a tiny alcove near the bar.

'You going to the little girl's room?' Najla asked. 'Wait, I'll come with you.'

Feeling trapped, Sara walked with Najla to the tiny rest room.

'What do you think of the beard?' Najla asked, as they crowded into the space between the door and the washbasin.

Realizing she meant Adrien, Sara grimaced.

'Yeah, he's not so hot. But Dave's okay. I might even take him home with me.'

'You hardly know him,' Sara protested.

'I can spot kooks. He's not one.' Najla looked into the mirror, fluffing her hair. 'Take a look at the back of my head, will you, Sara? It feels like something's wrong with my hair.'

Sara obliged. 'Either you've got a terrible hair stylist, or you did something to your hair that took out a chunk right here.' She touched the spot.

In the mirror, Najla's gaze met hers. 'I didn't do anything,' Najla said, reaching to feel the back of her head. 'And I haven't had my hair done lately.'

Sara shrugged. 'Well, there's a piece missing.'

'That's weird. What could have happened?'

'Who knows? Look, Najla, I think I'll leave, if you don't mind.'

'No, that's okay. I can tell you don't go for this place. But tell me one thing — do you think it's just the boobs? Do you think Dave sees *me* at all?'

Sara remembered how Dave had stared at Najla's breasts. 'I hope so,' she said.

'Maryann — she's one of my friends — says I let guys make out with me too soon. She says I should wait and be more sure.' Najla sighed. 'I always seem to wind up the same way when I meet a man I like. He wants to go to bed, so I do, 'cause I want to, too, you know? Maryann says you can't build a permanent relationship that way. She's going with a guy she met right here in Poll's. She says she didn't let him touch her for weeks, and now he respects her. But that seems so cold-blooded.'

'Don't look to me for answers,' Sara said. 'I don't have any.'

'But you're cool; you've got it all together.'

Sara shook her head. 'I didn't even give the beard my right name.'

Najla giggled. 'That's what I mean.' She reached for the doorknob.

'Wait,' Sara said. 'I do have one piece of advice. Make sure Dave doesn't have a tattoo with wings on his upper arm before you take him home.'

'Wings? Oh, yeah — the strangler. Hey, thanks, I didn't think of the tattoo. Not that Dave's the killer. But, like you said, it doesn't hurt to make sure.'

Sara scurried through the now crowded room, breathing easier once she was outside. She hurried to her car, the parrot's, 'Hiya, honey,' ringing in her ears. When she noticed the parking lot was lit only by the neon sign, she tensed again, glancing quickly around as she unlocked her car and climbed in. It made her uneasy to be driving alone at night. Why had she come out at all?

Not because she'd expected to find her dream man. He didn't exist. Any man she met would be just another man who wanted what every man wanted — if she was lucky. If not, he could be the strangler.

Sara drove home through the park, and as she swung onto Upas Street, she slowed to allow a man and a black dog to cross in front of her. The dog's eyes glowed red in the headlights, and she wondered if it was the lost shepherd she'd rescued.

She turned off on St. Hubert Street and drove the two blocks to her house. A single light shone from the living room; she'd left it on purposely. She'd also turned on the outside light, but it wasn't lit now. Was the bulb burned out? Or had someone unscrewed it? Someone who wanted the front of her house dark.

As she pulled into the drive, she stared nervously at the dark shrubbery beside the steps. Why hadn't she asked Bobo to prune in front while she was at it? A man could hide in there.

Stop it! she cautioned herself. You're making things worse than they are. Any man capable of hiding in those bushes would have to be a dwarf.

Still, the front light was out, and it shouldn't be. Sara forced herself to leave the car. House key in hand, she hurried toward the steps, eyes and ears alert for the slightest movement, for any whisper of sound.

She sighed with relief when she was inside, with the door locked behind her. But she'd hardly had time to relax when the phone rang. She couldn't bring herself to answer it, in case it was the breather, and it seemed to take hours before the ringing finally stopped.

When she climbed into bed, she left the lights on. Grandpa Saari used to call her his brave little girl, but any courage she possessed always fled in darkness.

The book she'd bought for the mythology class spoke of modern myths, and how all human cultures need a mythology to believe or to disbelieve. Religion. Science. The occult. What did *she* believe in?

Grandpa Saari often told her about the great *noitas* of Finland and the magic deeds of these wizards, but Grandma scoffed at the tales, asking him how anyone could believe in such foolishness. How could a man survive hanging by his neck for a week, then get down and walk away unhurt? How could he disappear into thin air?

'Ah, Mielikki,' grandpa would say, 'how about the bloodstopping, is that foolish?'

Grandma's father had been a bloodstopper, and she was quick to resent an implied slur on him. 'He was no *noita*, as you well know,' she'd snap. 'Bloodstopping is a gift, a healing gift, not a wizard's bag of tricks.'

Little Sara had pestered her grandmother to show her how to stop blood from flowing, but Grandma never would.

'I can't always stop it; I'm not as gifted as my father,' she'd say. 'As for you, child, you lack the true power.'

Sara had always resented her Scottish father, when Grandma reminded her she was only half Finnish. What had he ever given her except red hair?

'See yourself clearly and accept what you see,' Dr. Zimmer had told her. Easier to say than do.

'Myths are a way of facing reality,' the book insisted. 'Myths are also a way of evading reality.'

Didn't that mean you couldn't win?

She'd never go to sleep, if she kept on like this. Deciding to focus on Jamie and what they'd do tomorrow, her rebellious thoughts centered on Jamie's father instead. She went over and over the encounter with Ian.

She'd been right to reject him totally, of course, but since she claimed to prefer total honesty, why hadn't she mentioned the woman?

19

Sitting at the kitchen table with the dregs of his coffee, he told himself he didn't much care for Santa Anas. The desert winds kept the fog at bay, and he needed the fog. Usually the dry heat didn't last more than a few days; he hoped this time would be no exception. San Diego suited him fine. This close to the ocean it was hardly ever hot. He hated heat.

When he was a kid, he thought he'd die of suffocation in his tiny room in that crummy upstairs apartment of hers. He didn't like to let the poodle in his room when it was hot, because the damn dog always wanted to sleep curled up next to him. Who could stand fur, when it got over ninety? The poodle would whine and snuffle outside his door, until his sister would yell at him to for chrissake take in the dog.

He reached for the gold heart on the chain around his neck and fingered it absently. His sister always got what she wanted one way or another. Being first born she'd had over ten years start on him in having her own way. As a kid he'd thought he'd never catch up, much less pass her.

He smiled, remembering the first time he'd come out on top. He didn't realize it at the time, but when he took the gold heart from the jewel case — the heart he had as much right to as she did — and replaced it with the poodle's bloody heart, that had been the beginning. The start of his understanding what he'd been born to do in this world. Would keep on doing until the day he died.

He eased his forefinger over the letters incised on the back of the heart. He didn't have to look at them to know what they said: *Love lasts forever. E.L.R. to A.G.R.* His father had given the heart to his mother on their wedding day, and his sister would kill to have it back. He smiled. Fat chance.

It wouldn't have taken his old man long to discover that nothing lasts forever, neither love nor anything else.

He, personally, thought love was a truckload of bullshit.

He tucked the heart under his T-shirt, reached into his pocket for his prize of the day, and slid the shining red strands between his fingers. The hair clung to his skin as though it had a life of its own, both repelling and arousing him. The bitch hadn't noticed when he'd clipped it from her head. Would she notice tonight?

Maybe when she sat in front of the mirror

in her bedroom with a nightgown on, short see-through, her nipples erect as she pulled a brush through her thick red hair. And maybe she wouldn't even realize then, she'd be too busy looking at herself, admiring her white breasts and thinking of the men who'd touched them.

He rose and paced restlessly. Sheba lifted her head from her paws and stared at him. He hated the dog more than any bitch he'd ever had, but that didn't matter now. She had maybe a week to live. Next time he'd make sure to get a younger dog, a smaller one, one that didn't make him uneasy.

No other bitch had ever defied him like Sheba. Not fighting defiance, but in subtle ways, hesitating before she obeyed his orders, as though she had to decide whether she wanted to bother or not, her continuous surveillance, spying on him, raising her hackles as she stared.

He laughed, a short, sharp sound with no humor. Sheba growled.

'To hell with you,' he muttered.

But she was a big dog, and she might fight at the last minute. He'd better put more than one tranquilizer in her food, when it came time. No point in getting chewed up while he did for her. Yes, first Sheba. And then . . .

What was she doing now? He glanced at

his watch. Ten o'clock on a week night. She had to work tomorrow. Would she be in the shower, water glistening on her pale skin, sliding down over her hips, forming droplets on the springy hair covering her cunt?

He licked his lips and plucked a single red hair from the fly of his pants.

20

Friday morning dawned clear and warm. Since it was obvious the hot weather would last through the day, Sara decided to go ahead with her planned picnic for Jamie.

She walked across the park to Palo Oro, arriving just before ten. Mrs. Hodges intercepted Sara before she entered Jamie's room.

'I thought you'd like to know that Jamie's gained two pounds,' she said. 'He's eating so much better — he's even trying to feed himself finger food these past two days. I do hope you intend to continue working with him.'

Sara grinned. 'Just try and stop me.'

Mrs. Hodges nodded her approval, and Sara went on into the room.

Jamie's smile when he caught sight of her made her heart turn over. It was a full-fledged smile, not merely a twitch of his lips.

'I didn't bring the car this morning,' she told him. 'Instead, I'm going to push you through the park to my house. But you can't just sit back and do nothing. I expect you to take notice of everything we pass. I made a list, and when we get to my house, I'll ask you if you saw everything on the list, and I'll find out which you liked the best. After that comes the surprise lunch. Okay?'

To her amazement, Jamie nodded.

'Hey! You've learned something new.'

He nodded again, obviously pleased with himself.

'Can you shake your head for no, too?'

He turned his head to the right and back to midline, without turning it to the left.

'Half a no is better than none,' she assured him. 'I'm really impressed.'

With the plush monkey riding on the arm of Jamie's wheelchair, they set off.

'I looked up some information on that owl you saw in the zoo,' Sara said as they entered the park. 'No wonder he startled you. The Great Horned Owl is the mightiest of the owl clan — they don't call him the tiger of the air for nothing.'

She stopped the chair, moved to stand in front of him, and stretched her arms out to either side. 'The Great Horned Owl has a four-foot wingspread — that's almost as wide as this. Impressive, isn't it?'

Jamie blinked and nodded.

'Like most owls he's a night hunter, and he catches and eats a lot of mice and rats, so he's really a friend to man, even if he is scary-looking. Actually he avoids humans — he never attacks them unless they attack him, or if they come near his nest when there are little owlets in it. Even if the owl in the zoo could have gotten out of the cage, he wouldn't have hurt us.'

Satisfied that Jamie understood, Sara resumed pushing his wheelchair.

* * *

It wasn't that I was really scared of the Great Horned Owl in the zoo, Jamie thought. It was only because his eyes reminded me of the owl eyes in my dream — round and yellow and shining. I wish I could explain to Sara that I know owls won't hurt me. At least not real ones. Dream owls are different.

But he didn't want to think about what came at night, so he turned his head to look to the right. Palm trees lined the road side of walk running along the edge of the park, while oleander bushes with white flowers grew on the park side of the walk. He knew about oleanders, 'cause they taught in school that the leaves were poisonous if you ate them. It'd take a really dumb kid to eat leaves off bushes. Ugh. He'd never do it.

A guy with blond hair ran past bouncing a

basketball. Jamie decided there must be a place to practice shooting baskets somewhere around here. On the sidewalk to the right, a kid on a bike did wheelies. Over on the grass some teenagers tossed a Frisbee.

Ahead of them there was a daddy with a baby in a sort of a backpack. He'd see his own daddy tomorrow. Anticipation mixed with anxiety gnawed at Jamie. Would his father notice all the things he'd learned to do? Maybe he couldn't yet do enough to please Daddy, maybe he had to learn a lot more things first. If he could.

Off to the right a whole flock of pigeons settled onto the grass and began jostling each other, all trying to eat the same old grungy chunk of pizza. Birds liked really gross stuff — worms and bugs. Crows even ate dead things squashed by cars. He wouldn't much care to be an owl, either — rats and mice, yuck!

Coming toward them was a man walking a dog. A black German shepherd. Jamie tensed. Was it the same dog? Yes, and the same man; he recognized him as the man from his dream. The man with the flying owl on his arm. He'd seen him with the dog yesterday, too, near the zoo.

As they neared, the dog's gaze fixed on Jamie. She knows me, Jamie thought. I didn't think she saw me in the dream, but she must have, 'cause she knows who I am. He held his breath as dog and man came closer and closer and closer, then gasped when the dog broke free of the man, yanking the red leash from his hand as she ran to Jamie.

Sara stopped pushing the wheelchair, and the dog laid her head on Jamie's knee. Hesitantly he touched her, letting his hand rest on her head. I like you, too, he told the dog silently.

'Sheba!' The man's voice was gruff. Angry-sounding. He loomed threateningly over the chair.

Jamie glanced up at him and froze as the man's gaze passed over him, briefly meeting Jamie's eyes. No, Jamie begged, not now, please don't let it happen here. But he had no more control over the real dreams in the day than he did at night. They came whether he wanted them to or not.

In a gray fog, he saw the man kneeling with a long, sharp knife in his hand, saw the dog, Sheba, lying on a floor. The man lunged down with the knife, aiming for Sheba's heart. Jamie yelped in terror and rage, and the foggy dream was gone as though it had never been.

The man regained the leash and jerked Sheba away from him. She snarled at the man but he didn't pay attention, just pulled harder.

'I'm sorry if my dog frightened the boy,' the man said to Sara.

'I don't think it was the dog who frightened him.' Sara's voice was cool. 'You needn't have been so abrupt.'

The man nodded curtly and stalked on past them, keeping Sheba on a very short lead. The dog turned to look at Jamie, but was dragged on.

Sara knelt in front of the wheelchair. 'Are you all right?'

He nodded. He was fine. But something bad was going to happen to Sheba. If only he could tell Sara that the man meant to hurt Sheba. Kill her.

'The dog didn't scare you, did she?'

He gave a half-shake of his head. Not the dog. Just the man.

'Some people shouldn't be allowed to own dogs.' She rose and resumed pushing him.

Jamie couldn't agree more. As they walked on, he tried to concentrate on what he was seeing, but he was too disturbed by the real dream to pay attention. If he could tell Sara, he asked himself, would she believe him? The bad happenings he saw in them were kind of hard for even him to believe, but he'd learned the dreams came true. As far as he knew, no one else had real dreams. If they did, they never talked about them. He hadn't ever had one until after he got hurt. He hated the dreams.

By the time they reached Sara's house, the ugly menace of the dream had faded enough so he began to hope it wouldn't ruin his whole time with Sara.

She pushed him through a gate into the backyard, leaving him at the foot of the three steps while she unlocked the door. She propped the screen and the door open, then came back, untying him, lifting him into her arms, and carrying him up the steps into her house.

She'd already fixed a nest of pillows so she could prop him upright on the couch. Once he was comfortable, she went back for the monkey and brought it to him. He watched without understanding while she opened her shoulder bag, took out a gray felt mouse, and pinned it to the monkey.

'The mouse is stuffed with catnip,' she explained. 'I'm hoping to lure Violet with it. Did your cat like catnip?'

Jamie nodded, remembering the time Kiki tore her catnip ball to shreds and scattered the crumbly dried leaves all over the house.

Sara sat beside him on the couch, to his right so he could look at her. 'If we don't move,' she said, 'I think Violet's curiosity may overcome her fear of strangers. Meanwhile, I'll tell you one of my grandfather's tales.'

The story was about a boy named Jukka, and how he won a mouse with blue eyes and a white nose to be his bride. 'Course it turned out the mouse was really a fair maiden under an evil spell, but it was still a good story. Sara had just finished saying, ' . . . and so they lived happily ever after,' when a cat jumped onto her lap.

Jamie could see Violet was afraid of him, but also drawn to the smell of the catnip mouse pinned to the monkey on his lap. Inch by inch she crept closer. He scarcely dared to breathe. At last she decided he wasn't too much of a threat and pounced on the mouse, trying to worry it loose from the monkey. Enthralled by the catnip odor, she didn't notice when Jamie's fingers touched her soft fur.

Sara reached over and unpinned the mouse. Jamie expected Violet to run away with it, but she only pulled the toy into the space between him and Sara, and purring, eyes half-closed in pleasure, lay with her head resting on the mouse.

He enjoyed the feel of her warmth next to him, and he didn't mind that she wasn't pretty. Kiki, being a Siamese, had beautiful, perfect markings. Poor Violet didn't. She was far from perfect. Sort of like him. He wondered if Violet knew she looked sort of grungy, and that's why she hid from people.

Sometimes he wanted to hide, too. Only it was easier for cats than it was for people.

I bet if I saw her every day, he told himself, we'd be friends.

★ ★ ★

Sara brought Jamie into the backyard for the picnic, moving his wheelchair into the shade of the Brazilian pepper tree. She set out the food on a kitchen cart next to him — peanut butter and jelly sandwiches, carrot sticks, and strips of cheese, a simple meal of things he could hold in his hands and feed himself. She tucked a container of chocolate milk, complete with straw, between him and the wheelchair arm, so he could sip it whenever he wanted to.

Though he wasn't yet strong enough to feed himself an entire meal without tiring, she thought with time he would be. Meanwhile, for every mouthful he managed on his own, his confidence would grow.

After eating, Jamie rested on the couch with his monkey. When he fell asleep, to Sara's surprise, Violet jumped onto the couch and curled up next to him, kneading the monkey with her paws as she purred. Either Violet was becoming less fearful, or she smelled catnip on both Jamie and the monkey. As she watched the boy and the cat, Sara sighed at the realization that she'd soon have to return Jamie to the nursing home.

Tomorrow was Saturday, and that meant Ian would be going to see Jamie. At first she'd planned to arrange her own visit to avoid Ian, but, the more she thought about it, the more certain she became that she should arrive when Ian was visiting, so she could talk to him about his son. Looking at the sleeping boy, she made up her mind that she had to confront Ian about Jamie.

She wouldn't say a word about their own failed relationship.

After he woke, she carried Jamie outside to his wheelchair, sat on a lawn chair to his right, placed a small chalkboard on his lap, and handed him a piece of chalk.

'Can you draw a heart?' she asked.

Sara praised him when his second try produced a recognizable heart. 'Draw me something else,' she said. 'Anything you want.'

At first she could make no sense of the wavering lines he drew, but at last she decided, because of the four sticklike legs, he meant it to be an animal. Violet, she thought.

'A cat,' she said triumphantly.

He gave his negative half-shake.

'A dog?' she asked, the next logical guess.

He nodded, fixing her with an imploring gaze.

She understood Jamie wanted more from her, that he was trying to convey something he thought important.

Remembering what had happened in the park, she said, 'I'll bet it's the black shepherd who laid her head in your lap.'

He nodded, but his look still pleaded with her to go on. She had no idea what else he wanted from her.

'The man called her Sheba,' Sara said at random. 'Did you like Sheba?'

He gave another nod, but the intensity of his gaze didn't diminish. What did he want?

'I'm sorry, Jamie,' she said gently. 'I can't think of any more questions.' Reaching over, she erased what he'd drawn. 'Can you draw a letter of the alphabet? Or a number?'

He put the chalk to the board, but nothing happened. Whether it was because the accident had damaged that center of his brain, or whether he'd erected a block against communicating by the written word as well as verbally, she didn't know. An idea struck her.

'We'll try something else,' she told him.

Hurrying inside, she unearthed her old portable manual typewriter, and carried it back to Jamie. After setting the typewriter on the kitchen cart and moving the cart so he could reach the keyboard, she rolled in a sheet of paper.

'Have you ever used a typewriter? If you haven't, maybe you've used a computer. The keyboard is the same. You hit a letter, and it comes up on the paper, like this.' She typed *Jamie* in caps.

'Do you know what that word is?'

He pointed to himself.

Sara smiled. If he could read his own name, his cerebral language center must be functioning. She typed other words. Tree. Bush. Flower. Sky. Each time he pointed correctly.

'Now you try,' she suggested.

Hesitantly, Jamie lifted a shaking finger to the keys. Before he touched one, his hand dropped back into his lap, he ducked his head and began to cry.

Sara hugged him to her. 'It's all right, it doesn't matter,' she said. 'You've shown me you can read, and that's wonderful.'

As she consoled him, she tried to decide what his failure might mean in terms of actual brain injury. It seemed to her that he hadn't really tried, that his emotions had gotten between him and the attempt, preventing him from so much as touching the keyboard. He was afraid to try. Why? Fear of failure? She didn't think so, because he readily attempted other tasks she'd set, even though he couldn't be sure ahead of time that he'd succeed.

But if it wasn't brain damage that prevented Jamie from communicating verbally or by writing, what did? She needed to consult with his doctor, but that would be impossible without written permission from Ian.

When Jamie quieted, she wiped his damp face and offered him a miniature chocolate bar. While he was eating it, she went over her list of things that he might have seen in the park on their way here, and found he'd observed every one.

'Great,' she told him, happy to end on a positive note and restore his confidence.

Because he looked tired, she drove him back to Palo Oro instead of pushing the wheelchair across the park.

'I'll be here tomorrow,' she told him as she wheeled him into his room. 'Since it's Saturday, I expect your father will visit you, too. So we won't plan to go anywhere except outside, okay?'

He nodded.

Sara leaned down and kissed his forehead, proffering her cheek for him to kiss in return. '*Au revoir*,' she told him. 'That's French for goodbye. It means till we meet again.'

★　★　★

After the evening nurse tucked him into bed, Jamie watched the clock. He wasn't sure he wanted to think about everything that had happened during the day. He knew that if he began going over the visit to Sara's, he'd remember every last little thing, he always did. But the clock wasn't enough to distract him, by now he pretty well knew most of the pictures on it by heart.

Au revoir. He liked the sound of the words. And the meaning, 'cause it sort of promised there'd be another meeting, that Sara would come back like she said she would. Sometimes people went away and never returned.

He wished she'd understood about the dog. About Sheba being in danger. But how could Sara know, unless she was a mind reader? Jamie made a face. He didn't like to think *he* was a mind reader, but he guessed he sort of was.

Otherwise, how could he know that Sheba was afraid of the man, and how could he feel the evil surrounding the man like a fog? He wondered again how Sheba had known *him*. Maybe the dog could read his mind. That was okay, but he sure hoped the man couldn't. Jamie shivered and pushed the notion away.

Sara's house was nice. He wished he had a warm cat like Violet to sleep with all the time. Kiki had never been allowed to sleep with him; she'd been banished to her own bed in the laundry room at night.

The day had been fun, except for the man in the park. And the typewriter. He'd used a computer lots of times at school, and sometimes he used to play computer games at Ryan's house. So he knew how to work a keyboard, and he should have been able to type. But his brain somehow didn't connect with his fingers anymore.

It was getting dark outside. Pretty soon the nurse would come by and make him pee in the urinal, so he wouldn't wet the bed in his sleep. Then she'd shut off the light, and it would be night.

Owls hunted at night. They were night birds. Night hunters. Like the man. Jamie blinked, wondering how he knew that. Sara had told him about owls, but the thought about the man had just popped into his head, and he'd instantly been sure he was right.

A chill ran along his spine. What would a

bad man hunt at night in San Diego? In the park. Jamie swallowed. The park *was* where the man hunted — but how did he know? The real dreams were bad enough, but this was different than the dreams. Worse. Somehow he must be reading the man's mind. He clutched the monkey to him, wishing more than ever that it was a live animal instead of a stuffed one. Something warm and comforting.

Frantically, he searched for a way to stop thinking about the bad man. What had Sara taught him today, besides the French word for goodbye? He breathed a sigh of relief when he remembered the counting. He'd learned how to count to ten in Finnish. He already knew how in Spanish, but that was sort of like English. Finn was a lot weirder. He'd have to work hard to recall all those strange words.

Yksi. That was one. *Kaksi.* Two. What was three? It hovered at the edge of his mind, starting, he knew, with a *k* like two . . .

⋆ ⋆ ⋆

Sara turned over in bed for what seemed like the thousandth time, disturbing Violet, who took time to settle herself again.

Why had she said *au revoir* to Jamie? It had

brought back the time she'd said the words to Ian, and Ian had been in her thoughts ever since. Not in relation to Jamie, but to her. The night they'd met. In the fog at the beach. Their first kiss. She'd taken out every damn little thing — bad and good — that had ever happened between them, and examined each item minutely, over and over.

How could she possibly face him tomorrow, without any mention of their own failed relationship? Much as she wished to banish any and all involvement with Ian, her feeling for him remained.

Why couldn't she be like Najla? Why couldn't she go to bed with a man and, if he walked away without a backward glance, look for another? Why in hell did it have to turn out to be such a vast commitment? At least on her part.

Stop it. Go back to the distant past, when times were good. To Grandma and Grandpa Saari and the farm. To the tales of *noitas* and bloodstoppers.

Did blood really stop for her great-grandfather? Grandma Saari had, she claimed, seen it with her own eyes. And the time little Sara cut her leg so bad on the barbed wire, Grandma had pressed her fingers over the wound, chanted in Finn, and the bleeding stopped just like that.

Power of suggestion? Possibly. She'd never know for sure.

How could a person know *anything* for sure?

Had C.W. ever loved her, even at the beginning? Hadn't he married her because she wouldn't go to bed with him otherwise? She didn't think she'd deliberately held back waiting for marriage, but it was difficult to remember how her mind had worked eight years ago.

His need to conquer had pressured C.W. into marriage with her, and then he'd pressured her in return, squashing her into a doormat. But, as Dr. Zimmer had pointed out, she'd let him squash her for seven long years, before she finally revolted.

Ralph had tried to pressure her into bed with him when she didn't really want him, and she'd come damn close to going along with it. She knew better than to take more than two drinks — why had she?

Ian didn't pressure her. The pressure came from inside her, and that scared her. Why hadn't she asked him about the woman who'd answered the phone? Because it was safer to find an excuse to end their relationship?

'See yourself; know yourself,' had been Dr. Zimmer's expensive advice.

Bits and pieces seemed to be the best she could do. And she didn't much like what she saw.

The phone rang and she froze. Answer it and get breathed at, or pull the plug and wonder what she might be missing? It didn't have to be the breather.

Admit it, you hope Ian's calling or you'd never answer, she told herself as she groped for the phone. 'Hello?'

'Sara?' Najla asked. 'Thank God! I'm sorry if I woke you up, but I had to talk to someone. I just saw Otto Hammer's talk show — were you watching it?'

Sara stifled a yawn. 'No.'

'Otto interviewed that shrink who commented about the strangler for the paper. Oh, Sara, I wish I hadn't listened. I'm so scared!'

'What did he say that was so frightening?'

'This doc was talking about, you know, serial killers, and he mentioned how some of them follow the victim for weeks or months, sometimes stealing a personal belonging from her before — ' Najla stopped, her voice quavering.

'You mean like a pair of bikini panties?'

'Hair.' Najla moaned the word. 'The doc said some killers enjoy the challenge of getting close enough to the victim to clip a strand of her hair without her noticing.'

Sara's eyes widened as she remembered being in the ladies room at Poll's with Najla. She swallowed. 'You mean you think the strangler might have . . . ?'

'Oh, God I'm scared to death that's *exactly* what happened to me. You saw for yourself a piece of my hair was gone. And I'm a redhead. *He's* got it, I just know he has. What am I going to do?'

'Call the police.'

'They won't listen; they'll think I'm some weirdo. This shrink didn't say the strangler cut off hair, just that some serial killers did.'

'I'd call the police anyway. Or listen, do you have family around? It'll be Christmas in a couple of days; why not visit them? Then you'd be with people at night.'

'My folks live in New York, but they're on a Christmas cruise in the Caribbean. There isn't anyone else.'

Sara dredged up a name. 'How about Maryann?'

Silence on the other end. 'Maybe. If I didn't tell her why I wanted to stay. But she wouldn't take me in for more than a week.'

'If all else fails, you can move in with me for a while.'

'Didn't you say you live right next to the park.'

'Yes, but — '

'I don't want to be anywhere near that damn park. I mean, thanks, it's nice of you, but I'm afraid he'll find me if I'm close to where he — where he — ' Again her voice failed.

Where he kills. The unsaid words echoed in Sara's head.

'Call the police,' she urged again. 'Then move in with Maryann, while you decide what to do. How about tonight?'

'Tonight's no problem, Dave's here. You remember Dave.'

Dave, from Poll's. Sara frowned. If Dave was with her, why was Najla so upset? 'What does Dave think about it?' she asked.

'He fell asleep when the talk show was on, so he didn't get to listen to the shrink. He's told me before I overreact, and all he said about my hair was that I probably used too much hairspray or something.'

An unpleasant thought struck Sara. 'You did check Dave out for tattoos, didn't you?'

Najla giggled. 'The only one he's got is on his ass. A wolf, of all things. Men kill me.'

Poor choice of words, Sara thought grimly. 'Doesn't Dave have a place where you can stay?'

'No way, he's got a real picky roomie. Can you believe the guy made him sign an agreement about no live-in girlfriends, before he'd let Dave move in?'

'How about Dave sharing your place?'

Najla hesitated. 'I don't think so.' She lowered her voice. 'It's sort of petering out between us, like it does after a while, you know? I'm fairly sure he's already got another gal on the string. Anyway, he doesn't believe me about the hair.'

'I do. Call the police tomorrow, will you?'

'I'll think about it. Actually, I did try a new gel mousse lately, and I notice I'm shedding a lot more hair on the brush and in the shower. Maybe I'm allergic or something.'

Sara took a deep breath and was about to urge Najla one more time to go to the police, when Najla began giggling.

'Stop that, Dave,' she said, 'I'm on the goddamn phone.'

He murmured something Sara couldn't hear.

'Look, I've got to go,' Najla told her. 'Thanks for listening. I feel a whole lot better.'

Najla might, Sara thought as she hung up, but I don't.

Short of dragging Najla to the police herself, though, there was nothing she could do if Najla chose not to report the problem.

Sara spent the next hour worrying, finally

falling asleep on the couch with all the lights on.

She dreamed she was back on the Saari farm, but couldn't find anyone there. After she looked in the house, the barn, and the outbuildings without success, a big black dog appeared. She followed him into the woods, certain the dog would lead her to her grandparents.

Soon a ground fog gathered, thickening and rising until she could hardly see where she was going. The dog became only a vague dark shape ahead of her and Sara began to run, afraid she'd lose sight of the dog. She tripped and fell over a stone.

As she started to rise, she saw the stone was a grave marker. Other headstones loomed around her, and she realized, with horror, she'd been led into a cemetery. In the uncertain light she struggled to read the name on the stone she'd fallen over, hoping it wasn't her grandmother's.

It wasn't.

The name she spelled out, letter by letter, was her own.

21

The morning was cool with an overcast sky, when Sara arrived at Palo Oro. When she saw Ian's car in the parking lot, she tensed, bracing herself to face him.

No need to get flustered, she admonished herself. Never mind the personal; your concern is what's best for Jamie.

When she entered the room, Jamie, in his wheelchair, was watching his father leaf through a book she'd given the boy. His face lit up when he saw her.

'Hi, Jamie,' she said, tousling his hair. 'Ready for a game of catch?'

He nodded.

She glanced at Ian. 'Hello,' she said, keeping her voice carefully neutral. 'Won't you join us in the game?'

Ian stared at her for a long moment. 'How are you?' he said finally.

'Fine.' She had no intention of veering a hairline away from what she'd programmed ahead of time. They were both here because of Jamie; their meeting had nothing to do with Ian and Sara.

'Why don't you push Jamie outside, while I

find the ball?' she asked.

When he had difficulty releasing the wheelchair brake, she showed him how, understanding then that he'd never handled a wheelchair before, never once pushed Jamie out of the room in all the times he'd visited his son.

'One of the nurses told me you'd been coming to see Jamie every day,' Ian said as they walked along the corridor.

'Yes. We've been having fun. I've taken him to the park, to the zoo, and on a picnic. I didn't think you'd mind.'

'I don't mind but I *was* surprised.'

She decided not to ask why. 'In just one week Jamie's learned so much,' she said, laying a hand on the boy's shoulder. 'He's very bright.'

Ian said nothing, but she hadn't expected an answer. Showing, not telling, was the key to inducing belief. She directed him to the door opening onto the back patio, and the three of them ventured into the overcast morning.

'It looks as though the Santa Ana has curled up and died,' she said. 'Right, Jamie?'

He nodded.

After setting the brake on his wheelchair, Sara moved in front of the chair, backing away until she was several feet from him, the ball in her hands. 'Ready, get set,' she warned.

Jamie lifted his hands and spread his fingers. Sara gently tossed the ball to him, and he caught it.

'How about that?' she crowed. 'A perfect catch. See how your coordination is improving? As soon as you get a little more strength in your wrists, you'll be able to throw the ball back to me.'

'Uh, that was great, son,' Ian said belatedly, his gaze shifting from Jamie to Sara and back. He was, she thought with satisfaction, obviously shaken.

She ran through a quick list of questions that could be answered yes or no, finishing up with, 'San Diego is the capitol of California.'

Jamie, who'd gotten every one right, gave his negative half-shake.

She gave him a hug. 'One hundred percent. I guess I'll have to think up harder questions.'

Jamie grinned at her. He opened his mouth as though to speak. She froze, hoping against hope for a miracle. It didn't happen. Jamie mewed like a cat.

Sara covered her disappointment with a smile. 'Are you asking me how Violet is?'

Jamie nodded.

'I think she misses you. Or maybe it's your catnip-scented monkey. One thing for sure, she'll be as amazed as I am to know you can make cat noises.' She turned to Ian. 'This is a first for Jamie. Every day he comes up with something new he can do.'

Ian got down on one knee in front of his son. 'Would you like me to come and see you more often?' he asked.

Jamie's nod was enthusiastic. He reached toward his father, and Ian took his hand. Sara, watching, saw tears in Ian's eyes.

So he *was* moved. For Sara, that wasn't enough. How much did it take to convince him to bring Jamie home for good? What Jamie needed wasn't more visits, but to live with his father.

When she offered Jamie a miniature chocolate bar, Ian started to help Jamie tear off the paper, but she stopped him. Everything the boy did for himself, no matter how hard it was for him, built needed confidence.

'He can feed himself!' Ian blurted in surprise, when Jamie stuffed the tiny bar into his mouth.

'Finger food,' she said briskly. 'But soon he'll be able to manage silverware.' She glanced at Jamie. 'Sorry to be talking about you as though you're not here, but you've sort of overwhelmed your dad with what you can do, and I need to explain a little.'

Actually, she also wanted Jamie to hear what she had to say, because it would encourage him.

'Jamie's muscles are weak because he hasn't used them for so long. Now that he *is* using them, his muscles will gradually regain strength, and he'll be able to do more and more for himself.'

'I don't know what to say. I didn't believe — ' Ian broke off and rose. 'Thank you, Sara.'

She shook her head. 'Jamie's done all the work.' It was true. All she'd really done was to provide the opportunity.

Ian glanced at his watch. 'Maybe we three can have lunch together.' He turned to Jamie. 'How about a hamburger?'

Jamie frowned, finally shaking his head.

'Hot dog?'

Another no.

'Pizza?'

A smile and a nod.

Ian left and came back with milk shakes and a pizza big enough for them all, plus leftovers for the ground squirrels.

After lunch, Sara pushed Jamie back inside, knowing he'd need to rest. In his room, she hugged him and kissed his forehead. Ian watched her, then bent and awkwardly kissed his son's cheek.

'I'll see you tomorrow,' Sara told Jamie as she went out.

She was disappointed when Ian didn't set a definite date for his next visit with his son, and, when they reached the parking lot, she told him so.

'I won't make a promise I can't keep,' he said. 'I don't know when I'll be back. I have to think about it.'

Sara's tight control over her emotions let go abruptly. 'What is there to think about?' she cried. 'Have you forgotten Christmas is only three days away? I hope to hell you weren't merely planning a quick visit on Christmas Day. Jamie needs to be with you; he needs to go home. The least you could do is take him home for Christmas.'

Ian stared at her. 'Take him home?'

Exasperated, she snapped, 'If you won't take him for Christmas, I damn well will.' She turned on her heel and marched to her car.

Ian got there before she did, his expression clearly showing his annoyance as he blocked her from opening the car door. 'Stop condemning me. I admit I was wrong about Jamie's capabilities. What you've done with him is amazing. But he's far from normal. They can take care of him a lot better here than — '

'You're dead wrong! They keep him clean

here, they feed him adequately, they do range-of-motion exercises, but what Jamie really needs is missing. He needs love. Your love. He needs to live in his own house. With you. If you have to, hire a nursemaid for whatever you feel you can't do for him, but for God's sake take him home.'

'Damn it, Sara, I don't know. I need time. You make everything sound so simple. It's not. How do I know I won't backslide? Drink. Take reds again.'

'You didn't do either when you had people depending on you, did you?'

'That was different. Moira was alive and — '

Sara glared at him, angrier than she'd ever been at anyone. 'Damn Moira! She's dead. Nothing will ever bring her back. Why don't you climb out of her grave and take a look around? Your son's not dead. Try thinking about this situation from Jamie's point of view, instead of your own. If you can, which I seriously doubt. You're too fond of your role as the guilty, bereaved widower to try to understand how your son might feel. You — you make me sick.' In her fury, she shoved him, hard.

Taken by surprise, he stumbled sideways. She flung open the car door and slid in. Moments later she roared from the parking lot, eager to put distance between herself and Ian as fast as she could. She was too agitated to go home, so she drove to the beach, planning to walk along the sand until she calmed down.

The wisps of fog drifting at the water's edge reminded her of the day she and Ian had walked in the mist. That had been the first time he kissed her.

She'd blown it with him this time for sure. Since they didn't have much of a relationship anyway, it wouldn't matter to her, except for Jamie. She couldn't give up her visits to the boy; they'd become as important to her as she thought they were to him.

Now that she'd reamed Ian out good and proper, would he be likely to give his permission for Jamie's doctor to talk to her? She needed to know about the boy's injuries from the accident and what his physical limitations might be, to plan a complete program for him. After what she'd said to Ian, she'd be lucky if he didn't tell Mrs. Hodges she wasn't to visit Ian again — or take him home for Christmas. Since Ian hadn't agreed he would, she certainly meant to. Unless Ian refused to allow it.

Sara shook her head. No, she didn't think Ian would go that far. Whatever his faults, he wasn't vindictive.

Determined that Jamie would have a good Christmas one way or another, she stopped in Mission Valley on her way home to buy decorations and a small live pine tree. If it turned out she couldn't bring him home, she'd take the tree to Palo Oro and let Jamie help her decorate it there.

The stores and the freeways were crowded with last-minute holiday shoppers, so she didn't get home until the long shadows of evening darkened the day. As she pulled the car into the driveway, her headlights picked up a man opening the gate of her backyard and coming toward her car. She slammed on the brakes, heart pounding before she recognized Ian.

'You scared me!' she cried as she opened her door.

'I didn't mean to,' he said. 'I got tired of waiting in my car for you to come home, so I found a chair in your yard.'

Looking around, Sara spotted his car parked up the street.

'I don't have your new and unlisted phone number, so I had no choice but to come in person,' he said. 'Take a walk with me, Sara.'

When she hesitated, he smiled wryly. 'Come on, get it over with.'

She shrugged and fell into step with him as they walked along St. Hubert Street in the gathering darkness, fallen eucalyptus leaves crunching underfoot. She expected him to start talking, but he remained silent for so long she grew uneasy.

'It feels like autumn tonight,' she said at random. 'Like an October evening where I grew up. But by now they'd have snow. Snow for Christmas instead of fog.'

She thought he'd react to the word Christmas but he didn't.

'You talk a lot about your childhood,' he said. 'Was it so much better than the rest of your life? Than now?'

'Yes.'

'Yet you accuse me of living in my dead wife's grave, instead of facing what's now.'

His comparison left Sara momentarily speechless. Did her longing for her past happy childhood imperil her chance for a happy present?

'Before the accident,' he went on, 'I was afraid Moira was going to leave me for another man. Then she was killed. I know I'm still trying to work it through. Not only trying, damn it, but slowly getting there.

'I apologize for rushing you the other day, and then accusing you of playing games when you refused me. I admit I expected too much from you too fast. It won't happen again. Please don't give up on me. Can't we try again, you and I?'

He stopped under a street light and put his hands on her shoulders. His face, shadowed by the light overhead, seemed a stranger's face. Sara was suddenly conscious of the darkness and the silence around them. Of the park just across the road. Of being a woman, a small red-haired woman with no self-defense skills.

'Let's walk back,' she said.

'Not until I get an answer.'

This is Ian, she told herself. You're not afraid of him. And, while he's with you, you're safe enough from the strangler. Don't be foolish, say something.

'I don't know how to answer your question,' she admitted.

His arms dropped, letting her go. 'I suppose I can't blame you. But we ought to give ourselves one more chance. Neither of us can live in the past forever — and don't tell me you're not, because you're as guilty as I am. I hate to let you go. There aren't very many Saras in the world.'

Not many Ians either. Though they disagreed about Jamie, among other things, most of the time she liked Ian. He wasn't a spoiled hero like C.W. Or a manipulative Ralph.

'I'll think about it,' she said finally.

Before she knew what he meant to do, he brushed her lips with his. 'I'm trying to influence you any way I can,' he murmured, taking her hand.

She couldn't deny she felt something for him . . . whenever he touched her the wanting began. But she was afraid to let herself be betrayed by her physical yearning. Sex wasn't enough, and she was far from certain what other emotions might be mixed in with the sex.

They walked on, hand in hand, not talking.

'Do you really want to bring Jamie to your house for Christmas?' he asked at last.

'Of course!'

'Would you consider inviting me, too?'

Since she hadn't expected this, it took her a moment to reply. 'Jamie and I would love to have you. Dinner's at three on Christmas Day.'

'When do you open the presents?'

'On Christmas morning.'

'How about decorating the tree?'

'Christmas Eve. I thought I'd keep Jamie over that night, if you don't mind.'

'He'll enjoy it. So would I.' Ian's voice was wistful.

She decided to be blunt. 'We could use help with the tree, but I'm inviting only Jamie to spend the night. You'll have to go home.'

'And come back in the morning to help open presents.'

'If you like.'

'It'd be simpler all the way around, if I stayed over night.'

'You're wrong. It'd be far more complicated, and you know that as well as I do.'

'Maybe it's time we got into complications.'

Sara shook her head and changed the subject. 'What kind of a present did you get for Jamie?'

He sighed. 'I didn't know what to get. Any suggestions?'

'How about a small radio he could work himself? Or a small tape player? Nothing fancy, the important thing being that it's simple enough for him to manage on his own.'

'Sounds like a good idea. Thanks.'

Seeing they'd reached the house, Sara turned into her walk. Ian came with her, stopping her when she started up the steps.

'I'd like to take you to dinner,' he said.

'Not tonight.'

He gave her a twisted smile. 'Too much of a good thing?'

Despite herself, her lips twitched into a half-smile.

He pulled her down onto the steps, sitting

beside her. 'Humor me for a few minutes more.'

'I think you're hoping if I sit here long enough, I'll get so hungry I'll agree to dinner.'

'*Are* you hungry?'

'Don't push your luck.' She looked at the thickening fog and hunched her shoulders. 'You really ought to leave while you can still see to get home.'

'I like the fog.'

'I don't. Not anymore.' Sara sighed. 'I worry about the strangler. Even more since my new friend Najla called me. Najla's a redhead like me. Earlier this week she found a clump of her hair missing. Not just a little, but an obvious chunk. Last night she heard a shrink on a talk show say that serial killers sometimes steal a personal belonging from their chosen victim before the killing. Najla's afraid the strangler might have snipped off a piece of her hair without her knowledge. The trouble is, Najla's sort of an airhead, and I don't believe she's afraid enough. I told her to call the police but . . . ' Sara shrugged. 'What do you think?'

Ian took a moment to reply. 'With this serial killer on the prowl, if I were a red-haired woman, I'd take the loss of a strand of my hair seriously enough to make damn sure I had good locks on all my doors and windows. And I wouldn't go out at night alone. I'm not sure whether I'd call the police or not, though. In everything I've read about the murders, there was no mention of missing hair.'

'But mightn't the police hold back some of the evidence?' Sara asked. 'Keep it secret? It's been hinted he mutilates his victims, but no details are given.' She shuddered. 'Actually, I'm just as glad not to know.'

Ian put an arm around her and drew her close to his side. She leaned against his warmth for a long, comforting moment, before pulling away and getting to her feet.

'Go home, Ian. I'll see you on Christmas Eve.'

'I can take a hint.' He rose, then bent, plucked the evening paper from the shrubbery, and handed it to her. 'This yours?'

Sara nodded. 'The paper girl's aim is far from perfect. She'll never make a pitcher. Good night, Ian.' She turned quickly, dug her key from her pocket, and unlocked the door.

She didn't want to be alone. Worse, she specifically wanted Ian with her. If he kissed her again, she wasn't sure what might happen. Yet she was determined to be by herself tonight, both because she had to learn to deal with her fear of being alone, and because she wasn't certain whether or not it was wise to open her arms to Ian.

Just the same, she was disappointed when he made no attempt to kiss her good night.

In the kitchen, Sara first fed Violet, then fixed herself a bowl of chicken noodle soup, and sat down to eat it with crackers and cheese. She unfolded the paper to read while she ate.

She immediately focused on a composite picture of the rapist-strangler drawn by an artist. It was based on a description given, while under hypnosis, by the woman who'd escaped from him. Unfortunately, the drawing looked to Sara like Mr. Average Man.

The woman recalled that he seemed about forty and that he threw a jacket — khaki, she thought — over her head before he raped her. She still couldn't positively identify the bird tattoo. The killer had apparently talked continuously, gibberish about bitches in heat, the heart of a dog, and something about 'there came darkness,' that sounded as though it might be from the Bible. Nothing he'd said made much sense to her in or out of hypnosis.

While Sara wasn't a Bible reader, her Grandma Saari had been, and many's the verse she'd heard as a child. ' . . . there came darkness . . . ' struck a chord. She was positive she'd listened to her grandmother say those words, but she didn't own a Bible, so she couldn't try to find them. Wait, though, hadn't she saved Grandma's Bible? It must be packed away someplace in the room she used for storage.

Abandoning her half-eaten soup, Sara rummaged in the unpacked boxes stored in what was meant to be a second bedroom, but at present was full of things she didn't know what else to do with. Among other treasures of her past, she found the familiar scarred and tattered brown leather Bible. Sara opened it carefully.

Damn. She'd forgotten it was a Finnish Bible. She spoke Finn much better than she read it; she'd never locate those words. Was it possible there was a Bible packed away with the gift books C.W. had deliberately left behind? Sara bent over another box and began sorting through it.

When she came across a huge book in fancy ecru leather, she might not immediately have realized it was a Bible, except for the inset colored picture of 'The Last Supper' in the center of the front cover. With an effort, she lifted the book from the box and opened it.

'What a treasure,' she said approvingly, when she discovered a subject index giving chapter, verse, and page number for the reader. She looked up darkness, discovering the quotation that interested her was in the Book of Job, Chapter XXX.

'When I looked for good, then evil came unto me: and when I waited for light, there came darkness.' She read on, coming to a verse that chilled her very marrow. 'I am a brother to dragons and a companion to owls . . .'

Companion to owls. The deadly night hunters. Symbolized in the winged tattoo?

★　★　★

Jamie couldn't sleep. He watched the clock picture change at eleven — a boy asleep in a four-poster bed that was crowded with stuffed animals — and clutched his monkey to him.

At first he'd been really happy, because Daddy looked at him and pushed his chair and spoke to him. Daddy had even kissed him goodbye. But then he realized that, though his father had promised to visit oftener, he hadn't said when he'd come again. And it was almost Christmas.

He was pretty sure Sara would come to see him on Christmas, but, even if she did, he wanted Daddy, too.

Maybe he'd disappointed his father after all. Maybe the things he'd learned to do weren't enough. Maybe Daddy didn't like it that he hadn't learned to talk. But he couldn't talk. Just like he couldn't write. Or turn his head to the left. 'Cause if he succeeded, something awful would happen.

Something even worse than what was going to happen to Sheba. He wanted to save the dog in the worst way, but he hadn't been able to get Sara to understand how bad the man was and how he meant to kill Sheba.

Maybe even if he did make Sara understand, Sheba couldn't be saved. 'Cause his real dreams always came true.

* * *

Restless and unhappy, Ian paced repeatedly from one end of the living room to the other. 'Put yourself in Jamie's place,' Sara had admonished him. Ian shuddered.

Though he realized that, of its kind, Palo Oro was a well-run, clean facility, he hated the place — the smell, the sight of the deformed children and the senile elders, the sounds made by the disabled and the old, even the cheery voices of the nurses. How could he expect Jamie to like being there?

Yet he was afraid to bring his son home.

No matter how much he improved, Jamie would never be the healthy, normal boy he'd been before the accident. If it was agony for him to visit Jamie one day a week, could he face living in the same house with the boy?

What would have happened if, instead of Moira being in the car with Jamie, he had been? Where would Jamie be now, if Ian were dead and Moira alive?

He shook his head. Useless to speculate. Moira was dead, he was alive, and Jamie was his responsibility.

He thought of the way Sara had smiled at the boy, how she'd tousled his hair and kissed him. Her fondness for Jamie showed in everything she did with him, and it was obvious Jamie would do all he could to please her.

Sara, though she did happen to have a degree in special education, was no relation to Jamie. She had no reason, other than her interest in helping him, to spend so much of her time with the boy. While here he was, Jamie's father, doing nothing for Jamie except paying to keep him shut up in Palo Oro.

Ian's mouth twisted in disgust. What the hell was the matter with him?

He thought about taking a drink and shook

his head. There was no way out for him, except to face down his ghosts and demons cold-sober, and conquer them.

If he could.

22

Bitch! He crumpled the newspaper into a ball and flung it at the wall, startling Sheba. The dog leaped to her feet, her hackles rose, and she showed her teeth.

He glared at her, and she subsided, but watched him warily.

If he didn't have almost all the arrangements made for this new one, he'd sure as hell alter his schedule and go after that bitch who kept blabbing to the papers. He'd already had her once, the next time he caught up with her he wouldn't need to take her again, just finish her off. If he had the time, though, if conditions permitted, he might fuck her again before he offed her. After what she'd done to try to harm him, he had the right.

His eyes gleamed as he pictured her whimpering in fright as he slit through her clothes with the knife, the sound and scent of her fear readying him, making him rock hard. Hard enough to hurt her, to make her bleed.

He licked his lips, giving up the vision reluctantly. She had to wait her turn. He'd get to her soon enough. For all her carry-on in the paper, she'd given a lousy description of him. Even his fat slob of a sister down there in Chula Vista wouldn't recognize him from the artist's sketch. The man in the picture could be any man; he was perfectly safe.

Hank was the one who'd taught him the value of planning. Before he met Hank, he'd gone from one mess to another. If not for Hank, sure as hell sooner or later he'd have ended in the pen.

'Make a list,' Hank would insist. 'A list and a timetable. Then stick to both as much as possible.'

He'd begun doing bitches in Nam. Hank knew what went on, but he never talked about it. Never acted any different toward him, either. Except to teach him how to plan. He never touched Hank's women, of course. Hank's possessions were sacred.

He'd liked Hank's crazy dog almost as much as Hank had. He and the damn dog had been one hundred percent loyal to Hank. Unfortunately. The dog's loyalty wound up blowing Hank to hell and gone.

That soured him on dogs. They were all like his sister's poodle, Minx — eventually, in one way or another, they betrayed you. No different than women.

In Hank's memory, if for no other reason,

he'd stick to schedule. First the new one, as planned. His gaze fastened on Sheba.

Damn dog. She'd surprised him the other day by slipping her leash, running to that crippled kid and fawning all over him. He hadn't much cared for the look the kid had given him. Almost as if the little bastard *knew*.

He hadn't liked the redhead's snotty remark, either. For a minute or two he'd regretted his choice, because he'd had the chance to pick her instead of the other. Then he realized it didn't matter. She could wait her turn. Doing her would be all the sweeter for the delay.

Forget her. Concentrate on the current one. After each item on the list was checked off, Hank always made him ask himself what could go wrong. Time to do that.

As he thought about what might go wrong, he caressed the gold heart he wore around his neck. No one suspected him. The sketch in the paper, though annoying, wasn't likely to lead to anyone identifying him. As for the owl — he kept the tattoo hidden, no danger there. He'd dispose of the khaki jacket and buy a gray one.

Anything else? He frowned. That kid bothered him. But what danger could there be in a crippled kid? None, that he could see.

Unless — was it possible the kid had been around when he clipped the hair?

She'd certainly made it easy for him to cut the strands. He'd followed and watched her, until he knew that if she brought her lunch, she always tried to sit on a certain park bench to eat it, sometimes with a friend, sometimes alone. Conveniently, behind the bench was a large clump of hibiscus, where he was out of her sight. When he was walking Sheba, no one paid any attention if he slipped behind bushes.

He'd waited there several noons before his chance came. By now his technique was so deft that she hadn't felt a thing.

He thought he'd have seen a wheelchair in the area; it was the kind of thing a man noticed. He hadn't. The more he pondered, the more convinced he became there'd been no wheelchair. The kid hadn't been there. Hadn't seen him.

But then why had the brat looked at him so strangely? He didn't like things he didn't understand, they made him edgy. Especially this far into the plan. He'd better keep an eye out for the little bastard.

23

On Sunday, the sun broke through the overcast by eleven, making Sara decide she and Jamie would walk in the park. She brought along a pad of sketch paper and colored marker pens, in the hope that Jamie might enjoy drawing.

'Mr. Wilson called to say you were taking Jamie home over the Christmas holiday,' Mrs. Hodges told her when she arrived at Palo Oro. 'I'm sure Jamie will have a wonderful time. Is there anything you'd like to ask us about his care?'

'I don't forsee any problems,' Sara said, 'but if something does come up, I'll call here and talk to whoever's on duty.'

Mrs. Hodges nodded and asked what time Sara would arrive tomorrow to pick up Jamie. After that was settled, Sara went to Jamie's room, finding him ready and waiting, his eyes bright and eager. She noticed, though, there were dark smudges underneath, an indication he hadn't slept well.

A good reason to make today's visit short, so he'd be well rested before she took him home tomorrow.

'I have a wonderful surprise for you,' she told Jamie, kneeling beside his chair. 'Your father gave me permission to bring you home with me tomorrow. Not only that, but you'll be able to sleep at my house over Christmas Eve, so Santa Claus will be able to find you on Christmas morning.'

Jamie's pleased grin made her hug him. She was thrilled when, for the first time, he made an effort to hug her back.

Pulling away, she asked, 'You do believe in Santa Claus, don't you?'

His smile faded, and he gazed into her eyes for a long moment. Biting his lip, he gave his negative half-shake.

'I'm glad you're honest,' she said. 'It's okay not to believe in Santa Claus. But I like to think of him as the Spirit of Christmas. All of us can believe in that.'

Jamie nodded, patently relieved.

'Today we'll walk in the park,' she said. 'Maybe you'll be able to draw a picture while we're there. Perhaps a tree. A palm. Or a eucalyptus. Whatever strikes your fancy.' She had an ulterior motive she wasn't ready to reveal.

The day was truly beautiful — warm sun tempered by a cool ocean breeze. Sara found an unoccupied bench shaded by a fat date palm, pulled the wheelchair up next to it, and sat down. She set the pad on Jamie's lap, removed the pens from their pouch, and tucked them in beside Jamie. She'd tried the tip protectors and found them not too difficult to remove, so she left them on for Jamie to take off.

'When you're tired of drawing, we'll read,' she told him.

Jamie gazed into the distance for a long time before he chose a brown pen. She tried not to watch him too closely, in case she inhibited his sketching, but she did keep an eye on him, noticing he was drawing a series of parallel brown lines. Thick lines.

After a time he recapped the brown pen and picked up a green. She soon realized he was sketching the row of tall palms that bordered the park along the outer walk. He colored in green grass, put some squiggles of blue for the sky, and then looked at her.

She took the pad from his lap and tore off the paper. The drawing was so good she was amazed. He hadn't tried for a photographic likeness, his sketch was abstract and very effective.

'I see we have a budding Utrillo in our midst,' she said. 'This is excellent.'

Jamie smiled.

'Do you know who Utrillo is?' she asked.

To her surprise, he nodded.

'In fact,' she said, 'I think this is good enough so you can give it to your father for his Christmas present. I'll frame it for you. Okay?'

His nod was enthusiastic.

'Ready to read now?'

He shook his head, reaching toward her for the sketch pad. Keeping the completed drawing, she gave him back the pad.

Jamie didn't hesitate. With a black pen he drew what she immediately realized was meant to be a dog. Sheba? He lined in a leash in red, then switching to black again, connected the leash to the hulking figure of a man. Last of all, he swirled gray around both dog and man.

Fog, Sara understood. Sheba and her master walking in the fog. The figure of the man, though crudely drawn, seemed to exude menace. She glanced at Jamie, and found him frowning at his sketch as though dissatisfied. After a long pause, using the gray, he started to draw something pointed extending from the man's hand. He stopped abruptly.

Dropping the marker, with great effort he tore the sheet from the pad and tried to wad it up. When the stiff paper resisted him, he looked at Sara and pointed to a nearby trash can.

'You want me to throw this away?' she asked.

His nod was vehement.

Though she would have liked to keep it, she did as he wished. 'Shall we read now?' she asked.

He shook his head and pointed back the way they'd come. Toward Palo Oro.

'You want to return to Palo Oro, is that it?'

He nodded, his face pinched and pale.

Alarmed, Sara asked him if he felt all right. She wasn't reassured by his nod, and hoped fervently nothing was wrong with him except lack of sleep.

As she wheeled him from under the tree she saw Sheba and her master approaching and hastily turned the chair toward Palo Oro, keeping dog and man behind them as she hurried along, and praying that Jamie hadn't seen them. Something about the pair distressed him, that much was obvious. Perhaps it was the man's unkind treatment of the shepherd; she hadn't liked it herself.

Jamie's color returned before they reached the facility, and when she kissed him goodbye in his room, to her relief he looked more tired than ill.

'I'll be here at noon tomorrow,' she told

him. 'There'll be lots of surprises waiting for you at my house.'

She knew that for Jamie his father would be the biggest and best surprise of all, but she didn't mention him because she couldn't bear Jamie's disappointment if he expected his father and Ian didn't show up.

Ian wanted a good Christmas for Jamie, she assured herself as she got into her car. She needn't worry about his not appearing. Ian would be there and Christmas would be wonderful, the most wonderful since her childhood.

★　★　★

He'd watched them from the moment they entered the park, being careful to keep out of sight. When they settled under the palm, he'd slipped close enough to hear what she said. The crippled kid hadn't uttered a sound; he was writing or drawing something.

Eventually she threw a paper in the trash, and they left. He waited until they were out of sight before approaching the can.

While Sheba looked on, he lifted the crumpled paper from the waste can and smoothed it. At first he made no sense of the scrawled figures, but then he noticed the red line connecting the two. The red leash. He scowled. One had two legs, the other four. The brat had drawn him with Sheba.

What the hell was that in his hand? He squinted at the scribble and tensed. A knife? The longer he looked, the more convinced he became. That damn kid had put a knife in his hand. No one knew he had a knife — how could the kid know?

Was he making too much of a kid's drawing? He studied the sketch. The figure meant to be him was done in black, giving it a sinister cast. Hell, he was blacker than the Sheba figure. That kid had seen him and knew very well he was a white man — why draw him all black?

Hank was never without a hat or a cap — invariably black. 'You remember those old Westerns,' Hank had told him. 'You could always tell the good guys from the baddies, because the good guys wore white hats and the bad ones black.' He'd touched his black wide-brimmed Stetson. 'Well, I'm making a statement here.'

Black for bad guys. Is that what the kid meant? He stuffed the paper in his pocket and hurried off in the direction the redhead and the kid had gone, intent on following them to their destination.

*   *   *

Jamie was glad when Sara left, because he needed to be by himself for awhile, to try to understand what had happened to him in the park. He ate his lunch as quickly as he could, and sighed in relief when the nurse assistant put him to bed for his nap. Now everyone would leave him alone until the next shift began.

He was tired 'cause he hadn't slept well last night, but he needed to think before he could rest.

He'd had a good feeling, sort of like he was floating, when he'd drawn the palm trees. Then he'd started to draw Sheba, and something had happened. He'd been caught up in a real dream where the man who owned Sheba, the owl man, stalked someone through the fog, knife in hand.

The dream ended. He felt compelled to draw in the knife, but when he began to, he realized the man was watching him. He couldn't see the owl man but he was there, somewhere in the park, watching. And waiting. Overwhelmed by panic, Jamie had done his best to destroy the sketch. He was afraid it had been too late.

The owl man knew about him. Knew that Jamie recognized his evil. But the owl man didn't know where to find him. He was safe here in Palo Oro, safe here in his room.

Wasn't he?

★ ★ ★

Late in the afternoon, Sara was trying to decide where to put the Christmas tree when the doorbell rang. Violet, who'd taken quite an interest in the tree, immediately scooted into the bedroom. Sara set the tree down and went to the door.

Ian stood on her doorstep with packages in his arms. 'I know it's not quite Christmas Eve, but I thought you might let me in anyway,' he said.

She stepped aside and he entered.

'You're putting the tree in the middle of the living room?' he asked.

'Not really. You interrupted my very important decision as to where it would look best.'

He juggled the packages. 'Since I can't put these under the tree until you decide, I guess I'd better help you.'

She both wanted him to stay and wanted him gone. Shrugging, she said, 'Be my guest.'

After circling the room, Ian pointed to the corner by the front window. 'There's the best spot. I'll help you move the plants.'

She raised her eyebrows. 'What if I don't agree with your choice?'

'Why wouldn't you?'

Why, indeed? Just because it was his? Actually, the corner was the ideal place. 'I don't have anywhere to put the plants,' she temporized.

'How about the back porch? I'll set a plank kitty-corner from railing to railing for them. Always supposing you have a plank.'

'I think there's one in the garage.'

Working together, they transferred the plants, then Ian positioned the potted tree in the corner, turning it until Sara was satisfied the most attractive sides faced outward. Ian piled his packages on the floor near the tree.

'You know,' he said, 'when I first came in, I could swear I smelled something good baking.'

She rolled her eyes. 'I made Christmas cookies this afternoon.'

'You mean they're all done?' he asked ingenuously. 'Did I happen to mention I missed lunch? And that I'm extremely fond of Christmas cookies?'

Smiling at him, Sara capitulated. 'Never let it be said that I refused a starving man food, during this season of cheer and goodwill. I'll put on the coffee.'

'I saw Jamie today,' she said, when they were seated at the kitchen table with their coffee mugs and a plate of brightly decorated cookies.

'I imagine he's looking forward to coming here for Christmas,' Ian said.

'I'm sure he is. But I wonder if something's bothering him.' She told Ian about the drawing of the man and the dog, and how upset Jamie had gotten over the sketch.

'Now that I think about it, I believe what he drew in the man's hand was a knife,' she finished. 'Why a knife? It makes me wonder what's going on in Jamie's head.'

'Beats me,' Ian said. 'He always loved animals and hated to see one mistreated. Maybe that's it.'

Sara bit her lip. 'In that case, I'd think he would've drawn the knife sticking out of the man's back. I saw more than one revenge drawing like that when I taught. But the knife was in the man's hand. Wouldn't that mean Jamie feared the man meant to hurt someone?'

Ian shrugged. 'I suppose it could. He might be worrying about what will happen to the dog. Poor kid. What a bummer not to be able to communicate.'

'I was going to ask you, if you'd contact his doctors and get permission for me to either review Jamie's records or talk to them about him. I need to know what they think.'

Ian sighed. 'You *are* persistent. Two months ago I couldn't have talked about it, but you've convinced me to climb out of . . . ' He paused. 'Out of the hole I dug for myself. As best as I can recall, the doctors didn't agree. Dr. Brill insisted all Jamie's problems stemmed from brain and spinal cord injuries. Dr. Leminowski didn't disagree that there'd been damage, but he thought an emotional overlay masked Jamie's actual condition. He tried to prove his point, but, unfortunately, Jamie didn't respond. Yet he's certainly responded to you.'

'Maybe he wasn't ready until now.'

Ian smiled ruefully. 'Yes, timing is all. Too bad Jamie's old man didn't realize that earlier.' He brushed his forefinger back and forth over Sara's hand. 'Are you going to stay mad at me forever?'

'I'm not mad at you.' She moved her hand away.

'Oh yes, you are. About Jamie but about something else, too. Something that has to do with us. Let's not have any lies between us. What is it, Sara without the *h*?'

Sara took a deep breath. All right, he'd asked for it. 'Who was she?' she blurted.

Ian blinked. 'Who was who?'

'The woman, the one who answered the phone when I called. The one who said you couldn't talk to me right then.'

He stared at her. 'When in God's name was this?'

'During those four days you claim you were spaced out on reds.'

He ran a hand through his hair. 'Christ, I can't remember much about that time. The only woman who could possibly have been in the house was the one who comes in once a week to clean. Velma. She might have answered the phone. God knows I didn't even hear it ring. I certainly wasn't aware you called me.'

Sara swallowed, heat creeping up her face. Had she made something out of nothing?

'You didn't think I had another woman in bed with me, did you?' he demanded.

She ducked her head, horribly embarrassed, sorry she'd brought up the subject. Her 'Yes,' was scarcely audible.

'In the shape I was in? Jesus, I could hardly crawl to the bathroom.'

In for a penny, in for a pound, Sara decided, and forced herself to ask, 'Then there aren't other women?'

'There've been some since Moira died, but none since I met you.' His smile was one-sided. 'You're not just another woman.

It'd be a hell of a lot easier if you were.' He gripped both her hands in his. 'You make mouth-watering Christmas cookies, but that's not the real reason I'm here. I can't be without you, Sara. You're into my bones somehow. It's not just desire. Though that's there, too — you know it is. I'm wary of love; I don't think I really know what love is. All I know is how badly I need you in my life.'

She needed him, too. She wanted him in her bed. In her life. Why was she so afraid to confess she did?

Drawing her hands slowly from his, she said, 'I'm willing to start over if you are, but let's wait until after Christmas.'

'Why?'

Without admitting how her feelings for him threatened to overwhelm her, she tried to explain. 'I want Jamie to enjoy every moment of this Christmas. This is his Christmas, not ours. If I — if we — ' She paused. 'I can't concentrate on two things at once,' she ended rather crossly.

Ian shook his head, grinning.

'It's not funny!'

'Okay,' he said, 'we'll play it your way. But I'm damned if I'll be put off with cookies after the twenty-fifth.'

Jamie woke from one of the bad nightmares, the one with the sirens and bright lights. His frantic heartbeats slowed as he took in the familiar sight of his lighted clock. He wasn't in that nightmare place, he was safe in bed at Palo Oro.

Fifteen minutes after twelve. He'd missed the changing of the picture. This one showed a black and white mama cat and kittens, asleep on a frilly pink bedspread. Two of the kittens were black, one was white and one was black and white like its mama.

Something about the thought made Jamie's breath catch painfully, and he hurriedly looked away from the picture.

He thought he heard a strange noise and listened carefully. Palo Oro was full of noises at night, sometimes people even screamed, but this was a different sound. What it sounded like was a dog whining. But it couldn't be.

The noise reminded him of Sheba with her sleek black coat and soft brown eyes, eyes that told him she liked him. He could almost believe Sheba was outside whining. To warn him 'cause he was her friend.

The hair rose on Jamie's nape. Warn him about what?

But in his heart he knew. Sheba wouldn't be outside Palo Oro, unless the owl man brought her here. She was telling him the owl man was coming after him. Maybe even now he was creeping down the hospital corridor toward Jamie's room. Soon, very soon he'd open the door far enough to come inside. And then he'd tiptoe to the bed with the shiny pointed knife in his hand . . .

Jamie froze as the slanting light shining into his room widened. Someone *was* opening the door. Who? Maybe it was the nurse. Somehow he couldn't make himself believe it was. Danger, not a nurse, was in his room. What kind of danger? His heart beat so hard he heard a roaring in his ears. Who was it creeping toward him? If he turned his head, he'd find out. But how could he turn his head to the left?

* * *

Whatever her other faults, Sheba wasn't a yapping dog. He'd have had to leave her at home if she had been. As it was, he took her with him, because a dog on a leash made a good excuse if a man happened to be caught in the wrong place after dark.

Not that he meant to be caught.

He'd walked through Palo Oro in the

afternoon, during visiting hours. No one had paid him undue attention, and, by glancing into each room, he'd found the boy. Jamie Wilson. Luckily the kid had been sleeping and didn't see him.

The nursing home was built like an *H*, giving many of the rooms access to the outside via sliding glass doors. Jamie's wasn't one of them, but the room next to his was. Since neither bed in that room was occupied and there were no names on the door, he presumed the room was empty.

He'd stepped quietly inside, unlocked the glass door, and eased out again without being seen. Even if someone relocked the door, it wouldn't be too much of a problem, because there wasn't a locking bar in place. Ordinary locks were easy.

He'd waited until midnight to return to Palo Oro. Now, keeping Sheba on a tight lead, he slipped around the outside of the building to the glass door he'd marked as the one into the empty room. He drove the metal stake he carried into the ground and wrapped Sheba's leash around it tightly.

'Stay,' he whispered.

Sheba obediently sat down.

Evidently no one had checked the sliding door, because he found it unlocked. He inched it open, careful to make no noise, and crept into the room. As he passed the empty beds, he lifted the pillow from one of them before he reached the open door to the hall. Light shone dimly into the room he stood in. Hearing no voices or footsteps, he risked a glance into the corridor. Empty. The nurses' station wasn't visible from here, so, with luck, no one would see him.

With his back to the wall, carrying the pillow, he edged to Jamie's room, where he cautiously eased the ajar door open wide enough to slip inside. The kid lay on his back in the bed.

Easy enough to shove the pillow over his face and hold it there until the brat stopped breathing, then take the pillow away. No one would suspect the death was anything but natural. Easy enough.

Then why was he hesitating? He'd killed kids before, in Nam. Sure he had. They all had to, in order to stay alive themselves. But he'd never killed a kid one on one like this. Come on, get it over with, he urged himself. You can't afford to let this brat live, to blab to others about you.

He inched closer to the bed, holding the pillow in position. Suddenly he froze. Footsteps! Someone was walking along the corridor.

The sound must have roused the kid.

His head jerked, turning slowly to face the door. For a long moment the boy's green eyes stared into his.

'I hate graveyard,' a woman's voice said outside the door.

A second woman spoke. 'Yeah, but don't forget it pays more.'

'You missed checking Jamie,' the first voice said.

'No need to. He's never awake. Poor kid. I'd sure hate not to be able to talk. The docs say he never will talk. Or be able to write either.' The second voice was fainter now, as though moving away.

'I'll never live to see the day *you* can't talk.' The first voice came from even farther away.

Outside, Sheba howled, a long mournful ululation.

Damn the bitch!

He backed hurriedly away from the kid, darted from the room into the one next door, tossed the pillow onto the bed, and fled through the sliding door, shutting it hastily behind him. He jerked up the stake, grabbed the leash, and ran for his car.

When they were a safe distance from Palo Oro with no sign of pursuit, he breathed easier. He'd missed his chance to waste the kid, but at least he hadn't gotten caught.

Tonight had been a fiasco. All because he

planned too hastily, without thinking things through. Hank would be disgusted with him. He should have investigated the brat more thoroughly. If he had, he'd have discovered Jamie Wilson couldn't speak and couldn't write.

No matter what the kid knew about him, there was no way to pass it on to anyone. Jamie was no threat at all.

★　★　★

Jamie writhed in agony, awake but somehow back in the nightmare land of sirens and lights and blood. She was there, too. This time he'd seen her. He meant never to look, but he'd broken his vow. He'd looked to his left and she was there, her head shoved through the broken windshield. Blood was smeared all over her and the seat and him, too. She made awful gurgling noises, like she had something caught in her throat, but he couldn't help her, he couldn't even unhook his seat belt, much less move.

He could only watch and listen.

If only she'd put on her seat belt, like everyone was supposed to. She never would, though, and she got mad if he reminded her.

'Don't nag me,' she'd say. 'You're as bad as your father.'

He watched with horror as something green oozed from her head and slid down onto the steering wheel where it stuck, staring at him like an eye. Her eye. Only how could it be?

He tried to beg her to stop scaring him with the dreadful sounds she made, but he couldn't speak any more than he could move.

After what seemed to be hours, he managed to turn his head, so he looked straight ahead and not at her. After the noises stopped, he made himself believe she wasn't there, that he was alone. He didn't turn to the left, though. 'Cause something awful waited there. Something he couldn't bear to see.

The sirens and bright lights were gone. On a wall he saw a clock that looked familiar, but he couldn't place where he was, whether in the nightmare or in a bed somewhere. He was vaguely aware he'd been in terrible danger, but he couldn't recall what had happened. It didn't matter. He was all right now, he'd keep on being all right as long as he looked straight ahead.

But despite all he could do to prevent it, his head began to turn ever so slowly to the left.

Jamie screamed.

24

Ian strode toward the nurses' station, hoping he didn't look as nervous as he felt. Everything had seemed simple yesterday, when he'd insisted to Sara that he'd pick up Jamie and bring him to her house. Now, though, he was faced with the fact that he literally had no idea how to handle either Jamie or the wheelchair. Presumably it folded up to fit into the car. But how about Jamie?

'Is my son ready?' he asked Mrs. Hodges.

'Almost,' she told him. 'Actually, Mr. Wilson, we let Jamie sleep late this morning. Unfortunately, there was a disturbance last night that woke many of our patients. Apparently some animal was outside howling — a coyote, we think, after the ground squirrels. I'm sure you're aware coyotes have been spotted in many of San Diego's gorges.'

Ian knew all about suburban coyotes. 'You're telling me Jamie had a bad night?'

'I understand he was quite frightened. One of the nurse assistants had to sit with him until he fell asleep again. He's fine this morning, though he does seem rather nervous.'

'It's all right to take him out overnight?'

Mrs. Hodges smiled. 'Certainly. Christmas with family will be good for Jamie.' She handed him a paper. 'Would you sign this form, please?'

Jamie was in the wheelchair facing the door when Ian reached his room. His pinched expression changed to what looked to Ian like relief, and he relaxed his desperate grasp on the plush monkey in his lap.

'Ready to go?' Ian asked.

Jamie nodded emphatically.

The nurse assistant making Jamie's bed offered Ian a small case. 'Extra clothes for Jamie and his toothbrush and pajamas,' she said. 'And urinal.'

Ian pushed his son out the front entrance. As he started for the parking lot, they approached a slight, dark-haired young woman in a white uniform hunched over and leaning against a brick planter that held flowering shrubs. Ian glanced at her as he passed. To his dismay, he saw tears running down her cheeks.

He hesitated, then stopped. 'Is something wrong?' he asked.

She covered her face with her hands and burst into loud sobs.

Ian felt he couldn't just walk away and leave her, so he set the brake on the wheelchair, as Sara had taught him, and turned to the woman.

'Look,' he said, 'if I can help, I will. But I can't do anything for you, unless you stop crying and tell me what's wrong.'

She dropped her hands, still weeping. He offered her his handkerchief, but she shook her head, pulled a wadded tissue from her pocket, and wiped her face.

'I — my ride didn't show,' she said, sniffling. 'And I don't have money for the bus.' She raised her woebegone face to look at him. 'I don't have any money at all.'

She was too proud to borrow from those she worked with, he suspected. Her name pin told him she was Ms. E. Vasquez, Nursing Assistant. She didn't look any older than the high school students he'd taught.

'I'm Ian Wilson,' he said.

'I know Jamie,' she told him, and smiled wanly at the boy. 'I'm sorry to bother you like this.'

'It might prove to be a fortunate meeting for both of us. I haven't the slightest idea how to fold up a wheelchair so I can get it in my car. And I'd also appreciate advice on what would be the safest way for Jamie to ride with me. If you'll help me, in return I'll drive you home. Is it a bargain?'

Her smile brightened. 'Oh, yes, Mr. Wilson,

316

I'll be glad to help you.'

She showed him how to place Jamie on his foam cushion in the passenger seat, where the safety belt held him in position. While he was handing Jamie the monkey, she folded the wheelchair and stowed it in the trunk.

'Where do you live?' he asked when she was seated in back.

'I'm staying with my girl friend,' she told him, giving a Golden Hill address that wouldn't take him far out of his way.

'The one who didn't show this morning?'

'Yes. Her car probably wouldn't start. It needs work, but her husband, he's always too busy.' Her tone suggested she didn't think much of the husband.

It came to Ian that she must have been waiting for her friend ever since she got off the night shift at seven. Over three hours.

'Mrs. Hodges said everyone got a scare last night from a coyote howling,' he said.

Before she replied, Jamie made a noise. Ian glanced at him and saw his son shaking his head.

'Not a coyote?' he asked.

Jamie shook his head again.

'Well, it couldn't have been a wolf.'

Jamie shook his head.

'A dog, then?'

Jamie nodded.

'My son thinks it was a dog,' Ian said.

'I don't know, but it scared him awful bad,' she said. 'He screamed and screamed until I ran in and turned on the light. I had to stay right there and hold his hand before he'd even try to settle down.'

So E. Vasquez had been the nurse assistant who'd comforted Jamie. Ian warmed to her. 'What's the *E* stand for?' he asked.

'Elena,' she said shyly, giving the name its Spanish pronunciation of E-lane-a. 'Mostly they call me Lena.'

He glanced in the rearview mirror at her and noticed something that he'd failed to see at first. She was pregnant.

'Thanks for your kindness to Jamie,' he said.

'That's okay. Jamie and me, we're friends.'

From the corner of his eye, Ian saw Jamie nod.

'Do you like working at Palo Oro?' he asked.

'It's better than a lot of other places, even if some of the patients are kind of heavy for me to lift.'

'I'd think lifting wouldn't be good for someone in your condition.'

'The doctor says its okay for another couple months yet. My girlfriend's already got three kids and a husband to feed, she can't feed me, too. It's like, you know, if I don't work, I don't eat.'

No husband, then. Or, apparently, any man she could count on. No place of her own. And a baby on the way. Poor kid.

When he pulled up in front of her apartment complex, he turned to look at her, 'Lena, I want to give you a Christmas present from Jamie. He'll be hurt if you don't take it.' He offered her a ten-dollar bill, certain she'd flatly refuse a larger amount. Chances were he'd have to argue her into this much.

'I can't take your money, Mr. Wilson,' she said.

He frowned. 'Then I'll be hurt, too. Remember, this is the season for giving. You've given friendship to Jamie — that's far more valuable than money. But money's all I have to give you. Please accept our Christmas present, Jamie's and mine.'

'I guess when you put it like that — ' She smiled uncertainly and accepted the bill. 'Thank you. I hope you both have a good Christmas.'

Driving to Sara's, Ian found himself whistling 'Jingle Bells' and smiled inwardly. Nothing like lending a helping hand to soften the most recalcitrant Scrooge. He glanced at his son, so frail and vulnerable, and suddenly knew that Sara was right. He couldn't leave

Jamie at Palo Oro. Jamie belonged at home. With him. He *wanted* Jamie with him.

Sara hurried to the car the moment he parked in her driveway. 'I thought you guys got lost,' she said.

'We were dispensing Christmas cheer, weren't we, Jamie?'

Jamie nodded, smiling at Sara.

'In that case, you're forgiven.' Sara unbuckled Jamie and carried him into the house, while Ian lifted the wheelchair from the trunk and brought it along.

'Ready for lunch?' Sara asked when Jamie was settled into the chair.

Jamie shook his head.

'What, then?'

Jamie made scribbling motions.

'You want the drawing pad and the color markers,' Sara said.

He nodded.

After Sara brought them, Ian watched Jamie uncap the black pen and draw what resembled an animal of some kind.

'Sheba?' Sara asked.

Jamie nodded.

'Sheba's the black dog I told you about,' Sara told Ian. 'The one the man walks in the park.'

In other words, the pair who'd upset Jamie yesterday, Ian thought. He looked at his son and saw the boy was staring at him as though expecting something. What?

Did it have anything to do with last night's howling? 'Was it Sheba you heard in the night?' he asked his son.

Jamie nodded.

'So it was Sheba who scared you.'

Jamie frowned, shaking his head.

Ian looked helplessly at Sara.

'You'd better bring me up to date on what happened last night,' she suggested.

Ian told her what Mrs. Hodges had said, and how Jamie had refuted the coyote story.

'You're sure Sheba was outside Palo Oro last night?' Sara asked Jamie.

He nodded.

'Alone?'

Jamie shook his head.

'Why, Jamie,' Sara said, 'I just noticed you've learned to do something new. You can turn your head to the left now.'

Jamie's eyes widened, then unfocused. Suddenly he began a wild, high keening.

Shocked, Sara hurried to put her arm around him, but he remained rigid in her embrace.

'My God, what's wrong with him?' Ian demanded.

She pitched her voice to carry over the wailing. 'I think it is something to do with him being able to turn his head to the left. He couldn't before. Or maybe he was afraid to.'

'Why?'

She didn't answer. Freeing Jamie from the wheelchair and carrying him to her grand-mother's old rocker, she seated herself and began rocking him back and forth. 'Ssh, ssh,' she soothed. 'Sara's here, Jamie. Daddy's here. It's all right, you're safe with us.'

The wailing went on without pause.

'Is he in pain?' Ian asked, kneeling beside the rocker.

'I think the hurt is in his mind.' She leaned closer to Ian, her lips close to his ear. 'Have you ever talked to him about his mother?' she asked in a whisper. 'Told him she was dead?'

Ian jerked back. 'No! Why risk upsetting him?'

'He's about as upset at the moment as he could possibly be; you can hardly make him worse. What if not turning his head to the left has something to do with the accident and Moira? Not knowing is always worse than the truth, no matter what. Talk to him, Ian. Talk to him about his mother and what happened to her. Now.'

Ian sat back on his heels, his gaze shifting from the moaning boy to her, and then back to Jamie. 'You're sure?' he asked.

She shook her head. 'How can I be sure?

But he has to know the truth sooner or later. I realize how difficult it is for you, but try. Please try.'

Ian took a deep breath. 'Son,' he said, 'I think you know you were in an accident.' He leaned forward and put his hand on Jamie's head. 'You were riding in the front seat of the car, and your mother was driving. Another car smashed into your mother's car. She was killed.'

Sara felt Jamie stiffen against her. She kept rocking and stroking his back.

'Your mother is dead, Jamie.' Ian's voice broke, but he cleared his throat and went on. 'I hope you don't remember anything about the accident, but maybe you do. There was nothing you could have done to save her.' Ian swallowed. 'Nothing I could have done. Accidents happen; we have to accept that whether we want to or not. She's gone from us for good, son, and nothing can bring her back.'

Ian's voice was hoarse with unshed tears. 'But we still have each other.'

★ ★ ★

Jamie, his face buried against Sara, stopped keening as he listened to his father's words. He didn't want to believe them, but he knew his father wouldn't lie. All these months he'd tried so hard not to remember his mother, not to think of her at all, and now his father's words forced him to. Mama had been in the same accident he was in. And she'd died.

Mama was dead. Daddy said so. Mama wasn't ever going to come back. He relaxed in Sara's arms and began to cry.

Later, after his tears were dried and Sara laid him on the couch to rest, he remembered what else Daddy had said. They still had each other. But they had more. Didn't Daddy know they had Sara, too?

Groggy with fatigue, he heard Sara and his father talking softly in the kitchen, their low murmurs reassuring. He started when he felt the couch jar slightly. Moments later, Violet's rough tongue licked his cheek, then she curled herself next to his monkey, in the space between him and the back of the couch. Her warm, purring presence eased his grief, and he drifted peacefully into sleep.

★　★　★

What with one thing and another, they didn't begin to decorate the tree until late in the afternoon. Though Sara remained disturbed by Jamie's earlier insistence that the man and the black shepherd had come to Palo Oro the night before, he seemed to have forgotten about it. Not wishing to upset him anew, she left the subject alone.

As she watched Ian hold the ornament box within Jamie's reach while they decided which colored ball to hang next, she felt tears sting her eyes. Ian was learning to love his son all over again.

'Hey,' Ian said, turning to her, 'you're making us do all the work here. How about a helping hand?'

After Jamie plucked a bright pink ball from the box and held it out to her, Sara blinked back the tears and joined them.

When they decided the tree couldn't possibly hold one more ornament, Sara turned on the Christmas lights. By the lights' colored glow, they put the presents under the tree.

'Now all we have to do is wait for the Spirit of Christmas to arrive,' she said.

'What happened to Santa Claus?' Ian asked.

'Jamie and I changed his name to something we thought was more suitable.'

'I think the Spirit of Christmas sneaked in while you guys weren't looking,' Ian said. 'Can't you feel his presence?'

Watching Jamie's happy face as he nodded, Sara thought she almost could. She knew he'd still have to work through the loss of his mother, but for the moment he was wrapped in the insulating wonder of Christmas.

Ian caught her hand and tugged her toward the kitchen. She went with him, leaving Jamie content by the tree.

'You can't expect me to leave you two alone tonight,' Ian said in a low tone. 'I saw the rollaway you set up in your room for Jamie. That leaves the couch free. I'll sleep there.'

'But — '

'No argument. Whatever went on at Palo Oro last night, I can't be sure Jamie wasn't somehow involved. I'm taking no chances.'

What Ian said made sense. Since he wasn't proposing to climb into bed with her, there was little point in objecting. She nodded her agreement, aware they'd all sleep easier if they were under one roof.

★ ★ ★

Jamie woke to daylight, looking around in confusion for a moment before he realized where he was. At Sara's. With Violet curled on the pillow next to his head. He watched the cat yawn, her pink tongue curling in her mouth.

'Meow,' he said softly.

Violet sat up and regarded him gravely, as if asking herself what strange kind of cat he was. Jamie giggled.

'I hear someone laughing,' Sara said drowsily from the other bed.

'It's about time you sleepyheads woke up,' his father muttered from the doorway. 'I was getting ready to open the presents all by myself.'

At his father's appearance, Violet leaped to the floor and darted under Sara's bed. Jamie guessed it might take the cat a while to get used to Daddy. Like it would take him time to get used to not having nightmares. He'd slept through the night without waking, and he didn't remember even one bad dream.

He hoped he never had another. Maybe he wouldn't if he could stay at Sara's house. The idea of going back to Palo Oro scared him so he pushed it away. He wouldn't think about the owl man at all. He frowned, certain he'd forgotten part of what had happened the night before he came to Sara's. Something important.

Sheba had been outside in the dark with the owl man, and then the nightmare with the sirens came. Or was there something in between? He couldn't remember. Didn't want to remember. Not on Christmas.

'Is that scowl for me?' his father asked, rubbing his stubbly face as he stood over the bed. 'I know I scared the cat, but I didn't think I looked bad enough to scare you.'

Jamie smiled at him.

'That's better.' He lifted Jamie into the wheelchair. 'Jamie and I will use the second bathroom,' he told Sara. 'Us men have to stick together.'

It turned out that his dad didn't know the best way to help him, but Jamie didn't care. He'd rather have Daddy take care of him than the greatest nurse in the world.

By the time they washed and dressed and all, and his father pushed him into the living room, Sara was already there. She wore the prettiest red dress he'd ever seen. His father must have thought so, too, 'cause he gave a wolf whistle.

'Breakfast?' she asked.

Jamie shook his head.

'I can't believe you'd rather open presents than eat.'

He nodded, grinning.

'Believe it,' Daddy said. 'He's a chip off the old block.'

A minnow of fear darted along Jamie's spine. ' . . . just like your father . . . ' his mother had said.

He bit his lip. Mama was dead. She wasn't

here this Christmas. And wouldn't be, ever again.

The lights of the tree blurred as tears wet his eyes. He blinked, then his attention was caught by the sight of a white face peering through an opening between the stacked presents. Violet was hiding underneath the tree, behind the presents. He wished he had a present for her.

He did have one for Sara. His dad had given it to him in the bathroom, something in a little red box with a gold ribbon. He had the present tucked between him and the chair, so she couldn't see it and would be surprised.

'You get to give out the presents,' Sara told his father.

Jamie watched as his father stooped to choose one, smiling when he saw by the silver bells on the paper it was his present to Daddy — the drawing of the palm trees in the park that Sara had framed and wrapped for him.

'From Jamie to me,' his father said. 'I wonder what this can be.' He shook it. 'Doesn't rattle.'

Jamie's smile faded as his dad peeled off the wrapping. What if daddy didn't like the picture?

'An original!' his father exclaimed, holding up the framed drawing. 'My very own original Jamie Wilson picture.' He reached over and hugged Jamie. 'Thanks, son. I had no idea you could draw this well. I know exactly where I'm going to hang it.'

Reassured, Jamie relaxed. He was pretty sure he couldn't draw that good before his accident. He guessed he saw things different now.

Then the presents came so fast he didn't have time to think. From Daddy he got a radio small enough to keep in the wheelchair with him and earphones to go with it. And a tape deck that was bigger but easy to use. He could work it himself, after his father showed him how the cassette of Christmas carols went in.

Sara gave him a book about cats and one about a baby whale. And a book holder that made it easier for him to read. Plus an adjustable easel, along with brushes and stuff for painting.

When every other present had been opened, he held the red box out to Sara.

She opened it carefully. Inside was another box of dark green velvet. When she lifted the lid, her eyes widened, and she didn't say anything for a long time.

'From Jamie and me.' Daddy sounded sort of hoarse.

Finally she lifted a golden heart on a gold chain from the velvet box. In the center of the heart were two smaller hearts, with a green stone in the center of one and a red stone in the center of the other. Jamie thought it was really neat, 'cause it was like the three hearts meant he and Daddy were a part of Sara.

He noticed his father's hands shook when he fastened the chain around Sara's neck. Why was Daddy nervous? The gold hearts looked really cool against the red of her dress.

'It's beautiful. Thank you both.' Sara's voice was husky, like she might cry. She kissed Jamie's cheek.

'How about me?' Daddy asked, so then she started to kiss his cheek, too, but his dad turned his head and Sara wound up kissing him on his mouth instead.

'I'm going to run home and change into some clean clothes,' his father said when they got through kissing. 'You two go ahead and have breakfast. I'll grab something at the house.'

'Dinner's at three,' Sara told him.

'I'll be back long before three,' he said.

Only he wasn't. Sara had dinner on the table by the time his father returned.

'Sorry to be late,' Daddy said, 'but I had to make a few arrangements, and it took longer than I thought.'

'Arrangements?' Sara asked.

Instead of answering her, his father turned

to Jamie. 'Do you like Lena, son?' he asked.

Surprised at the question, Jamie nodded. Didn't Daddy remember that he and Lena were friends?

'That's what took me so long,' Daddy said. 'Arranging for Lena to come and help me take care of you. Because I'm taking you home with me, Jamie. You won't be going back to Palo Oro. Ever.'

25

He still didn't know what had gotten into Sheba the night before — howling loud enough to wake the dead. She'd screwed him right and proper. What with the racket she made, it was just dumb luck no one saw him run out of Palo Oro.

The kid had seen him, of course, and the kid was still alive. But he was safe enough; Jamie Wilson couldn't tell anyone one damn thing.

Scratch Jamie Wilson.

But even with the kid eliminated as a problem, he couldn't get on with the game because it was Christmas. He hated Christmas. He always had. Everything closed, no place to go, nothing to do. This year Christmas was even more of a bummer than usual, because it disrupted his plans.

It was one holiday where everyone stayed home. Maybe not their own home, maybe they'd gone to visit relatives, but wherever they were, they stayed around the house.

He'd allowed for the holiday in his schedule, but just the same it irked him to wait. He had no choice. She wouldn't show today because, like him, she had nowhere to go. Poll's Cage was closed, and that was the only singles bar she went to.

She'd be surprised if she realized how much he knew about her. Her latest pick-up wasn't in town; he was spending Christmas in Arizona with his folks, and wouldn't be back until after New Year's. She hadn't met a new man yet.

He smiled. Chances were she never would. Except for him.

He'd watched her long enough to understand that she couldn't bear to be without a man. But he was sure she wouldn't venture out tonight — where would she go? Tomorrow night, though, Poll's would be open. By then she'd be really hot to trot. And she'd be alone. At least until she arrived at Poll's. With luck and a little fog on his side, she'd never get there.

He slid the knife from its sheath and caressed his palm with the flat of the blade. Glancing at Sheba, he smiled. 'You first, old girl,' he said. One bitch before the other.

He hadn't fed her tonight, so she'd be good and hungry when she ate tomorrow. A hungry dog was less likely to pay attention to any taint of tranqs in her food. Sheba was a big dog, he had to make sure to give her enough to knock her out, because he didn't care to struggle with a dog her size. The next bitch would be a hell of a lot smaller than Sheba.

He didn't use poodles. Not after Minx. He never would've killed the damn little bitch, if she hadn't bitten him. Turned on him like every other bitch in his life.

His mother had died when he was six. Before that she'd been sick in bed for two years, so occupied with dying inch by inch, that she had no time for him. When Ma died, there was just him and his sister and Pa. But pretty soon Pa had started fucking Sis, and any attention he paid to either of them was to her.

He didn't figure out what was going on between them till he got a little older, but even before then he blamed his bitch of a sister. She had other guys when their father wasn't home, older guys who paid her.

Then Pa came home and found her with one of them and took a knife to the guy. Killed him. When the cops came for him, he jumped from the tenth-floor window and broke his neck. Took him a week in the hospital to die.

He put down the knife and pulled the golden heart from under his shirt, smoothing it between his thumb and forefinger. After Pa died, Sis had cried and carried on like crazy, turning this same damn heart over and over in her hands, and blubbering on about how much Pa had loved Ma and how he never was the same after she died.

'So now they're both gone, and I'm stuck with you,' his sister had said after she calmed down.

Did she think he wanted to live with her, for chrissake? At nine he didn't have any damn choice, that was the trouble.

There hadn't been any good Christmases he could remember before that, and there sure as hell weren't any afterwards.

What was Sis doing today down in Chula Vista? One thing for sure — if she was eating Christmas dinner, it wouldn't be one she cooked. Amazing how, sloppy and lazy as she was, she always found a man. She didn't know zip about his whereabouts, but he always kept up on where she was living.

Sometimes after he did a redhead, he was tempted to cut the headlines from the paper and send the clipping to her. To scare the hell out of her. But he didn't dare. Much as he hated her, she wasn't stupid. Chances were she'd catch on to who'd sent her the clipping, and begin to wonder what else her baby brother might have done.

He had no doubt she'd turn him in if she

knew. And she'd laugh just like she had when she'd watched that bastard bugger him. Damn her, he hoped she'd fry in hell's hottest fire.

26

Sara had little doubt what was wrong with her. She missed Jamie. And Ian, too, for that matter — why not admit it? The house seemed too quiet. Too empty. Even Violet prowled from room to room, as though searching for something she'd lost.

Naturally she was thrilled and happy that Ian had taken Jamie home for good. But only now was she realizing that she could hardly drop in to see the boy every day, as she had when he was at Palo Oro. Her daily visits with Jamie were an event she'd come to look forward to.

She glanced at her watch. Nearly noon. What she needed was a brisk walk in the park to get her out of the day-after-Christmas doldrums.

As she strolled along St. Hubert Street, she noticed a telltale line of gray creeping up the sky. Soon high fog would shut the sun away. And tonight, when she was alone, the fog would lower. She quickened her pace, as though walking faster would somehow keep the fog at bay.

The park held the usual assortment of sun

worshippers, serious joggers, parents with children, and those Sara had come to think of as lost souls — people without homes. Wanderers. She strode along the paved paths, remembering how she'd pushed Jamie's wheelchair in the park, and she wished he was with her now. Thinking of him reminded her of how he'd insisted Sheba and her master had been prowling outside Palo Oro several nights ago. Could Jamie be right? Apparently both nurses and patients had heard an animal howl that night.

Sara glanced around, looking for the man and the black shepherd, but they weren't in sight. The man's behavior toward Sheba had disturbed Jamie — perhaps the boy had a nightmare triggered by the howling.

Coyotes in the city gorges, possums in backyards — it seemed wildlife was infiltrating San Diego.

She heard someone call her name and whirled around. Najla, wearing short shorts and a long T-shirt, pounded up to her.

'I've been yelling at you for blocks,' Najla said breathlessly.

'Sorry — I guess I wasn't expecting to meet anyone I knew.'

'Did you have a good Christmas?' Najla asked.

Sara smiled. 'The best in years.'

Najla made a face. 'I wish I could say the same. I watched TV all day. Bor-ing. Are you busy tonight?'

'Yes.' Sara lied without compunction. She liked Najla, but their life-styles were too different for them to do much together.

Najla sighed. 'I was hoping you'd maybe like to stop by Poll's Cage with me.'

Sara shook her head. 'Sorry. Anyway, you know that's not my thing.'

'Yeah, so you said. I guess I'll have to go alone.'

'How about Dave?'

'Didn't I tell you he was away for the holidays? Besides, I've got my doubts I'll see much of him when he gets back. It's time to investigate what new talent's around.'

'Do you think it's a good idea to be out alone at night? Especially after someone hacked off a chunk of your hair?'

Najla shrugged. 'My hairdresser fixed it so you can't see the place anymore.' She twirled around to show Sara. 'Anyway, I met this gal at the hairdresser's who's studying psychology. She says guys who steal women's hair are mostly harmless perverts — hair fetishists, they call them. You know, these guys take the hair and, like, jack off with it or something.' She giggled. 'It's kind of funny to imagine some nerd wrapping my hair around his prick while he whangs himself.

'Besides, you know I'll only be alone till I get to Poll's. Ten to one I won't go home by myself.'

Aware nothing she could say would dissuade Najla, Sara merely warned, 'Be careful, okay?'

'I'm always careful.'

Sara walked with Najla until she came to St. Hubert, then they said goodbye.

'Have a good New Year's,' Sara said as they parted.

'You, too. The best.'

Sara ate a lonely lunch and spent the early part of the afternoon in the backyard, trimming straggling branches from the shrubbery while Violet chased the occasional moth that fluttered from the bushes, disturbed by Sara's pruning. When she finished around three, the sky was overcast.

'There's always TV,' she told Violet, as the cat slipped through the door and into the house ahead of her.

The phone rang. Sara hurried to pick it up. 'Hello?'

On the other end somebody breathed heavily.

Both chilled and angry, Sara slammed the phone down. Damn! It'd been so long since he'd bothered her, that she'd almost forgotten about the breather. She started to pull the plug and then shook her head. No. Not unless he kept calling.

She turned on the TV, but the call had upset her and she couldn't relax and get into any of the programs. Finally she clicked it off and went to the kitchen to make coffee. She'd just started to measure the coffee when the doorbell rang.

When she saw Ian in the doorway, her heart flipped. Whether she was willing to admit it or not, she'd been more or less waiting for him all day.

'Where's Jamie?' she asked.

'He and Lena are home watching *Star Trek V* — or is it *VI*? I forget. So far things are working like a dream. I should have done this a long time ago.'

'I miss Jamie,' she confessed.

'And not me?'

'W-e-l-l — ' The phone rang, cutting off her reply.

She glanced toward it but made no move.

'You're not going to answer?'

She shook her head. 'It might be the breather. He already called once today.'

Ian hurtled across the room and grabbed up the phone.

'Hello?' He listened a moment, then

scowled ferociously. 'Listen up, you son-of-a-bitch,' he said. 'If I ever find out who you are, I'll kill you. You hear me, you perverted bastard?' He set down the phone with coiled control.

'How long has this been going on?' he demanded.

'I told you that's why I had my number changed and unlisted. But somehow he found me anyway.'

'Who has the new number? I know you took your time giving it to me.'

'I — well, Ralph has my number.'

'MacDuffy.' There was a speculative note in Ian's voice that disturbed Sara.

'Come on, Ralph's surrounded by eager female students, why would he make breather calls? He doesn't need to.' But even as she defended him, she recalled the sequence of events that had led to Ralph almost sleeping with her. First the call from the breather that scared the hell out of her, then a call from Ralph. Had he set her up? Would he do a thing like that?

'I wouldn't put it past MacDuffy to get his jollies by calling up women he knows and enjoying their panic and helpless anger. I can almost see him talking to them about how they feel when he sees them next.' Ian's eyes were cold. 'I don't like the bastard. Haven't from the beginning.'

'But calling and breathing into the phone — that's sick.'

'So?'

'He seems normal enough.'

'I damn well intend to let him know how I feel about it,' Ian snapped. 'Where's your phone book? Or do you have his number handy?'

'Ian,' she protested, 'you can't accuse him without any proof.'

'Watch me. Where's the phone book?'

No one answered at Ralph's place.

'Doesn't prove a thing,' Ian insisted. 'He could have called from a pay phone. Or he might well have recognized my voice and decided not to answer his phone, maybe figuring I've tumbled to him. He sure as hell didn't expect me to pick up your phone and ream him out.'

'No one's ever been here before when the breather called.'

'What does MacDuffy know about us?'

Sara looked at her hands. 'He thinks I'm not seeing you anymore.'

'So you did have a thing going with him?'

She shook her head. 'I told you about making tapes of my grandfather's stories for him. He believes he can interest a publisher.'

'That's all?'

'I don't really like Ralph.'

'How about me? Do you like me?'

She smiled slightly. 'You're different.'

He cupped her face with his hands. 'I came here to ask you to dinner. I wanted to do everything right. Take it slow. None of this slam, bam, thank you, ma'am stuff. But the way I feel about you doesn't make it easy to slow down.' He bent his head and kissed her.

What started as a gentle, sweetly persuasive kiss soon began to demand. When her lips parted, welcoming him, he groaned and gathered her close, deepening the kiss.

Ian's touch, his body pressed hard against hers, made her weak with longing. Slow? Forget slow. She already knew Ian could take her higher than she'd even been before, and she urgently wanted to go there with him again. Fast. And now.

She showed him her need with her lips, her hands, and her body, but she thought she'd die of longing before he lifted her into his arms and strode down the hall to her bedroom.

'I don't want to rush you, Sara,' he murmured, as he eased her onto the bed.

'Much longer and I'd have picked you up and carried you in here,' she told him, her voice husky.

They undressed themselves and each other,

flinging clothes with abandon, eager to lie flesh to flesh. She'd never desired any other man with such intensity; she couldn't imagine wanting anyone but Ian ever again.

Lips, hands, bodies caressed in a frenzy of need until at last he raised himself over her, and she arched to meet him, uniting them. He took her beyond thought, took her where there was no one but Ian and Sara and their shared passion.

When they finally drifted back into real time, spent, he held her, murmuring her name.

'Sara, Sara, you don't know what you do to me.'

She smiled at him lazily. 'I like those words a lot better than 'Thank you, ma'am.''

Ian grinned. 'You're the one who insisted on speed.'

She nuzzled his cheek. 'With you, I'm afraid any way at all suits me.'

'Why afraid?'

'You make me forget everything, even who I am.'

'Sara without the *h*, are you hungry?'

'I don't feel like going out, but there's nothing in the house to eat except Christmas dinner leftovers.'

'I have nothing against leftovers. Especially since they tasted so good the first time.' He ran his hand over the curve of her hip.

'I'm talking about food,' she said.

'Why?'

When she thought about it she couldn't find one good reason, so she kissed him instead and one thing led to another . . .

It wasn't until after nine that they got around to eating turkey sandwiches and coffee at the kitchen table. When Ian finished, he rose. 'Time for another phone call.'

Realizing he meant to call Ralph again, she said, 'Why not let it drop? What if Ralph's not the breather?'

'He is. I feel it.' Ian's voice was grim.

This time Ralph answered. Sara hovered nervously behind Ian.

'Listen, MacDuffy, I know damn well what you've been doing. If you want to get it off that way it's up to you, but if I ever hear of you calling Sara again, I'll break your slimy neck. Understand?'

He listened for a moment, then took the phone away from his ear and looked at it blankly before setting it down. He stood without moving or even glancing her way.

'What's the matter?' she asked. 'Did he deny calling me?'

'No. All he said was — ' Ian turned and looked at her. 'What he said was, 'She's not that good in bed anyway.''

Sara swallowed to relieve a suddenly dry throat. Why hadn't she explained that night to Ian? Whatever she told him now would sound false. Damn Ralph. He was a despoiler, a destroyer.

'Well?' Ian said.

She took a deep breath. 'Nothing really happened. It might have, because he set me up but — ' She paused. 'It was when you — when we weren't seeing each other. The breather called. How was I to know he was Ralph? I was frightened. I'd been reading in the paper about that woman who'd escaped from the strangler and I've got red hair, too. You don't understand how it feels to be afraid someone's after you, you're a man and you don't know.

'I was alone and scared and Ralph called just after the breather did. He said I shouldn't be alone, and he'd take me to dinner. We had to wait at the restaurant and I had three drinks, and then we never did eat because Ralph brought me home instead, saying we'd get hamburgers on the way. I went to sleep in the car, and I didn't realize until later he never did stop for food.

'After we got here I was afraid to be alone, and he tried to get me into bed. I was pretty damn fuzzy-headed, but not completely zonked. I had barely enough wits to lock myself in the bathroom, where I passed out on the floor. I admit it's not a pretty story, but the bastard did *not* get into my bed.'

'You could have told me.' His voice was stiff.

'What was the point? Nothing really happened.'

'It shouldn't matter that you didn't tell me, I suppose. But it does.'

She stared at him. 'You don't believe me, do you?'

'I don't know.'

Anger began to simmer inside her. 'I believed your story about the cleaning woman, because I trust you. If you don't trust me, if you can't trust me, then you and I are finished here and now. I refuse to be involved with a man who thinks I'm lying to him.'

He picked up his jacket. 'I'll call you,' he said, his voice tense.

'Don't bother!' she snapped.

He strode to the door and let himself out into the night.

Sara sank onto the couch, tears of rage and loss gathering in her eyes. He'd never understand how afraid she'd been that night. Only a woman would. Another woman who knew how it felt to be in terror because darkness surrounded you, and there was no one who cared whether you lived, but there might be someone who cared whether you died, who might be planning your death there in the lonely darkness.

Death or defilement or both. Someone bigger and stronger, who might have a knife, and you hadn't taken any of the karate courses, any of the defense classes, and probably you'd be so paralyzed with fright if you were attacked, that you couldn't try what you'd learned if you *had* taken the damn class.

Men wanted to own you, make you a possession, a thing. C.W. never could understand she was a separate person. But C.W. was the past.

She'd thought maybe Ian was the future. But even if he got over this, would he always be watching her? Watching and waiting for another man in her life? Is that what he'd done with Moira — watched, suspected, but never knew for sure?

'I can't bear it!' she cried.

Violet, who crept onto the couch next to her, sat up in alarm. Sara lifted the cat onto her lap and hugged her, tears dripping onto the pale fur.

'Never mind,' she whispered to Violet. 'Who needs him?'

★ ★ ★

Jamie liked being back in his own house. Sara's house was nice, but his felt like home. He liked having Lena living with them, too. She'd been his favorite of all the night nurses. Besides, home was safe. The owl man wouldn't find him here.

The clock Sara had given him hung on his own bedroom wall now, and he lay in bed watching the big hand edge toward twelve. The little hand was on nine, and he didn't want to fall asleep yet. Daddy had promised to come in and say good night to him, when he got back from Sara's. But his eyelids kept drooping shut, no matter how hard he tried to keep them open.

He wished he could remember exactly what happened at Palo Oro the night of the owl man. It was like the accident — he knew something had happened, but he couldn't bring back what it was.

Thinking of the accident reminded him of his mother and made his throat ache. He wanted to forget she was dead, but he couldn't, not anymore. He cuddled the monkey to him and tried to pretend it was Violet. He wished she was here. Daddy had given Kiki away, so they had no cat at all. He liked cats, liked to play with them and to hear them purr. He tried to imitate the sound, but wasn't satisfied with the noise he made.

351

It was lots quieter at home than in the hospital. Lena's room was across from his, the guest room. She'd gone to bed after she tucked him in.

'I get tired awful easy, 'cause I'm going to have a baby in April,' she'd told him.

That's why her stomach stuck out, 'cause babies grew inside their mamas. He could hardly wait for the baby to get big enough to be born. It wouldn't be exactly like having a brother or a sister, but almost as good. April seemed a long way off, a long time to wait.

He was glad she'd left both doors open and the hall light on, plus the Mickey Mouse night-light he'd had since he was a little kid. Not that he was scared, but he didn't trust the dark. This way, even with his eyes closed he could tell there was some light.

He would've liked to listen to his new radio with the earphones, but his dad had told him night was for sleeping and the radio was for daytime.

He managed to stay awake until nine-thirty, before his lids got so heavy that no amount of willpower could force them open.

He wasn't sure whether he dreamed that his father came into his room and kissed him good night or if Daddy really did, but it left him with a good feeling.

Until the sirens began to wail. Jamie knew

the bad dream was starting, but he couldn't stop it. The sirens and the lights, red lights shining on him, going away, coming back, the broken glass all over, and to his left Mama with her head through the windshield.

This time he couldn't protect himself, this time he'd have to watch her die, 'cause his head turned to the left now. Jamie whimpered in protest but the dream continued, the dream that was always the same, the dream he never saw the end of. The dream where Mama made terrible sounds, and her eye squeezed out of her face onto the steering wheel, and there was blood on her and on the seat and the windshield and on him, too.

He couldn't bear to watch her die, but his head wouldn't turn away from the dreadful sight, so this time the dream was different. He had to keep looking, had to keep listening.

She stopped moaning and the terrible bubbling sound began, blood gushed from her neck, some of it spraying onto him. Finally it all stopped, the noises, even the blood.

The dream was over. Mama was dead.

Instead of terror, a strange peacefulness enveloped him.

Until he heard the dog whimpering. He struggled to wake but the darkness held him fast. Sheba was warning him about the owl man, the owl man was coming to get him, he had to wake up.

He couldn't.

There was no light where he was, but owls didn't need light to see, 'cause they had night vision for hunting. Owls were night hunters, swooping on silent wings to kill with their sharp talons.

The owl man had a sharp knife. He meant to kill Sheba with his knife, but first he was coming for Jamie, slipping through the darkness, unseen, unheard, coming to kill Jamie, 'cause Jamie knew what he was.

Evil.

The owl man eased inside the door, and Jamie turned his head to the left to try to catch a glimpse of him. He saw nothing. No one. But the owl man was there, waiting. A long way off Sheba howled and howled, but the owl man didn't move. In his mind Jamie could see his evil eyes staring into his own. Death gleamed in those eyes. The owl man meant to kill him, and there was nothing Jamie could do to stop him.

He tried to scream but no sound emerged; he tried to reach for and ring the bell tied to his bed, but couldn't move so much as a finger.

The owl man inched closer and closer. Panic throbbed through Jamie.

Suddenly Sheba was between him and the owl man. But she was hurt, she had a great gaping hole in her side. Blood oozed from her and dripped onto the floor. In the deadly silence Jamie could hear the drops as they fell.

Then the bad dream was gone, and he was in a real dream, no longer in his bed or even in his house. He was in the park watching Sheba stagger toward the street, leaving a trail of blood behind her. She was hurt, she was dying, and he couldn't help her.

It was worse than the most horrible nightmare, 'cause he knew this was what would happen to Sheba. He couldn't stop it from happening. He feared no one could. 'Cause his real dreams always came true.

'Jamie, Jamie, don't cry.' Lena's voice.

He opened his eyes. The light by his bed was on, and Lena was sitting beside him, holding his hand.

'Do you hurt?' she asked, wiping away his tears.

He shook his head.

'How about if I pull up a chair and sit here next to your bed?' she asked. 'Would you like that?'

He nodded.

'I'll stay with him.' His father spoke from the doorway. 'You go back to bed, Lena.'

'I don't mind — ' she began.

'I know, but I'll stay with him anyway.'

Lena said good night to him, rose, and left the room. His dad pulled up a chair and sat down.

'Did you have a bad dream, son?'

Jamie thought about it and didn't know how to answer. He finally nodded and then shook his head. It was the best he could do.

'A bad dream along with something else?'

Jamie nodded.

'Is there something I can do for you?'

Slowly and sadly Jamie shook his head.

His father sighed. 'Maybe you can draw me some pictures in the morning and explain. In the meantime, I'm here with you, and nothing bad can happen. Try to sleep, Jamie.'

His father's large, warm hand closed over his, comforting him, making him feel secure enough to close his eyes. He felt safe with his father.

But it hurt to realize there was nothing Daddy could do to make Sheba safe, anymore than he'd been able to keep Mama safe.

Sheba was going to die.

27

Fog swirled around him and he cursed. Fog was his friend, but at the moment he could use a little more visibility. He had to find the damn dog. Nothing would go right without her. He couldn't go after the woman until he finished with Sheba. Couldn't begin without the heart of a dog. In this case, Sheba's. And he damn well meant to get it.

He'd mixed the tranquillizers into her food, but he should have known Sheba would be suspicious. Since he hadn't fed her the day before, she was hungry enough to eat the mixture, but when he wasn't watching, she'd gone behind the couch, puked half of it up, and then gone back to lie down near the door.

When he saw her head droop and her eyes close, he'd figured the tranqs had hit her. He waited awhile to be sure, but she didn't move, so he decided she was too zonked to give him any problem. If he'd seen her upchuck earlier, he damn well wouldn't have come at her with the knife.

He'd gotten one good slash at her before she went for him. He knew how to protect himself, but when he'd tried to slip out the door, she'd rushed him, slid past him, and took off into the early evening dusk.

He'd tracked her into the park, where he lost her trail in the thickening fog.

Cursing again, he admitted to himself that he wasn't going to find her tonight. Injured animals tended to go to earth; she was hiding in the bushes somewhere in the park. He stroked the sleeve covering his tattoo — too bad he didn't share the owl's night vision.

He'd search tomorrow. As badly as she'd been bleeding, he ought to have no problem tracking her by day.

Her running off was something he hadn't figured into his plans. How could he? Even though Hank was always warning him to be on the lookout for wild cards.

'Just when you think you've got it cold,' Hank would say, 'that's the time some guy's going to clobber you with the joker.'

Now that he thought about it, the joker for Hank had been a dog, his brown and white Nam pup. Old Hank would still be around, if he hadn't befriended that pup.

A dog turned out to be his joker, too — Sheba. He didn't like her, but he'd never thought she'd foul him up. Damned if he'd let her ruin everything. She'd been nothing but trouble from day one, but zero hour wasn't here yet, he still had time. Sheba wouldn't get the best of him.

No dog was smarter than a man. Smarter than he was. He'd find her, and that would be the end of one bitch.

One heart coming up. After that the fun could begin.

28

When she woke the next morning after a restless night, Sara decided that the best way to stave off the blues was to keep busy. She dismantled the Christmas tree, storing the ornaments and lights away carefully. She wrestled the potted tree onto the back porch and replaced the plants in the corner of the living room. Then she cleaned the house. Thoroughly. After that, she sorted through her clothes and other belongings, setting aside what she didn't wear for the Salvation Army. It took her most of the day.

Near six her doorbell rang, and her heart began to pound. But it was Najla, not Ian, on her doorstep.

Najla carried a pizza box. 'I come bearing gifts,' she said. 'Care to have dinner with me?'

Sara summoned up a smile. 'Sure, come on in. I'll put on the coffee.'

Najla made a face. 'Nothing goes with pizza except beer — I've got a sixpack in the car. Wait, I'll bring it in.'

When they sat at the kitchen table with the pizza between them, Sara said, 'How was Poll's?'

'I didn't go.' Najla took a bite of pizza and chewed thoughtfully. 'I'm not sure why. I wanted to, but I kept thinking about what you said about being careful, and I guess I got cold feet. So I watched TV. Ugh. Believe me, I've had it up to here with TV.'

Sara sipped her beer. She didn't much care for beer, but since Najla had taken the trouble to bring it, she'd drink one can to be polite. Actually, it wasn't too bad with the pizza.

'I hate eating alone,' Najla said. 'Don't you?'

Sara nodded. 'Thanks for coming by — and bringing the food. Next time it's my turn.'

'I could've called first — I guess I should've — but I took the chance you'd be home.'

And alone. As she was. And apparently would continue to be.

'You look kind of down,' Najla observed. 'Man trouble?'

'In a way.' Sara didn't want to talk about Ian to Najla. Or to anyone.

'Bastards, every one of them.' Najla shook her head. 'Beats me what I see in men. I guess hope springs eternal, so I always figure the next man I meet will be different. To date I've been one hundred percent wrong.'

Sara smiled wryly. So had she.

'Maybe now you're ready to give Poll's another try?' Najla's voice was hopeful. 'Like, I sort of thought I might drop in tonight, since I'm already out and all.'

'Sorry, but no. I don't know when, if ever, I'll be ready to meet another man.'

'What'd he do — split?'

'Not really. It's just that I can't stand not being trusted.'

Najla nodded. 'Yeah, the real jealous type's a drag. Never gives a gal any peace.'

'He isn't exactly jealous . . . '

'Ha! They're all possessive sons-of-bitches. Some are worse than others, that's the only difference.' Najla glanced at her watch.

'I've got some Christmas cookies for dessert,' Sara offered.

'I shouldn't, but what the hell. What's Christmas for if you can't gain a couple of pounds?'

Around eight-thirty Najla went to the bathroom. When she emerged, Sara saw she'd freshened her lipstick.

'Time to hit the road,' she said. 'You keep the rest of the beer, okay?'

Sara shook her head. 'I'm not too crazy about beer; I'll never drink them. Thanks anyway.'

Sara walked Najla to her car. 'Please be

careful,' she told her.

'Yeah, I will. But if being careful means staying home alone all the time, I swear I'd die of boredom. Like, I need a little night life, you know?'

Fog had begun to drift in from the ocean, and swirled in white patches across the road in front of Najla's headlights as she drove off. Sara started to turn toward her house when, from the opposite side of the street, a dark shape lurched from the sidewalk into the road, stumbled, fell, and lay still.

An animal of some kind. From the size and shape, it looked like a dog. What was wrong with the dog? Warily, she advanced toward the stricken animal, hesitating when it staggered to its feet, whimpering. Definitely a dog. The poor thing must have been hit by a car.

'Here, boy,' Sara called tentatively.

The dog weaved toward her, and she saw it was a German shepherd. A black shepherd. Could this possibly be the one she knew?

'Sheba?' she said, reaching to touch the dog.

The dog lifted its head to her hand, and she ran her fingers over the head and along the shepherd's side. She gasped and pulled her hand away, her fingers sticky with blood.

Staring into the thickening mist, she saw no

sign of Sheba's owner. Or of anyone. What should she do?

The dog leaned against Sara's legs, as though convinced she'd found help. Sara knew she'd have to try. 'Come along, Sheba,' she ordered, turning toward her house.

She didn't have a veterinarian anymore — the one who'd given the cats their shots had moved to LA. Not that any vet was likely to be in his office after nine at night during the holiday season. Still, she'd have to find one.

The dog whimpered low in her throat as Sara half-dragged, half-carried her up the stairs and inside. When Sara saw the wound along Sheba's side and neck, she bit her lip. Hair and skin opened away from a long gash, blood matted the black fur and trickled down Sheba's left foreleg.

Aware she had to check the bleeding, Sara wished she'd inherited her grandmother's bloodstopping talent. Since she hadn't, she'd have to do the best she could. After coaxing the dog into the kitchen, she told her to stay.

Rummaging in the bathroom cupboard she found a box of gauze squares, brought the box into the kitchen, and laid the gauze over the open wound. Then she wrapped a beach towel around the dog as tightly as she could without hurting her, pinning the towel into place. When she finished, Sheba slumped onto her side on the kitchen floor.

Sara watched her anxiously. Was she dying? When Sheba's eyes opened and gazed into hers, she was somewhat reassured.

'Okay, girl,' she murmured, 'I'll do my damnedest to save you.'

On the third try she found a vet who'd talk to her on the phone.

'Sounds like you've given appropriate first aid,' Dr. Charnley said. 'As long as you've got the bleeding stopped, she can wait until morning. Bring her by at nine, and I'll evaluate her.'

'She's lost a lot of blood,' Sara said dubiously, 'And the cut looks awfully deep. Do you sew up dogs like doctors do people?'

'It depends. With animals, it's sometimes best to leave a wound open. I'll check her tomorrow. A move now might start her bleeding again. Let her rest, keep her warm, give her water. You have no idea how she got hurt?'

'As I told you, I found her in the road, so I assume a car hit her. I know she got away from her owner once before, but, as I said, I don't know what his name is or where he lives, because I've only seen him walking her in the park. She's not wearing any identification tags.'

'What did you say her name was?'

'Sheba. At least I think so. She does look at me when I say the name.'

'All right, then, we'll see what we can do for Sheba in the morning.'

Sara thanked Dr. Charnley and hung up. She returned to the kitchen, where the shepherd lay sprawled on the floor. The dog raised her head when she saw Sara approach.

Sara knelt beside her and stroked her head. 'I'm doing all I can, pretty girl,' she told the dog. 'I'll find you a blanket and get a dish of water for you. I'll take good care of you, poor baby.'

The dog's tail thumped against the floor. Sara rose, her eyes filled with tears.

Sheba knows I'm trying to help her, she thought, as she tucked an old quilt she'd salvaged from the Saari farm around the dog. I must have hurt her, tugging and pushing to get her up the steps, but she never once growled or snapped at me.

As she filled a bowl with water, furtive sounds told Sara that Violet must be huddled between the refrigerator and the wall. There was no way to get her out, and Violet would never appear on her own as long as the dog was in the kitchen. In fact, Violet might never forgive her for bringing a dog into the house.

＊　＊　＊

Since he'd spent the night beside Jamie's bed, after breakfast Ian fell asleep in a chair in his study. He woke near noon, logy and irritable. Not with Jamie or Lena. With Sara. And with himself.

He had an uneasy feeling the two of them were behaving like a pair of adolescents, quarreling over trivia. Yet he was determined to stay away from her, determined not to involve himself in another destructive relationship. If he'd learned anything from Moira, it was that women can't be trusted.

Sara was no exception.

Ralph MacDuffy, that miserable son-of-a-bitch. Didn't she have better sense?

The more he thought about MacDuffy, the angrier he got. He was sure the bastard was even going to profit by the story tapes she'd made.

Before Jamie took his nap, Ian brought his son the drawing pad and colored markers. Jamie drew a black animal.

'Sheba,' Ian guessed, remembering other drawings.

Jamie nodded and proceeded to draw something disturbing, a man stabbing the dog. The mere act of drawing the picture obviously upset Jamie. Ian wished he understood what his son meant.

'Is this the bad dream you had last night?' he asked.

Jamie shook his head, leaving Ian even more confused. He gazed at his father intently, as if willing Ian to understand.

Ian spread his hands. 'I'm sorry, Jamie.'

Jamie frowned, then laboriously tore off the paper and began another drawing. A person. Evidently a woman because she wore a skirt. When Jamie used the red marker for her hair, Ian realized who she was.

'Sara,' he said.

Jamie nodded vigorously.

Ian was afraid he did understand this drawing. Jamie wanted Sara. He wanted her with him, because she might be able to interpret the meaning of what he drew, and probably also because he missed her. No, not probably. Ian knew damn well the boy missed Sara.

'Sara can't come to see you today, son,' he said uneasily, knowing he meant he wasn't going to ask her.

Jamie's green eyes clouded, making Ian feel like hell. Was he right to deprive his son of Sara's company, just because *he* didn't want to see her?

'In a day or two, maybe,' he temporized, and was rewarded when Jamie's expression cleared.

Later, as Ian busied himself in the neglected yard — mowing, pruning, clipping — his next door neighbor, Len Quigley, hailed him.

'How're things going?' Len asked.

'Better since I brought Jamie home,' Ian admitted. They talked for a few minutes about the boy. About to end the conversation, Ian remembered Len was a lawyer. He was still annoyed about MacDuffy and the tapes, so he decided to get a professional opinion.

'As an attorney, what would you recommend in this case?' He told Len about the tapes Sara had made, and what MacDuffy meant to do with them.

'She certainly ought to safeguard her interests,' Len said when he finished. 'If you like, I'll write up a contract for her, that will guarantee her a share in any profits.'

'Fine. Thanks. I'll pay any fees.'

Len waved a hand, they chatted for a while longer, then Ian returned to his yard work. By the time he quit, exhausted, he'd come to the realization that however he felt, Jamie had the right to be with Sara. In fact, to exclude her was to deprive his son of what he needed most — someone he not only loved, but a person who understood his needs far better than his father did.

What was he going to do about it? When he

finally kissed Jamie good night that evening, he was no closer to making a decision.

★　★　★

Jamie watched the clock picture change at ten to Winken and Blinken and Nod in their wooden shoe. He was afraid to go to sleep. His father had asked him if he wanted him to stay in the room again and he'd shaken his head no, but it was a lie. Lena had kissed him good night and asked if everything was all right, and he'd nodded. It wasn't.

But he knew neither his dad nor Lena could help with what was wrong. It had to do with Sheba and the owl man. If only Sara was here, she might understand. His father had sounded odd about Sara today. As though he didn't want her around. Jamie had thought they liked one another. Why had his dad given Sara the heart, if he didn't like her?

Something was going to happen tonight. Something bad. Jamie watched the clock apprehensively. Just as the big hand reached the three — fifteen minutes after ten — to his horror, he saw the clock blur and disappear . . .

The owl man stalked through the park, fog swirling around him like a gray cape. Sheba wasn't with him, but Jamie knew she wasn't

370

dead, either. For a moment he rejoiced, but then he saw into the man's mind and terror choked him.

The owl man was going after Sheba. He'd tried to kill her the night before, but she'd escaped. He'd spent the day tracking the dog by the trail of blood she'd left, and finally he'd found her. In the night and the fog, he was going after Sheba; he was going to kill Sheba.

That was awful enough, but there was worse. Sheba was at Sara's. As the real dream faded, Jamie suddenly remembered where he'd seen the owl man before. In another real dream before Sara came to Palo Oro with his father; before he ever met her. Owl man was the evil in the pink oleander bushes with the dead woman at his feet. Jamie shuddered, horribly certain the owl man meant to kill Sara, too.

Lying in his bed, Jamie stared at the clock — hardly a minute had passed. He had to do something — but what? He couldn't let the owl man kill Sara. Real dreams always came true, but this real dream hadn't showed Sara dying. Did that mean he could stop it from happening?

But how? Jamie thought frantically. He could draw pictures, but his father might not understand them. Daddy wasn't good with pictures like Sara. Lena was even worse.

He couldn't let Sara die. He had to stop the owl man from getting to her. But he was helpless. Unless —

Jamie swallowed. He cleared his throat. Opening his mouth, he tried to call. Only a croak emerged. Tears filled his eyes, but he blinked them back impatiently. He didn't have time to cry. Besides, crying wouldn't save Sara.

He pictured a word in his mind, spelled it silently, letter by letter. Closing his eyes, with all his will he imagined the word going from his mind to his throat and then out of his mouth.

'Daddy!' he called. Then again, louder, 'Daddy!'

Lena and his father reached him at the same time.

'You spoke!' His father's voice quavered.

Jamie had no time to think about what he'd done. Closing his eyes again, he shaped the next word carefully in his mind, and the next and the next and the next. He went limp with relief when the words floated from his mouth as clearly as the first one had.

'Sara. Owl man. Danger.'

His father leaned over him. 'What are you trying to say, son?'

Didn't Daddy understand he *was* saying it?

Gathering all his strength, Jamie tried again. 'Save Sara. Danger.'

'You want me to go to Sara's?' Daddy asked.

Jamie nodded, finding enough strength for one final word. 'Hurry.' He gazed at his father, pleading silently.

★ ★ ★

Sara scrubbed the dog's blood from the kitchen floor, then, as best she could, from the living room rug. No doubt there was a trail of blood leading from the road along her walk and up her steps, but that would have to wait until tomorrow.

She'd never understood how people who'd hit a dog with their car could drive away without even stopping to see if they could help the dog. To be fair, though, it was foggy tonight, and perhaps whoever had injured Sheba didn't realize they'd struck a dog.

No doubt Sheba's owner was worried about her. Sara tried to picture him, but all she remembered was his cold gray eyes and his stocky build. He hadn't had any other distinguishing features she could recall. Jamie hadn't liked him, had even seemed to be afraid of him.

When the man had walked Sheba in the

park, she'd worn a collar. She wore none now. Where was it? Had she managed in some way to slip it over her head? Perhaps that's how she got loose.

At the moment Sheba seemed to be sleeping naturally, but Sara wasn't at all certain she'd know the difference between natural sleep and unconsciousness. If she went to bed, she'd worry for fear the dog had started bleeding again, and yet she could hardly sit in the kitchen with her all night.

She could sleep on the couch. There, she'd be able to hear any sound the dog made. Yes, that's what she'd do. She clicked off the light, leaving the kitchen illuminated only by the living room lamps. As she started away from Sheba, the dog's eyes opened and her head lifted. Her gaze shifted from Sara to the back door, her hackles raised and she began to growl.

Goose pimples rose on Sara's arms. Did Sheba sense something in the backyard? Someone?

'What's the matter, girl?' She tried for a calm tone, but her voice shook.

Sheba, her gaze fixed on the back door, paid no attention to Sara. Her lips drew back over her teeth and she snarled.

Someone was outside!

Who? Was he trying to get in? Sara gathered her courage, edged to the window, and peered out. What was that shadow? Had it moved? Was it a man?

Should she call the police? Sara tried to make up her mind. Sheba could be reacting to a stray cat, she told herself. Or maybe the possum was back. The dog wasn't used to this house, or what went on in the backyard at night. It could well be an animal rather than a man.

Sheba stopped snarling, and her head swung around so she was staring into the living room toward the front door.

What now?

The doorbell rang.

The dog tried to get to her feet, evidently intending to go to the front door. Sara, afraid Sheba would begin bleeding again, put a hand on the dog's head.

'Down, Sheba,' she said firmly.

Sheba growled, deep in her chest, still looking toward the door, but she eased down again.

Who could possibly be at her front door at this hour? Sara asked herself. She entered the living room and glanced through the entry window. Wasn't that Ian's car parked in her drive? In the fog it was difficult to tell. She hoped to God it *was* Ian.

The doorbell rang again. Sheba gave a short, sharp bark.

'It's all right, girl,' Sara called to her as she approached the door.

'Who's there?' she demanded.

'It's Ian. Let me in.'

Sighing with relief, Sara opened the door and Ian stepped inside. 'Are you all right?' he demanded.

In the kitchen, Sheba snarled.

'What the hell is that?' he asked.

'I rescued a hurt dog.'

Ian's eyes widened. 'The black shepherd?'

'Yes, it's Sheba. She — '

'Never mind about the dog. Are you all right?'

'I'm fine. Why?'

He put his hands on her shoulders. 'I worried all the way over here, driving through that damn pea-soup fog at a crawl. Go ahead, tell me I'm the world's worst fool.'

'For driving in the fog?'

He smiled crookedly. 'You know why. For ever doubting you. If nothing else, those honest eyes of yours have told me the truth ever since the first time I met you.' He dropped his hands. 'Do you still want me, Sara?'

'Yes.' She gazed at him, making no effort to touch him. 'Even with the problems. But

I don't know if — '

'We'll talk about the ifs, okay?'

As badly as she wanted to talk to Ian, wanted to have things clear between them, Sheba's continuous growling distracted her. 'You weren't around in back before you rang the bell, were you?' she asked.

'No — why?'

'The dog seemed to think there was something or someone at the back door before she heard you. She's still upset.'

'To hell with the dog.'

'But she — '

'I swear you're going to drive me right out of my mind. I'm trying to tell you that I love you, damn it, and all you can do is worry about a stray dog.'

Sara, the breath knocked out of her by his words, could only stare at him. 'Did you say you loved me?' she whispered finally.

'If it isn't love, I don't know what other name to give it. When Jamie called to me tonight and insisted I — '

'*Called* to you? Jamie?'

'Yes. I'll tell you about that later. He spoke a few more words, something about the owl man and telling me that you were in danger, and he wanted me to get to you pronto. I suppose he had another bad dream, and it scared him. But I realized then that if anything did happen to you, I couldn't bear the loss.' Ian caught her to him. 'Sara, we belong together.'

His lips covered hers, and Sara was about to lose herself in the kiss, when she felt something brush her leg and jerked away. Sheba was staggering toward the front door. When she reached it, she collapsed on the small rug in the entry. Sara hurried to her, Ian trailing behind.

Sheba gazed from one to the other of them, then put her head on her paws and closed her eyes. She didn't seem upset nor did any fresh blood stain the towel. Sara had no idea why the shepherd had decided to choose the entry rug as a place to sleep.

Ian tugged Sara away. 'I'm beginning to think the dog's more important to you than I am.'

'Well, for one thing, you're not hurt.' She smiled at him. 'Don't get your nose out of joint. I'll make some coffee, and you can explain about Jamie to me. I can't believe he really spoke!'

Ian gave an exaggerated sigh. 'So much for romance. She loves dogs and kids, but not me.'

She rose on tiptoe and kissed him. 'Coffee and explanations first,' she murmured.

As they went into the kitchen together,

Violet, who was peering from behind the refrigerator, made a mad dash for Sara's bedroom.

'I'd better shut my bedroom door,' Sara said. 'I wouldn't want Sheba to go after her.

When she returned, she found Ian closing the front door. There was no sign of Sheba.

'The dog stood up and put her nose to the door — she obviously wanted out,' he said. 'I obliged.'

'Oh, no!' Sara wailed. 'She isn't supposed to get chilled or move around too much, because she's lost so much blood. What if she wanders off?'

'Why should she run off? She's probably been well-trained, a dog who knows not to make a mess in the house.'

Biting her lip, Sara opened the door. She could see nothing but fog. 'Sheba,' she called. 'Here, Sheba.' When the dog didn't come, she ran down the steps, the fog enclosing her in its damp embrace. 'Sheba,' she called, 'where are you? Come here, girl.'

The fog muffled sound, her words seemed to stop inches from her mouth, and not penetrate the grayness at all.

'Sheba!' she cried.

Was that a whine by the road?

Somewhere in the fog a dog began to bark, yelped, then there was silence. What had happened? Sara hurried toward the sound, calling the dog's name. The fog roiled thickly about her, hiding all landmarks, making her miss the curb. She stumbled and fell forward, her ankle twisting as she went down.

Damn!

Sara sat up. To her surprise, she couldn't see the lights of the house along St. Hubert Street. Of her house. In fact, close though she must be to home, she wasn't all that sure exactly where home might be.

When she tried to stand, a stab of such acute pain shot through her right ankle that she was thrown off balance again. She sat down hard. She was going to need help getting back to the house.

'Ian?' she called, certain he must have come after her. 'Here I am, Ian. I need help.'

After a long minute, a dark figure loomed over her and she raised a hand to him, so he could help her up.

'I thought you'd never come,' she said.

'I always show up sooner or later,' he said.

But it wasn't Ian's voice.

29

I'm wrong, Sara told herself as a strong arm pulled her to her feet, this must be Ian, it has to be. When her right foot touched the ground, she yelped with pain.

'My ankle,' she moaned.

'Lean on me,' he said.

She had no choice, her ankle wouldn't bear her weight without excruciating pain. But the man clearly wasn't Ian, the voice was wrong, and he was too short to be Ian.

'Who are you?' she asked.

'That's not important. Getting you out of the street is.'

As she hobbled along, the pain in her ankle made her light-headed, but she had enough sense to know she couldn't trust a stranger. 'Who are you?' she asked again.

'We've never been introduced, but I'm a neighbor. Leighton's my name. Bob Leighton. I'll take you to your house.'

She'd never met anyone named Leighton. But it was true, she didn't know many of her neighbors. It was so foggy she couldn't see any of the houses, and she wondered how he could.

'I heard you calling your dog,' he said. 'I didn't realize you had one.'

Sara was in no condition to explain. 'I'm afraid she's lost,' she said.

★ ★ ★

The man who'd called himself Leighton smiled, confident that she couldn't see his face. Lost was right. He hoped he'd finally done for that bitch Sheba with the kick. He was almost certain he'd got her in the head; he knew he'd hit bone. With any luck, she'd bought it.

Against all odds, despite the mistake he'd made, luck was still with him. Sheba had chosen this woman from the beginning, and he hadn't understood. He'd gone ahead and made his choice. The wrong one. He should have paid more attention to what Sheba was trying to tell him. To the omens. Everything had pointed to Sara from the first.

He should have marked her for what she was when she first said hello to him in the park, but he wasn't accustomed to having his prey chosen for him. That creepy little brat she'd befriended had known, though. So had that damned Sheba; she'd not only known, but had run off, found Sara, and tried to protect her from him. Trouble from day one, that was Sheba. She'd failed — no dog could outsmart him. He hoped he'd done for her once and for all.

If not dead, the dog was out for the count. And he had the woman named Sara, Sheba's choice, where he wanted her. She'd swallowed his story hook, line, and sinker. His heart speeded with anticipation as he led her toward the park. She made no resistance, trusting his word that he was taking her home. Women were fools. If he'd had the sense to pick this one from the start, he'd have saved himself a lot of trouble.

After a day's search in and around the park, he'd found the trail of blood the dog had left, followed it to her house, and then waited for his chance. He'd brought the knife to finish Sheba, but now that he knew Sheba meant him to have this woman he'd do her first, and then drag Sheba's body to the park, cut out her heart, and transfer it to the woman's chest, giving her the bitch's heart she deserved.

His free hand came up to touch the gold heart nestling under his T-shirt against his chest. His good luck piece. After he'd nicked it from his slut of a sister, things went better for him. The heart, along with the owl, were what Hank had called talismans, things that shielded you from danger. Hadn't they carried him safely through the hell of Nam? Lucky, that's what he was.

Luck brought the fog to him tonight, billowing in to shroud the park, letting him move unseen. He'd slipped into the woman's backyard like a ghost. Sheba'd known he was there, but the woman hadn't spotted him. Neither had the man.

He jerked his head around, aware that the man was looking for her. The fog was a dense cover; he couldn't see anything. Nor could he and the woman be seen. His luck held.

His sense of direction had never let him down. They were heading straight for the park — slowly, it was true, because she'd hurt her ankle. He meant to lead her into the very heart of the park, where they wouldn't be disturbed while he enjoyed himself with her very slowly and thoroughly. Let the man search all night. He smiled. The man wouldn't find her.

Until afterward.

★   ★   ★

Something was wrong. Now that she'd grown accustomed to the pain, Sara's mind began to function more clearly. She hadn't wandered very far from the house; they ought to have reached it by now.

384

'Are you sure you know where we're headed?' she asked.

'Positive.'

Why did he sound amused? The hair rose on her nape as Jamie's warning to Ian, ignored when she first heard the words, now rang in her ears. *Owl man*, Jamie had said, connecting him to Sheba. She swallowed, suddenly terrified. There was only one person the owl man could be. But was he also Sheba's owner?

Was the owl man the one she leaned on, the one helping her walk? Walk where? A dreadful suspicion slithered into her mind.

A scream burst from her throat, as she wrenched free of him and hobbled away as fast as she could.

'Sara!' The call was faint. Faraway. Ian, she was sure. He shouted her name again.

Sara tried to hurry toward the sound, but she couldn't tell where it was coming from in the fog, and her throbbing ankle slowed her. She opened her mouth to call to Ian and checked the impulse. The owl man would hear her, too. And he was closer to her than Ian was.

Panic clogged her chest. She breathed in fear along with the dampness of the mist. Though unsure where she was going, she hobbled on, hoping she was headed toward the safety of Ian. But the grayness, thick and soft and silent as an owl's wings, covered all landmarks.

She blundered into a parked car, not her own because it was in the garage. Not Ian's car, either, parked in her drive. Whose was it? Where was she? Had she gone past her house? Worse, was she so disoriented she was headed for the park?

Shivering in the chill, the damp penetrating her T-shirt, she stifled a sob. It wasn't safe to make a sound, or the owl man might find her. The stranger. Add one more letter to stranger, and it became strangler.

She saw him in her mind's eye as she'd first noticed him, wearing a khaki jacket as he walked Sheba in the park, a stocky, fortyish man, ordinary enough looking, but curt to the point of cruelty with the dog.

Sara remembered Jamie's picture of the dog and the man carrying a knife. Sheba's wound could well have been a knife slash. Why would the owl man try to kill his own dog?

Oh God, he must be carrying the knife. Pain shot up Sara's leg as she increased her pace. Her mind spun in a whirligig of terror.

She blundered into another car. A car meant a house, didn't it? She had to find the house, find it and pound on the door until they let her in.

But what if he reached her first? He'd hear the pounding, he'd drag her away before anyone could answer the door. Sara moaned and half fell as her ankle gave way.

Can't keep going. Hide. She found a curb and stepped up. There ought to be houses, shrubbery. Her eyes searched the grayness frantically, and she saw a thinner patch of fog to her right, where a house was barely visible, a light shining from its porch.

If she ran for the house, he'd see her. Slow as she was, he'd catch her before she got there. Instinctively she crouched next to the car. The fog thickened again, hiding the house. Belatedly, she realized that she recognized which house it was, and the thought chilled her. It was the one near the end of her block, the one where a Siamese cat perched on the porch railing and that meant, oh God, that she was almost to Upas Street, almost to the park. She'd gone the wrong way.

Upas. Poison tree, that's what a upas was, no, don't clutter your mind with trivia, he's out there, he'll drag you into the park, he'll find a ravine, and —

No! Stop it! Think.

Sara knelt to ease her right leg and leaned

her head against the car fender. She couldn't go any farther. Sooner or later the fog would thin and he'd find her here, she had to go on. But she couldn't force herself to move. Long shudders shook her, making her teeth chatter.

Ian, please find me, Ian, come to me, help me.

But how could he? If the fog thinned enough for Ian to locate her, then so could the owl man. She didn't dare approach a house and try to hide in the shrubbery, because if the fog lifted she'd be trapped. If she stayed near the road, she'd have a chance to get away. How far, though? She couldn't run. Better to chance hiding by a house than staying here. Wasn't it?

Sara tried to stand, and found she couldn't put any weight on her right leg without the pain making her dizzy and faint. She crouched by the side of the car again. Try the car door? If it was unlocked, she could slip inside, she'd be safe there after she locked the doors. Safe. She fumbled for the handle, paused. What if this was his car? He'd have a key; she'd be trapped. She slumped down.

She thought she heard her name and held her breath, listening.

'Sara, Sara.'

She opened her mouth to answer, then closed it abruptly. Why was the person calling so softly? Wouldn't Ian shout? Was the strangler close by her, did he know her name? Yes, he must, he would have heard Ian. He knew her name. She swallowed a moan and listened.

What if it was Ian? If she didn't answer, he'd go past her without realizing it. While if she called to him, he'd come and carry her home, hold her in his arms where she'd be safe.

She couldn't take the chance. Sara put her hand over her mouth to prevent any sound from escaping, feeling like Violet hiding between the wall and the refrigerator, hiding from the good as well as the bad. Yet Violet was alive, and the two other cats were dead.

Terhan Neiti, she thought. The Fog Maiden. If I believed in her like the old Finns, would she come and lift me in her damp embrace, carry me away with her? But the Fog Maiden couldn't save her, the Fog Maiden was only a myth. Nothing could save her, except her own wits.

Did the owl man find me by tracing Sheba to my house? she wondered. Or has he been stalking me for weeks, waiting for the right time? How does he decide the right time? Sheba knew he was outside tonight, she tried to warn me. She's afraid of him, too.

If I'd stayed inside, I'd have been safe. Now

and forever. No, not forever, he'd wait for another time. I wouldn't have known he was after me, and he'd have found another time.

'Sara.' Her name drifted softly in the fog, but it was death to answer.

★ ★ ★

Ian cursed as he ran up against a low fence, banging his shin. Damn the fog! Where was Sara? What had happened? Nothing after that one scream. She'd had this fear of the strangler, could it be — ?

No, that was impossible. She'd fallen and hurt herself, that's all, she was lying unconscious maybe in this damn fog.

'Sara!' he shouted and tripped, falling across something soft and warm. For a moment he thought he'd found her, but then he felt the dog's muzzle under his hand. It had to be the black shepherd. Sheba. Was she dead?

She stirred under his fingers. Sticky fingers, he realized. Sticky with blood? But the wound had been in her side, and all he'd touched was her head.

'Sheba?' He spoke the word tentatively.

The dog shifted position, trying, he thought to get her feet under her. Ian's nape pricked with unease. Why was the dog lying here with a bloody head? What had happened to her? What was going on?

'Sara!' he called again. He heard the scrabble of dog's claws on cement, and realized Sheba was getting to her feet. He grasped the fur along the back of her neck.

'Find Sara,' he ordered, wondering why he'd said it. The dog was dazed and injured, and wouldn't understand what he told her even if she was in good shape. But she was better equipped in the fog than he was. If she moved, he'd follow her.

Feeling slightly foolish, he ran his hand along her back to her tail and held on to it, hoping she wouldn't snap at him. Sheba growled low in her throat but tolerated his grip. After a moment she began moving slowly. Ian wasn't sure of the direction, he might have gotten turned around in this damn fog, but he thought they were heading away from the house. He'd left the door open in his hurry to go after Sara, not that it mattered at the moment. If only he'd stopped her. Or gone with her.

He ground his teeth together, seeing Moira rushing from the house, angry with him, hurrying toward her death. Now Sara.

Not Sara! It wasn't the same, couldn't be the same.

But why had the dog been lying there with a bloody head? Who'd done that to her, and why? Where was Sara? She couldn't have gone far. Why didn't she answer his calls?

The dog walked a few steps and paused. Was she going to collapse? He touched her with his free hand and found she had her head down. In pain? Or trying to find a scent? Damn this fog, he couldn't even tell what the dog was doing. He had no better choice than to wait until she continued on.

What was that? Had someone spoken? Sara? He opened his mouth to shout her name and then held, listening. Had the voice said, 'Sara?' Fear caught him by the throat. Who else would be calling her?

He strained his ears, but all he heard was the dog's low growl. At what? She wouldn't snarl at Sara, who'd taken her in and tended her. He remembered Sara telling him the dog had been growling by the back door before he came, and now it took on a sinister significance. Who else was out here?

Sheba leaped forward suddenly, so fast Ian lost his grip on her tail. He heard her snarl and flung himself after her, but she was lost in the grayness.

A shout. Barking. A man swore. A man! Where was Sara?

'You son-of-a-bitch,' Ian yelled as he

groped toward the sound. 'If you've hurt Sara, I'll kill you!'

★   ★   ★

The commotion jerked Sara to her feet, her heart beating wildly. She balanced on her left leg, holding herself erect by leaning on the car. Was that Sheba barking? She heard her name — was that Ian? Yes, he was shouting.

'Ian!' she screamed. 'Here I am! Ian!'

'Sara!' His call intermingled with Sheba's snarling barks.

Where was he? She couldn't be sure which direction his voice was coming from. 'Here, Ian, here!' she cried.

The barking grew muffled. Sara thrust herself away from the car, trying to balance without putting too much weight on her right ankle.

A figure loomed out of the fog beside her. Ian? She couldn't tell and she shrank away, unsure. Too late. He hooked his arm around her neck, choking her, then pulled her backward and inside the car. The dog barked. Ian shouted. As soon as the pressure on her throat let up, she tried to scream, but before she could, his hand fastened over her mouth. He shoved her sprawling onto the back seat. She felt the prick of a sharp point at her neck.

'It's a knife, you bitch,' he muttered.

She went limp with terror.

'Thought you'd outsmart me; no slut can do that.' His voice was low and angry. 'No redheaded whore ever got the best of me. Move and I'll kill you, bitch.'

Was this his car? She didn't think so. Otherwise wouldn't he be driving her away from Ian and Sheba, taking her into the park? But she was helpless nonetheless, terrified of the knife at her throat. He could so easily kill her.

He pushed her onto the floor and lay atop her, his weight half-smothering her. The knife point was gone from her throat, but her face was pushed into his chest and she couldn't call out, she couldn't get her arms free, she could hardly even breathe.

He was quiet. She could feel his arousal and bile came into her throat, making her afraid she'd choke, but he did nothing to her except lie there with his weight crushing her, so she couldn't move or speak.

Where was Ian? Surely he'd look inside the car. She hadn't heard the door slam, it must not be closed completely. That meant it was unlocked. If Sheba led him to the car, all Ian had to do was open the car door and he'd find her. Hurry, please, Ian, she prayed.

The hump on the car floor hurt her back,

she fought for breath, her leg was twisted and pain rolled upward from her ankle in continuous waves.

He whispered to her, his words stirring the hair above her ear. 'They won't find us, I'm lucky, I'll never be caught.' His hand moved and he gripped her hair hard, hurting.

'Red. Hot, you're all alike, hot pants. I'll give it to you, you won't ever need another man after me, you bitch, in heat all the time, the men running after you like dogs, following you, all of them fucking you one after the other, but now I have you, and I'm the last.'

The hand tangled in her hair pushed her face harder against his chest, while his other hand fumbled at her clothes, unzipping her jeans, pulling them down. She tried to fight him, but there was no room, she was trapped. She moaned, gagging on the bile in her throat.

He snarled like an animal, his fingers on her bare flesh. What had he done with the knife? If she could get a hand free, if she could find the knife —

But his weight pinned both her arms. He growled like a dog, he was an animal, a beast, he was evil, he was going to rape her, and then kill her. She was going to die.

'A bitch at heart, that's what you are.' He

chuckled, a indescribably evil sound that froze her very marrow. 'With Sheba's help I'll make it come true. Bitch heart, yes. Do you hear me?'

She couldn't speak.

'Answer me!' he snarled.

Paralyzed with fright, she had no control over the words that burst from her. 'Owl man!'

He stilled for an instant, as though what she said had surprised him.

'Yes,' he whispered at last. 'The death bird.'

He yanked at her jeans, forcing them down, her bikini panties with them. In another minute he'd be forcing himself into her.

No! she screamed inwardly, No! Never again. Strength she didn't know she possessed flowed through her, and she struggled violently, managing to free one hand. She clawed at his face with her nails.

He let go of her and hit her hard across the side of the head, dazing her, then caught her again. When she tried to scream he stuffed a cloth into her mouth and halfway down her throat, gagging her. As she fought for breath, he grabbed both her hands, holding them above her head with one of his. With the other, he fumbled at his pants, the slithering snick of the zipper mingling with his hoarse breathing and a terrible low-pitched growl.

Like an animal. Panic gripped her.

Suddenly he stopped moving, stopped trying to shove himself into her. The growling, though, continued, the animal sound. Gradually she realized the sound wasn't coming from him, it couldn't be; his face was just above hers and he was talking.

'Damn you, Sheba.'

Sheba!

Sara twisted her face to the side, but the cloth in her throat still gagged her. He released her hands, then his weight shifted, freeing her. Certain he was reaching for the knife, she yanked the cloth from her mouth and screamed and screamed.

Claws scratched against the car door, then damp air streamed over her. She sat up groggily to find he'd opened the other door and fled into the fog. She rested her head on the back seat, too weak to try to get out of the car, fumbling as she tried to pull her clothes straight, listening as the dog's snarls faded into the fog.

Sheba had gone after him.

Lights flashed, bright haloes in the mist, voices, a siren rose and fell in the distance. Then Ian was there. His arms around her, lifting her out, holding her.

'The owl man,' she mumbled. 'The

strangler. Sheba belongs to him, she hates him. He — '

'Ssh, take it easy, you're all right, you're safe,' Ian murmured.

She clung to him, still afraid. He carried her into a house, not her house — where was she? He laid her on a couch, and she tried to hold onto him, but he eased away.

'You're safe here,' he assured her. 'I'll be back in a minute.'

A gray-haired woman she'd never seen before brought her a blanket, and Sara huddled into its warmth and tried to stop shivering. The woman handed her something warm to drink. Coffee? No, tea. The heat felt good inside her, and she made an effort to smile at the strange woman, but her lips were stiff. Where was Ian? Why didn't he return? She whispered his name.

'He's outside with the police, dear,' the woman said. 'Just you rest.'

'Sheba?' she asked. 'The dog?'

'We heard her barking, such terrible sounds, and Arthur called the police because of all the commotion out there in the fog. We're so close to the park, you know. Oh dear, of course, you know. That horrible man . . . ' Her words trailed off.

Sara closed her eyes, only to open them quickly and pull herself to a sitting position, clutching at the blanket. 'Did you lock the doors? He can't get in, can he?'

The woman's face paled. 'No, he wouldn't try to get inside. Why there are all those policemen out there, and Arthur and Joe Sanders, he lives next door, and — ' Again she stopped. Hurrying to the front door, she snapped the lock. 'Just to be sure,' she said. 'I'll check in back, too.'

The front doorknob rattled, and then someone pounded on the door.

'Who — who is it?' the woman quavered.

'Ian Wilson. Let me in.'

He knelt beside Sara and took her hand. 'How do you feel?'

'Did they catch him?' she demanded.

Ian hesitated, then shook his head. Behind him, a policeman waited.

After Sara told the police as much as she could remember, she turned to Ian. 'Take me home, please,' she begged. 'To your house. I'm afraid to stay in my own.'

'We'd like to talk to you again, Ms. Henderson,' the policeman said. 'If you could come to headquarters tomorrow, we'll take a deposition there.'

Sara nodded numbly.

'She'll be staying with me,' Ian told him.

Before he carried her to his car, he called home, telling Lena to reassure Jamie that Sara was safe.

When he stopped to lock her doors, Sara insisted on going inside with him, afraid to stay in the car alone. He started to carry her into the bedroom while he packed an overnight case for her, but she shook her head.

'I can't leave Violet here alone,' she said.

She told him where the cat carrier was, and he left her with it in the kitchen.

Sara hobbled to the cupboard, opened a can of catfood, and set a large spoonful of it inside the carrier.

After a few minutes, Violet's head poked out, sniffing the air. Seeing no one except Sara, she made a dash for the carrier and started gobbling the food. Sara snapped the door shut, trapping Violet inside.

'Don't worry,' she told the cat. 'You'll like it at Ian's, once you get used to the change. It'll be better than you can imagine.'

Ian drove slowly through the foggy streets. Sara couldn't see much of his house when they pulled into the drive. He helped her inside and onto the couch, sat down and took her into his arms.

Sara leaned against his warmth. 'What do you think happened to poor Sheba?' she asked.

'I don't know. She took off after him.'

'She saved me. Sheba and you.'

'Sheba led me to you. Thank God I found you in time.'

Sara shuddered. 'I'll never be free of him. Never. I know he's out there somewhere watching. Waiting for me.'

Ian stroked her hair. 'They'll find him, Sara.'

'How? From my description? It isn't a good one.'

'The police have his jacket. He threw it over the dog's head there at the last, so he could get away from her. She tore it some but — '

'I heard one of them say there was no identification in the jacket, and it was a cheapo, dime a dozen kind.'

'Sara, you need to rest. You can have my bedroom tonight. I'll take you — '

'No, not yet. I can't. And I want you in the bedroom, too. I can't bear to be alone. In the car with him — it was awful. He hated me, not just me, every woman, and he was going to, he wanted to, he almost — '

Ian stopped her with a kiss. 'Sara, it's all over. You're safe. I'll keep you safe.'

She looked into his eyes, trying to believe him, but fearing she'd never be safe again.

'I love you, Sara. So does Jamie. You're here with us, and we're not going to let you go.'

Tears filled her eyes. 'I'm afraid, Ian, I'm so afraid. Of him. Out there waiting. And you. I'm afraid of you, of what will happen if we let ourselves love each other. And there's Jamie, I couldn't bear to fail Jamie.'

'Jamie's strong. You won't fail him; he won't let you.' He cupped her face. 'I don't have all the answers, but I do know that because of you and Jamie, I've stopped being afraid of tomorrow. I — ' He stopped, glancing to his left.

Sara turned her head and saw Violet ease from the open carrier and look fearfully around. She slunk over to the nearest wall, followed it to the door, and disappeared down the hall.

Ian smiled. 'You see that? Violet's begun her move to adjust. If she can, we ought to be able to make it, wouldn't you say so?'

Sara relaxed into his arms. Though she could do nothing to relieve her fear of the owl man, Ian was right about the rest. Just as she'd told Violet, it was going to be better here with Ian and Jamie than she could imagine.

30

He could no longer hear the sirens. He ran on the grass, he was somewhere in the park, he thought he knew about where. The fog was no worse than the Nam jungles, you had to have a feel for direction.

As he stopped to orient himself, he heard her snarl. That damn bitch Sheba was trailing him. She'd been out to get him since the day he brought her home, watching and waiting for the right time.

'Sheba!' he called. 'Heel!'

He hoped the command would confuse her. She'd been trained to heel, and he'd been her master, the one she obeyed. She'd have to ignore her training to keep coming after him. He figured she would, by now she hated him. But he wanted to buy time to locate a tree and get his back against the trunk for a good fighting stance. She didn't have a chance against him once he did. Not only was she injured, but he'd worked too long with attack dogs to be killed by one. He knew all the moves.

The whitish trunk of a big eucalyptus loomed ahead. He sprinted to it and took up a defensive position. All right, Sheba, he thought, come on, I'm ready.

She growled and he saw her, a dark menace in the gray mist, remaining just beyond his reach, hesitating to rush him. He stripped to his T-shirt, rolling his outer shirt around his forearm for padding, keeping the knife in his other hand.

She attacked without warning, leaping for his throat. He thrust the padded arm in her mouth, and brought the knife up into her belly with his free hand. Somehow she pulled away, and he grunted with pain as her teeth raked his upper arm.

She lunged again. He threw himself sideways. Felt a burning pain in his neck. Something snapped as he scrambled to his feet to face her next rush. She didn't come after him. He heard her whimper. Then silence.

He looked for her in the fog, knowing she must be dead or dying. He couldn't locate her body. Men shouted off to his left. Were the cops searching the park?

He plunged his knife into the ground a couple of times, before putting it back in the sheath. His shirt was gone. No loss. The shirt, like the jacket, was nothing special, the kind that could be bought in hundreds of stores. No name anywhere, nothing in the pockets.

Time to split, go home, clean up the bite on his arm — damn bitch — and say *adios* to San Diego.

At his apartment he hastily taped up the bite, put on a clean shirt, and threw open drawers. He lived spartan, so packing took little time. One duffle bag, a box of miscellaneous junk, and his sleeping bag. He stowed them in the car.

That little redheaded bitch didn't know his real name, but she knew his face, because she'd connect him with Sheba. He couldn't hang around and risk her spotting him, so he'd go on up to LA for awhile. Maybe grow a beard, let his hair get long enough for a ponytail. With luck he'd get a job in a kennel there, he was good with dogs, he could handle them. He shrugged. If worse came to worst, he could always wash dishes or flip hamburgers.

He drove carefully through the fog; this was no time to risk an accident.

What he'd do, he decided, was mail the key and a note to his landlord in a week or so. Not from LA. Depending on his finances, maybe he'd take a bus to Vegas for a weekend, and mail the letter from there. He'd say he and the dog were going back East, and wouldn't be returning. Mention the dog was with him. They'd find Sheba sooner or later and, though he was pretty sure the landlord had never seen Sheba, he didn't want any connection made between the dead dog and him.

Since he got his mail through an accommodation postal drop in downtown San Diego, the retirement check would go there. On the first he'd have to come back for it, because he'd need the money. Safe enough, no one knew his real name except the government agency that sent him the check.

When he returned to LA, he'd get some kind of a job to tide him over, stay around for awhile, then maybe later he'd move on up the coast. Lots of fog around Frisco. Big cities were always the safest.

But he'd be back. Sooner or later he'd look up that little bitch who'd gotten away from him tonight. He owed her, her and the other one, the bitch who'd written to the paper. He wasn't through with either of them, not by a long shot. He'd be back all right. They'd wait.

The fog dissipated when he hit the freeway, and the sky was gray with morning by the time he reached Santa Ana. He pulled onto an off ramp and into a Denny's parking lot. Damn, his shoulder ached from the bite. He'd done for Sheba once and for all, but she'd come too close to doing him in. She sure as hell was his last big dog.

'No bitch can get the best of me,' he muttered aloud. He smoothed his hair as he left the car, and then felt to make sure the heart on the chain was tucked safely under his T-shirt . . .

★ ★ ★

A jogger and his Irish setter ran through the park as morning lightened the grayness, the fog thinning to swirls between the ghost trunks of the eucalyptus.

The setter paused, head in the air, and came to a perfect point facing one of the trees. His owner looked, gasped, and stopped, remembering what he'd heard about the strangler on the early morning news.

Had the strangler claimed another victim?

Heart slamming against his ribs, the jogger glanced around apprehensively before hurrying toward the dark mound under the eucalyptus. He let his breath out in a long sigh, when he realized that it wasn't a human, but a dog. A black German shepherd. Dead.

He leaned over the stiffening body. Between the animal's teeth he saw the glint of gold. A heart on a broken chain. He eased it from the dog's mouth to examine it, and noticed an inscription, with initials, etched on the back of the heart.

His setter whined uneasily.

'Good dog, stay,' he muttered absently.

Could the dead dog be the black shepherd mentioned on the news? The dog belonging to the strangler? He stared at the heart in his hands. The strangler's?

The quicker he got out of here and gave this to the cops, the better. For all he knew, the heart might be enough to identify the bastard.

He looked around again, then, the heart clenched in his fist, turned, and, followed by the setter, ran back the way he'd come, toward the nearest pay phone.

31

On a sunny January morning, Jamie, propped in a lounge chair on the patio, watched a gray and white mockingbird land on a branch of the jacaranda tree. He noticed Violet, curled up beside him, raise her head to look at the bird, too. The tip of her tail twitched, and she made a funny noise deep in her throat, a hunting noise, Jamie guessed. But he knew the mockingbird was safe from Violet.

The bird seemed to know he was safe, 'cause he stared down at the two of them with a harsh challenging cry like a blue jay's. Mockingbirds could imitate every bird call there was, making Jamie wonder if they had any song that was theirs alone.

For the moment he and Violet were alone on the patio, 'cause Lena had gone inside to get something, and Sara and Daddy were still sleeping.

Sara had been here a week, and he really liked having her at his house, but he wished he could find some magic to banish the fear he saw in her eyes. The owl man hadn't been caught yet, and Jamie knew she was afraid he'd come after her again.

Yesterday's paper was lying on the umbrella table next to the lounge chair. The paper was open to the article about the heart the police wanted identified. Jamie craned his neck to look at the picture of the heart, and decided it wasn't nearly as pretty as the one he and Daddy had given Sara.

The heart in the paper was sort of a mystery, 'cause the police didn't say where it came from or why they had it. Jamie stared at the picture and wondered.

The picture and the print around it blurred, as Jamie recalled the real dream he'd had two nights after Christmas. In that dream Jamie had seen a heart like the one in the paper, a gold heart caught in blood-smeared teeth. Sheba's teeth. She'd been lying dead under a tree.

Sadness gripped him as he remembered. Poor Sheba. He laid his hand on Violet's soft fur for comfort.

Then suddenly he couldn't feel her fur under his fingers, he wasn't on the patio anymore, he was somewhere else — it seemed to be a downtown street — and he knew he was in another real dream.

He saw three men getting into a car. Two of them were handcuffed together, and the scowling one, Jamie realized with a spurt of apprehension, was the owl man. The others were policemen. They were arresting the owl man.

'It makes no difference what this woman might have identified,' the owl man said. 'I didn't lose anything.'

Jamie knew he was lying, 'cause he could see into the owl man's head. The heart in the paper, the heart in Sheba's teeth, was his. The woman he mentioned was his sister, she lived in Chula Vista, and he'd stolen the heart from her a long time ago.

The men and the car faded from view, and the next thing Jamie saw was newspaper headlines: PARK STRANGLER NABBED. Below, it said: Chula Vista Woman Identifies Heart.

He was reading on when the headlines wavered and vanished, and he was back on the patio with Violet. Jamie blinked, trying to order his thoughts. The owl man had been caught, because he lost the golden heart he'd stolen from his sister. His sister had seen the picture of the heart in the paper and called the police.

He couldn't wait to tell Sara. After a moment, though, he decided maybe he'd better not. He knew his real dreams always came true, but no one else did. Sara might want to believe him, but she actually wouldn't until she read the headlines for herself. Then she'd believe him. But then she'd know he could sort of read minds.

Maybe she wouldn't like him anymore. Real dreaming was weird. Maybe no one would like him, if they knew about his real dreams.

Jamie sighed. It'd be hard to wait till the paper came with the headlines he'd seen. The newspaper story wasn't completely right, though. 'Cause the paper said the owl man's sister was responsible for him being caught. He knew different, and it made him feel a little better about the dead dog.

Sheba was the one who'd really caught the owl man.

THE END

We do hope that you have enjoyed reading this large print book.

Did you know that all of our titles are available for purchase?

We publish a wide range of high quality large print books including:
Romances, Mysteries, Classics
General Fiction
Non Fiction and Westerns

Special interest titles available in large print are:
The Little Oxford Dictionary
Music Book
Song Book
Hymn Book
Service Book

Also available from us courtesy of Oxford University Press:
Young Readers' Dictionary
(large print edition)
Young Readers' Thesaurus
(large print edition)

For further information or a free brochure, please contact us at:
Ulverscroft Large Print Books Ltd.,
The Green, Bradgate Road, Anstey,
Leicester, LE7 7FU, England.
Tel: (00 44) **0116 236 4325**
Fax: (00 44) **0116 234 0205**

Other titles published by
The House of Ulverscroft:

NIGHTINGALE MAN

Jane Toombs

During World War I, Luke is recruited by the British Secret Service from the American pilots flying with the French Air Force. His mission is to rescue Nurse Edith Cavell, captured by the Boche, imprisoned in German-occupied Belgium and doomed to be shot as a spy. All too soon it becomes a challenge to stay alive. Who's double-crossing him? Can it be the English gal he's falling in love with? Or is it the spy-master back in England who's set him up as the fall guy?

HARTE'S GOLD

Jane Toombs

Carole Harte had never dreamed that she could be so attracted to a man or that any man could be so perfect. Trouble is, she's never heard of Jerrold Telford! What kind of a film company casts an unknown actor in a leading role? Could this be an elaborate scheme to con her grandmother into parting with her money?

TO CATCH A SPY

Stuart M. Kaminsky

Hollywood gumshoe Toby Peters finds himself working for movie star Cary Grant. The assignment seems simple enough. Grant merely wants him to deliver a package and pick up an envelope at Elysian Park in the middle of the night. But at the critical moment of the exchange, a shot rings out and Toby finds himself with a corpse on his hands, a lump on his head, grass in his mouth and a dying man's words on his mind. Now in pursuit of a murderer, Toby and Cary Grant follow a trail of clues that leads them to a second dead body, a nest of Nazi sympathisers, and finally to a night-time confrontation with a determined killer . . .

PERFECTLY DEAD

Iain McDowall

Chief Inspector Jacobson hates drug-related cases. Not least because it means he has to work with the drug squad. But there's no alternative when a local dealer turns up burnt, battered and dead. Just another hopeless, pointless sink estate incident. But even so, Dave Carter's torched body is the stuff of bad dreams. Death doesn't get any grimmer, Jacobson thinks. But that's because Jacobson, DS Kerr and Crowby CID are still forty-eight hours away from the 'Perfect Family' killings — five dead in a leafy suburb where bad things aren't supposed to happen. And the only witness may never speak again.

WINTER'S END

John Rickards

They have the body of a slaughtered woman. They have a half-naked man standing over her. They have no idea how to make him talk. And so they call in ex-FBI interrogator Alex Rourke to the traumatized Maine town of Winter's End. The Boston Private Investigator knows the place well — it's where he grew up. But as Rourke probes the mind of the enigmatic 'Nicholas', he is forced to re-examine his hometown and his own past — and what he finds is a place built on secrets. And if the man in custody does hold the answers to crimes both present and past, then Alex will have to get to them — and quickly. Because what Nicholas has been waiting for from the beginning is Alex Rourke . . .